Free Falling

A SKYHAVEN SERIES

M. J. Sullivan

FREE FALLING

A SKYHAVEN SERIES

© M. J. Sullivan

First published June 2021

ISBN: 978-0-6485089-7-7 Paperback

ISBN: 978-0-6485938-0-5 E-Book

Published with the assistance of :

ANGEL KEY PUBLICATIONS https://angelkey.com.au

Acknowledgements

This book has taken some time to write, and I have a few people I need to thank. To my husband and my two children, who have put up with me saying, it's almost done, it's nearly done, for the past few years. To me, it was never done and never good enough. But I think they finally believe me when I say I've finished, and I am going to put it out there for all to read.

I want to thank all those who read the draft and told me that they enjoyed reading it and asked when I will publish it. I want to thank Kim, who endured my begging to ask the geek squad to see who would like to do my cover art. I would also like to thank Luke for my Skyhaven tree. (Which will feature at the start of every book). To my mum, who double-checked my work and told me of all the mistakes I made, here's hoping I didn't miss any.

Thank you to all who have read my book.

Note from the author

I have so many stories sitting in my head, and it has taken me many years to finally get to this stage, where I can share these stories with all of you.

Free Falling is the first in the Skyhaven series; each book will tell a different story about one of the many residents of Skyhaven. So be on the lookout for the second book in the series.

I have had fun writing Free Falling, and I hope you enjoy reading it.

Until next time, happy reading.

(Look for the Skyhaven tree)

1

Layla

Breathe, just breathe. I keep saying this over and over; I keep trying to tell myself that everything will be all right. But will it?

"Where do you want this?" I turned to stare at these men who were carrying another box across my yard into the house. Both men were large, beefy with scruffy hair. One man had red hair, and the other man had brown hair. They were both wearing matching blue overalls with braces to hold them up.

All I wanted them to do was unpack the moving truck and stop looking at my ass. At this moment, the redheaded man was staring at my breasts. The brown-haired man was waiting for my reply.

"In the lounge room with everything else," I replied.

"Don't you want this in the bedroom? I just don't understand why you want everything in the lounge room." One of the men asked. I was starting to get annoyed.

"No! It's just that, if it is all in one room, I won't miss anything, and it also means that everything will get unpacked."

How do they not understand that, but they just continue to stare at me? They probably think that I am crazy or what they would do to me if they had the chance. Why can't they empty the truck and leave? I wish to be left alone; this is my first time away from everyone and everything. I don't want to be near anyone;

1

I want to feel how it truly feels to be free. I stood quietly, just waiting for them to get back to work and leave me in peace. After another minute, they start working again, and I am free to stare at my new house.

Finally, I'm free of my family, well, at least free of my father, and am starting a new life right from scratch, and I mean from scratch. I know how crazy it sounds, leaving home with nothing more than the clothes I wear and a bag in each hand. Still, leaving was the best thing I have ever done. I mean, it was hard to leave my mother and sisters, but there was no other way. I needed to get out of the tyranny. I needed to get away from my father but leaving did mean to leave certain things behind and start again. Now that I have done it, I feel that I am now finally breathing freely.

So, I have left the family home. I have bought my own home and buy everything that goes into it. I mean everything, a lounge suite, electronics, kitchen appliances and cutlery, lawn mower and everything in between. I know I might be crazy, but I had to get out from under my parents' rule. There was only one way to do that, and that was pretty much to run away and start again.

Now I have this beautiful one storey, four-bedroom, two-bathroom, two-car garage home. I don't know why I sound like a salesperson, but there are no front gardens to speak of, just weeds and long grass. I have a large patio in the backyard that spans most of the house's back wall and a massive, beautiful oak tree in the back-left corner, with weeds, weeds, and more weeds. The gardens are overgrown with weeds. However, I am more than happy to spend my days cleaning them out. I know most people would not have seen the beauty in buying this rundown house, but to me, it's perfect, especially that beautiful oak tree in the backyard. My thoughts are interrupted by those two sweaty, perverse gorillas.

"We have only the garden equipment left; do you want that in the lounge room as well?" One of the removal men asked.

Oh, how I'm not fond of sarcasm. It's such a corrupt form of humour; well, I would not say I like it from this joker. I keep staring at my house as I answer.

"Thank you, no, in the garage will be fine, and the case of beer in there is for you too," I replied.

I hear them thank me for the gesture, their mumbles of how if they knew earlier that there was beer in it for them, they would have been quicker. I highly doubt that, in any case. I think they were taking their time so that they could stare at me. I know I had many things that needed moving. Here I was guessing that leaving them a case of beer was a nice gesture. But I think what respectful behaviour from them would be to stop staring and just work. I impatiently wait for them to finish up working. If you could, call staring at me working. I haven't gone inside yet; I want them to go before setting foot in my house.

Ten minutes later, they leave. I am free to go inside and start unpacking. But first, I will need a glass of wine to help with the unpacking. I am glad I stole some of the family wine as I left, among a couple of other things.

Now there is a knock on the door. Knock! Knock!

I have been unpacking for about ten minutes. I am about halfway through my first glass of wine. I put my drink down and head for the door.

"Hello!" Knock, knock! Once again. "Woohoo!"

Like I didn't hear you the first time. As I reach for the door, I see a middle-aged woman with red hair, a plump figure, dressed as if she has just stepped out of a fifty's magazine. I haven't opened my door just yet, but I can see she has a basket in her hand.

"I have brought you a welcome basket," she said.

She holds it up to me. I reluctantly open the door and let her in. She hands me the basket. There were coffee beans, a couple of small jars of jam, biscuits and other odds and ends.

"I am Mrs Davis, and I live across the street," she said. She turns and points to the house across the road.

"If you need anything at all, dear, just pop on over," she said.

"Thank you for the basket and the offer, but I am okay for the moment." I smile and try to guide her back out the door.

"If you would like, I could send my son over when he finishes work."

Oh great! Not here for more than ten minutes, and she is trying to set me up with her son. I hope that is not what she is implying. 'Time to get her out, I thought'.

"Again, thank you, but no. I wish to do this myself," I exclaimed.

Oops, not what she wanted to hear. I can see the anger welling up inside her. However, I wonder if she was upset by me trying to get her out of the house or telling her I don't want her son's help. I want to be left alone. I don't want anyone around me. I wish to be free. I can tell that this woman wants to push her way in and push her son onto me in more ways than one. I can see her eyes are burning up even more. Mrs Davis is a woman you do not want to make angry or be on her wrong side. However, I think I have already done that within two minutes of meeting her.

"Humph, well, miss?" She leaves the question open. I guess she wants to know my name.

"Layla Dixon," I replied with a respectful smile on my face.

Mrs Davis doesn't say anything else but turns on her heels and storms away. That is fine now, but perhaps I should have acted more polite, but I got prickly when she wanted to send her son over. I could tell Mrs Davis wanted us to be together. It sure came across that way to me. I take a deep breath and place the basket on the bench and pick my wine glass back up and get back to unpacking again.

Knock! Knock. Once again, another knock on my door.

Again! I managed to achieve three hours more with the unpacking since my last guest. I don't want any more people visiting. I just want to be left alone. I don't want to answer the door. I nearly don't, but something inside me tells me to answer it. I put down my second glass of wine and head for the door. I'm glad I didn't ignore the knocking this time.

This guest standing in my doorway is a rather handsome man. He is tall and muscular and looks to be around the same age as me late twenties, maybe early thirties. He had short brown hair and piercing blue eyes; I could stare at those eyes all day. He was wearing jeans and a blue-buttoned shirt. He smiled when he saw me. I swear I went weak at the knees. It was the most delightful smile I have ever seen. It was warm and inviting. With those blue eyes, you could just lose yourself, and that was just what I wanted to do.

"Hi!" I said. Oh yes, very much weak at the knees, I grab the door frame to hold myself upright.

"Um. I'm Eric, from next door. I was, um, wondering if you would, um," he stuttered nervously.

Oh, why is he so nervous? I was thinking. He is the one that is making my legs go out from under me. I mean, I'm not that unique, not pretty. I'm five foot four, about sixty kilos. My most striking features are my waist-length brown hair and grey eyes. I also have pale skin, but people still stare.

"I'm sorry, I'm no good at this," he said. He had a shy smile as he said it and waves his hand to say this was a mistake coming here.

"At what, please tell?" I say with a laugh trying to make it easier for him not to be nervous.

"Never mind," he said as he turns to leave, pulling the doorknob behind him. No! Don't go; my brain screams at me. I want to keep looking at the fantastic smile. Before I knew what I was doing, I opened the door and reached for his wrist.

"Would you like to come in?" I asked. 'Please say yes, please, I was thinking'. "I rejected Mrs Davis's offer of sending her son over, but now I think I might need the help, and I wouldn't mind if you wanted to help. If that is what you were going to ask me." I said. He just stared at me, but it's now his blue eyes staring at my grey eyes. Still, I could see his nervousness. He started to smile at me.

"You said 'no' to Mrs Davis? That's a bit dangerous," he laughed.

I could not tell if his eyes, smile, or laugh were his best feature, but either way, I wanted him. The thought came out of nowhere.

"Yes, I didn't like her implications about sending her son over here to help me. I could sense that she had an ulterior motive."

I had left home to get away from this kind of thing. I was tired of having people pushed at me. So, I went; I just wanted peace and wanted to find my own heart, my way. When I looked at Eric, I started to see a worried expression come across his face. Oh, I'm an idiot. He was concerned that I was talking about him as well. But I was referring to Mrs Davis and her implications of pushing her son on me. But I wanted Eric to stay, and I want him.

I am not liking these thoughts that were screaming at me. I didn't realise that I had loosened my grip on Eric's wrist, and he turns to leave again. But just then, I had a flash of a thought. 'Oh my, what if he is Mrs Davis' son'. That's what the look is. He is Mrs Davis' son. Great, what a fool I have made of myself. I hang my head, and I feel the heat creeping up along my neck. Oh, but wait. He said he was from next door, not from across the road. How is he already mixing up my thoughts? How is he doing this?

"I am sorry to have disturbed you."

"Please don't go," I pleaded. "I want you to stay. I will buy dinner if you say yes to help me," I said.

Great, I sound like a crazy person were my thoughts.

"I'm sorry, I didn't mean for it to sound that way," I said. Why am I trying hard to get his approval? Maybe I realise I can't do this unpacking by myself, and I need help, his help. He just stands there staring at me like the crazy person that I am.

"If you keep talking like that to your neighbours, people are going to think you are off your rocker," he said. I couldn't help but smile.

"Okay, I will help, and I will buy dinner," Eric said. I stand aside and let him in. I inhaled as he brushed past me. I could smell the earth, fresh air and soap. I had to hold onto the door frame again. He turned and stared at me. I could feel myself going red.

"Where shall we start?" he asked. I look around and see box after box after box. I look at the bench and see my wine glass.

"Share a glass of wine with me while we work," I said.

"I don't drink the stuff, but I will if I can play my iPod," he said.

His iPod sounds scary, not too sure if I'm going to like his taste in music.

"Yes, but with limitations," I explained.

"Oh no, I am not going to drink some mysterious unlabelled wine and then have you make me skip all the cool songs. That's just not going to happen."

"It's a family wine, and for that, no songs," I said. He thinks about it for a minute.

"Family wine? So, I guess it is going to be strong? Strong enough to put hair on a bald man," he said.

Cheeky bugger, I don't answer him. I grab another glass and pour him one, and I hand it over. He smells at it and stares at the blood-red colour of it. He takes a small sip of it, then smiles.

"Wow, strong is an understatement, but damn that's good." He takes another small sip and shakes his head. "I think I'm getting drunk already; that stuff is wickedly strong," he said.

"I wouldn't know, I have grown up on it, and I guess I am just used to it," I said.

"Can I have my iPod on?" He smiles, asking politely.

'Anything, you can have anything you want as long as you keep smiling at me'. Again, with these thoughts?

I smiled at him and nodded my head in agreement.

After four hours and two bottles of wine later – I only took a couple of bottles when I left, but I got more from my uncle when I bought this place. We had the TV unit set up and had the TV, Blu-Ray, Play Station and the sound system set up. We also had the coffee table and the lounges in place.

I had a queen bed for the main room and one double bed for one spare bedroom. There were a lot of naughty looks and innuendo going on while we were setting the foundations up. I will admit, I didn't think so much would get done in such a short period. I guess we were so busy laughing and talking that time just flew by.

Eric was also singing along with his iPod in between our communication. He doesn't sound too bad either, but I liked it when he sang along with some of the more romantic songs. 'I think I blushed when he did.' I made him repeat all of Gin Wigmore, Blink 182 and Garbage. He also caught me dancing on a few occasions when I thought he wasn't looking.

I became all red and embarrassed. No one has ever seen me dance.

Our upbringing was a rigorous non-negotiable strict line to follow. My sisters didn't have to live the life or the path that I had to. My eldest sister lived by the same rules that I did. But she was the pride and joy of my father and could stray as often as she liked. My younger sister had no strict line to follow and could do and get away with anything. Then there was me, the middle child, the outcast who wasn't allowed any fun and must always follow the rules to the letter of father's law. At least that's the way it came across.

I felt so empty and yet so full of emotions that I thought I could never be free, forever trapped, with no one seeing my elusive cage but me. It got to the point where I could no longer take it. So, I packed a bag and left. I knew my uncle was on the outs with my family, so I went for his place, hoping he wouldn't turn me away. As a result, I stayed with him until I got this house, and it's starting to look and feel like home already. Plus, with such a handsome guest, things are looking better by the moment.

I'm leaning up against my kitchen counter, watching Eric sitting on the floor playing with the TV. His brown hair is all messed up from him running his hands through it all afternoon, he has his top buttons undone, and I can see his tan chest. His shirt sleeves rolled up, muscles everywhere; what a view, such muscular arms. Drool, wiping my mouth.

His shirt almost looks to be straining to stay on his frame. I wouldn't mind if his shirt came off or if his body just ripped it apart. My mind goes blank, then starts to play a movie of Eric's shirt just ripping apart and falling to the ground. I watched him stand up from the lounge and walk over to me. He pulls me close to his chest, I feel his fingers tilting my chin up, and our eyes lock. I shake my head at the thought, but then again, those cobalt blue eyes, I could stare at them all day, and that smile, every time he smiles, I swear I go weak at the knees. I start to babble.

He is so adorable and funny. Now and then, he would show a sign of nervousness around me, which would make me smile. Most people don't get shy around me. Most people are intimidated by me because of who my father is, but he gets nervous around me. I don't know why really, he is the gorgeous one, not me. He must have sensed that I was staring at him because he turns and smiles at me. He goes slightly pink. I think I do as well. He stands up and moves to the lounge.

"Um… do you…" he clears his throat and tries again. "Do you want to come and sit?" he asked.

Our conversation was strange as it had been free-flowing and light all day, but now, he is getting nervous when it comes to just sitting with him. I have a feeling that I will start to babble. I mean, I have never felt uncomfortable around anyone; a little shy, but never painful or nervous. These feelings I don't understand. It's not natural for me.

Eric pats the spot next to him. He moves down the lounge to make room for me. I push off from the counter and walk towards him. I was about to sit next to him when there was a knock on the door. Eric stayed seated. The look on his face clearly states his disappointment at someone being at the door. I walked over to answer the door. There in the doorway is a man in his late twenties with red hair and a rumpled grey suit from being worn at work all day. He is slender; by the looks of it, he is shorter than Eric. He is cute to look at, but he is no Eric. I doubt anyone could look as handsome as Eric.

"Good afternoon Miss Dixon," he said.

Wait, how did he know my name? The next thing I knew, Eric was beside me. I could feel a dominant aura around him, almost possessiveness around him.

"Davis!" said Eric, oh great, Mrs Davis's son. So, she did send him over after all. The young man was glaring at Eric and Eric at him.

"What do you want, Davis?" Eric asked.

I could feel Eric go to raise his arm and place it around my waist but thought better of it. I wouldn't have minded if he had, but the venom that was in his voice as he addressed Mrs Davis's son was astounding.

"I'm here to see Miss Dixon," he said.

"Did mummy send you over?" Eric said rudely.

What the! What has gone on between these two to spit so much venom at each other?

"If you weren't cowering behind that door, I would kick your ass Walker," he said.

"I highly doubt it. I am not the one cowering behind anything; it is you that hides behind your mum's dress," Eric said.

I watch as both boys, not men behaving like children, balling their hands into fists and glaring at each other. It is only the door that keeps them from hitting each other, not me standing here because they have forgotten that I am here. I cleared my throat. Being ignored already, that must be a record. That was even worse than being at home.

I wasn't going to have it happen again, and not in my own house. Both boys turned and looked at me, and both said 'sorry' at the same time.

"I don't give a damn what has gone on between you two, but this is my house," I yelled at them.

The two men said 'sorry' again.

"I'm going to open the door. Do you think that you two can be civil because if not, I would be more than happy to toss both of you on your arses?" I said.

Eric laughed, but Mr Davis said nothing. He just glared at Eric. I opened the door and gestured for both to take a seat, but neither one did. They just stood about five metres apart from each other, still throwing daggers at one another.

'I don't want this, I don't need anger, and I don't need hostility around me. Getting away from this type of behaviour was my goal in the first place. I never wanted to feel empty and trapped again; this was my new start', were my thoughts.

It's just that - how could Eric not see the pain on my face? Eric must have heard my silent pleas because he looked at me with a featured softened stare and looked apologetic. Finally, Eric moved back to the lounge and sat down, patting the spot next to him. I did as he wished, and I then sat next to him. Rather a bit closer than he or I thought I would because our legs were touching.

A broad smile spread across his face, and at that, I was glad I was seated because I got all weak at the knees, and a red flush was starting to creep across my face. If I didn't hear the cough, I would have thought that the world had dropped away. All I wanted to do was stare into those blue eyes and watch that smile all day and night long without moving, for fear of blinking and watching it all vanish and finding myself back at home being miserable and unhappy. But I pulled myself away from Eric, and I focused on Mr Davis.

"I'm sorry, I'm Layla," I said as I stood and held out my hand.

"Derek," he said. We shook hands; his grip was firm, but his hands were soft and gentle, but the thing that amazed me was that my heart didn't stumble. I did not go weak at the knees, nor was there a blush. It seems to only happen around Eric.

I released his hand and gestured for him to sit—this time, he did. I sat back down next to Eric and turned to face Derek. I put my right hand behind me to support me. I felt it encounter his left hand, but neither one of us moved our hand away. I found myself closing my fingers around his.

"Derek, what brings you over here?" I asked. 'As if I didn't know.'

"My mother," Derek said.

Eric snorted at his comment, so I let go of his hand. As I looked at him, I could see the hurt in his face.

"She said that you might need some help moving in. But she didn't mention that Walker was here," he said.

I ignored the last part of his statement due to it being very snippy.

"You are more than welcome to stay and help," I would appreciate that, I exclaimed.

"Thank you, but no, I only came over to introduce myself. I have somewhere I need to be, and I didn't want to take up too much of your time," Derek explained.

"Got a girl you don't want mummy to scare off?" Eric snarled.

'What is going on between these two?'

"Not that it matters to you, Walker, but are you jealous of the fact that I have a girl unlike you?" Derek said with a sharp tone.

"Jealous! Why would I be jealous of you? At least I don't have to hide my girlfriend."

"Must be able to keep one before you can say that, Walker."

"But I don't have to keep mine away from my mother," Eric said.

I can't believe what I am hearing.

"That's the thing; I am getting somewhere as you aren't getting anything, not unless you…" he doesn't get to continue because Eric stands up and gets up in Derek's face.

"But I don't have to hide mine," Eric said.

They just won't stop. And the conversation seems to be going around and around in a circle.

"I'm not trying to sleep with every female in the estate or Skyhaven, not with those blue eyes, award-winning smile and that fat overflowing wallet because that's the only reason and the only way you are getting any."

Both men had their fists clenched, ready to hit each other. I stood; neither one of them noticed that I stood up. I tried to drown out what they were shouting; instead, I moved to the door and opened it. I cleared my throat, grabbing their attention; they both relaxed and stared at me.

"Thank you, Mr Davis, for stopping by. I hope you have a pleasant night," I said.

He took one look at Eric before leaving, saying a somewhat embarrassed sorry. I stare at Eric a moment longer before I steady myself for this next part.

"I thank you for all your help today, Mr Walker. I greatly appreciate it and would not have gotten so much accomplished without your help, and for that, I thank you," I said.

He didn't move, I could see the hurt in his eyes, or maybe his eyes are trying to plead with me. I hope he will learn from this and note that I will not tolerate men being Neanderthals around me. I have had my share of that already.

He stands there looking at me, pleading with his eyes. 'Please don't do that, or I will lose all my conviction and ask you to stay. And I don't want to do that, not yet anyhow', were my thoughts. He gives me one last desperate pleading look before grabbing his iPod and coming over to me. He reached out to take my hand, but I pulled it away.

I watched as he walked out my door and across my yard. I closed the door, and as I did, my heart sank. Maybe that would be the last time I will see him; I hope not though I would love to see that smile again.

2

Eric

'She threw me out! After all the help I gave her today, she threw me out. I can't blame her, however. I can feel her eyes on my back as I walk away. Suck it up and walk next door; at least next door, I can feel something in the comfort of my own home,' was his thoughts.

As I walked back inside, I toss my stuff onto the coffee table and throw myself on the lounge. 'Don't stare out the window; don't stare at the house,' I thought. I close my eyes and try to quieten my inner voice. Still, it doesn't work; my mind goes back to the start of the day.

Here I was, turning on my TV. That's when I saw her standing there, staring at my house, as moving men unloaded the truck. I could see them staring at her ass and breasts every chance they got. But I couldn't stop staring at her face. Not long after the movers left, the lady from across the road came over – Mrs Davis – more than likely - she was trying to offer her son to her. Damn was all I thought. I couldn't believe that I was already getting jealous that she was over there trying to pimp out her son when the new girl was to be mine.

I couldn't fathom from where these emotions were coming. But the worst part was that I couldn't do anything about it; I had to leave in a couple of hours for work. I would go over and offer to help when I finish work; I just hope Derek wouldn't be there when I get back.

15

I had arrived home from work, showered, changed and headed over to Layla's house. I couldn't believe how nervous I felt. I was afraid somebody would recognise me, and that I did not want. As I got to the door, I could hear someone humming a tune I didn't know; the voice sounds sweet.

I knock, then I listen to her groan. I guess after Mrs Davis visited, she didn't want any more company. I was about to leave when she came to the door. She was beautiful; I think my heart stopped. So beautiful, her eyes were amazing; you wouldn't think grey could look stunning. But there was more hidden amongst the grey; they are the colour of a storm over an ocean. I couldn't help but smile. I could have sworn I saw her jaw drop and her hand reach for the door frame.

I don't think she recognises me, and that is a good thing. I don't want her to know that part of my life just yet. I want her to see the real me, but as a result,

I got nervous. Realising Derek wasn't there, my nerves settled.

It was fun and light-hearted. I was enjoying the company, and I even caught Layla dancing on a few occasions. She turned a lovely shade of pink. I will admit that when I saw her dancing, all I wanted to do was put my hands on her hips and move with her in more ways than you would think. But it all turned to shit because Derek turned up. While I was berating Derek, I was making her mad. That was one thing I didn't want to do as I was trying to impress her. I managed to fix the problem by asking her to sit next to me. When she did, our legs were touching.

Turning a pretty shade of pink, she placed her hand down next to her. It encountered my left hand. Her long slender, delicate fingers wrapped around mine. My head and my heart stuttered. Heat flooded my entire body. All I wanted to do was kiss her and feel her body beneath mine. It didn't last long because it all turned to shit again. I found myself walking back home.

Now sitting here trying not to look over at her house, I find myself thinking about how she moved her hips when she danced and her sweet singing voice when she thought I wasn't listening. I felt that I wanted to be sitting next to Layla with our legs touching and holding hands. I would pull her towards me. I would run my hands through her hair and kiss her, picking her up and carrying her to the master bedroom. My thoughts would soon turn to how I ruined it. Just thinking about her makes me want her even more. Maybe I should go back over there and try to make it right.

The phone ringing interrupts my thoughts. I pick the phone up and look at the caller ID; it is Gareth Flannery. A large, well-built redheaded Irish man, but without the Irish temper and almost no accent. I didn't feel up to talking to him, but I answered it straight away.

"Hey, Gareth," I replied.

"E-man, you coming to The Cavern tonight. Becca wants to see you," he asked.

I don't feel up to going out, especially to see Becca, were my thoughts.

"E-man, you there?" he exclaimed.

If I don't go, he will come over and drag me out of the house. I don't want to go but going to have to go. I don't want to be around Becca.

"Yeah, I'm here. What time?" I replied with zero enthusiasm.

"What's the matter?" he asked.

"Nothing much, just messed it up with the new girl next door," was my reply.

"Well, get your ass over there and bring her with you. You can have dinner and then go downstairs. You can take her back home, and it will all be sweet. Not to mention it may just get Becca off your back," he explained.

"Nah, messed it up too much, and I feel I have to give her time to cool down. I highly doubt that it would get Becca off my back," I said.

"Cool, I'll send a car to pick you up at nine," Gareth said, and he then hung up.

I go back to daydreaming before I have a shower. Dead at nine o'clock, Gareth's car turns up.

As I was heading out of the house, a car pulls up at Layla's. Not just any vehicle either; a black Bentley Continental 3 WGT sports car, worth nearly four hundred thousand dollars. A guy in his twenties jumps out to greet Layla with an embrace, and she kisses him. Jealousy surges within me and simmers as I remember she isn't my girl. I should have known someone as beautiful as she was would already have a boyfriend.

Just get in the car Eric and go. I get into Gareth's car, and as I open the door, I inhale the scent of Chanel No 5, Becca's perfume.

"Good evening Bec." I said.

As we left my driveway, Becca put her strappy six-inch black stiletto in between my legs. She pressed the toe of her shoe into my crotch, demanding my attention. I looked at her feet and glanced along her slender tanned legs that seem to go on forever to the bottom of her short mini black dress. I feel nothing for her. She has a tiny waist and full breasts that were almost bursting out of the strapless dress.

Feeling nothing, I make myself look at her face. She was busy looking for split ends in her long blonde hair. Her fingers were working each strand when she noticed I was looking at her.

Becca smoothed her hair out and looked at me with those big brown eyes. I still feel nothing for her. I have never felt anything for her, but again she presses her toe into me.

"My darling Eric, how have you been?" she asked.

Her voice drips with fake sugary sweetness. She could have any man she wants, but now she wants me because of who I am.

"I swear it feels like a lifetime since we last saw each other, let alone being seen together." Oh, it's going to be a trying night.

"Who was that girl who had your attention? She looks rather dull," she said.

I wanted to snarl at her. How dare she say Layla's dull were my thoughts? Breathe in, breathe out, and calm down. Ooh did these comments touch a nerve! Smarmy cow. Damn, from where did that come?

"She is my new neighbour; that is all I'm going to say, anything else, and you will splash her life all over social media, telling the world how you are much better than her," I said.

"Is she your girlfriend?" Becca asked abruptly.

"No, she is just my neighbour," I replied.

"Good, then I have nothing to worry about," she said.

I pick up her shoe from between my legs and gently push her leg back. At least she cooperated and put her leg down. But it doesn't last too long because she tries to put her foot back. I cross my legs over and move further away from her.

"Damn it, Becca, there isn't, and never will be anything between us," I explained.

Crap that is not what she wanted to hear; she glares at me, pulls out her phone and starts typing. Now here comes the trash talk on all forms of social media about me. As I said, it's going to be a trying night.

3

Layla

It's been a week since I moved in, and it's starting to feel like a home. But something is missing. Something doesn't feel right. Maybe it's the fact that I haven't seen Eric in a week. I felt bad for throwing him out that day, and I shouldn't have. It was petty, and he did help me so much that day, but I didn't want any form of confrontation in my house.

To make up for how I had behaved, I would invite him over tonight for dinner. But I will have to get some groceries for dinner. Before I do that, I must see my uncle. There's no doubt that he will solve my problem with the house, not feeling right.

After getting lost once or twice, I found myself driving up the kilometre long gravel driveway of my uncle's house forty minutes later.

I pull up out of the front of his house. I get out of the car and look up at the five-storey mammoth of a home. I can see gargoyles lining the roof and ivy climbing up and over the walls. My uncle's house sits on at least one thousand acres – but that could be an exaggeration - and more than half of it is forest.

He seems to have his fingers in an assortment of pies, but his most outstanding achievement is the jewellery he makes. He told me once that the cheapest piece was a pair of earrings that he sold for six hundred thousand dollars. His jewellery is fantastic and original, and no two are alike or can be copied, no matter how hard you try. It just doesn't work.

I walk up to the door and pull the rope bell, standing for about a minute, before my uncle answers the door. He doesn't have too many staff members. I stare at my uncle, who is the same height as me, with longish salt and pepper coloured hair that covers his ears which seems scruffy after running his hands through his hair about ten times a day.

He always looks smashing; today, he is in a dark grey suit with a dark purple shirt and a pink and purple striped tie. His green eyes stared at me, with his face lit up at the sight of me.

"My darling! What a lovely surprise. I do hope that you will stay for dinner?" he asked.

"Sorry, Uncle, but no," I replied.

His face dropped a little, and I just couldn't have that. "But I will have a cup of tea," I said.

"Smashing, we will have tea in the library. Please come in, dear one. I do hope you are enjoying the car. How is the house looking, and are you settling in okay?" he said as he clapped his hands together. He stepped aside and let me in, and we walked through the halls.

"That's what I wanted to talk to you about," I said.

As we walked towards the library in silence, I couldn't help but remember the day I first knocked on my uncle's door. It was about three months ago that I had walked from my home to my uncle's house. I think I had walked for nearly six hours, maybe longer, carrying a bag in each hand and one case on my back. I had walked up to my uncle's driveway to his front door, hoping that he would not turn me away. I tried to brush myself and my hair down to try and make myself look presentable. Pulling the rope bell, I waited. My uncle came to the door dressed in a black suit, blue shirt, and no tie. He stared at me before he recognised me.

"Layla darling, is that you? What happened to you? You look different. Why are you here?" he asked in a worried tone.

I couldn't say anything. My mouth opened, but nothing came out. All that I did was cry with tears streaming down my face.

"Oh, darling." He pulled me into his arms and hugged me close to him. "Come, you can stay here," he said. He walked me through the house. It looked better than I thought it would. He had nice looking plants throughout the house, lots of plants and vases sitting on small tables and paintings on all the walls. He had suits of armour decorated through his home; it felt like a mishmash of items.

Still, it felt warm and inviting; this feeling caused even more tears to stream down my face. My uncle grabbed hold of my hand and gave it a gentle squeeze. He led me through a massive set of double doors when the bright sunlight blinded me. Once the spots had faded from my eyes, I stood facing an extensive library that takes up three floors.

There are books, books, and even more books in there. There had to be thousands of them, but that wasn't the only thing in there. There were heaps of plants, a lounge suite, tables and glass cabinets with objects in and on them. Some held books; others had swords and other weapons. I was amazed at the splendour of it. Uncle led me to a lounge where we sat down. A few minutes later, a lady with a tea tray came in, set it down in front of us, and then left. My uncle poured our tea. We sat in silence for several minutes before either one of us spoke.

"Do you want to tell me what's going on?" he asked. I smiled at my uncle but didn't say a thing.

"Very well, my little Layla, you may stay here for as long as you like. When you are ready, you can tell me, but for now, we will have our tea and get you settled into a room," he said.

Again, I just smiled at my uncle. I felt grateful that he didn't turn me away.

Here I was again sitting on one of the soft lounges drinking tea.

"So, little Layla, what's the matter?"

'Where do I start? There are many things bothering me; the house, the yard, my neighbour Mrs Davis trying to force her son's presence on me and the biggest, my neighbour Eric, but I start with the easy things.'

"My house isn't right, and I don't know what it is, but it's not right," I explained.

"How do you mean, darling?"

"Not sure," I replied.

My uncle gives me a quizzing look and raises one eyebrow. It takes a split second to realise that he is referring to home, but it's not that, but maybe it is.

"Darling, do you have plants, paintings, anything to make it look like a home? What about the gardens? I know you still don't have a hobby, have you met your neighbours? Are they nice?" he asked.

So many questions, and I only have answers to some. My uncle is correct. I don't have any of those things he said, no plants, no paintings, I still don't have a hobby, and I haven't even attempted to start creating gardens. I have only just finished unpacking, and maybe, therefore, I don't feel a hundred per cent. My house feels sterile.

"You are right; I don't have any of those things, you know, I don't have a hobby. I never had one back at home either."

"I know you like to sew." I do like to sew. After all these years, I can't believe that he remembers that he puts his tea down and clasps his hands together.

"Good, it's settled. I will have James send another truck with plants and other items. Francis will rearrange one of your spare rooms into a sewing room, and I expect to see a gown in two months. I have a masquerade ball to go to, and I would like your company," he said.

I am sitting there with my mouth slightly open, but he doesn't seem to notice. I don't know what was more shocking: he is sending even more things over or the fact that he wants me to go to a ball with him.

Going to these things has never been my idea of fun. I don't want to go. I love my uncle, but this is going too far.

He is pushing like my father, and I don't want that; my father would be the same.

"I want you there at noon and not a minute late or else," he said.

"I want an uncle, a friend. Not a father," I said.

"Uncle?" he said, looking startled.

I stared at him with sad eyes; my uncle's face softened.

"Oh, I'm sorry, darling, I only want what's best and what will make you happy."

My father would say the same thing, and nothing he did could make me happy. I knew that everything he said was and will always be a lie. I don't want to go back to living like that.

I agreed to let my uncle buy the house, furniture, and clothes, only because he said he wanted it as an investment property. I could live there, rent-free for as long as I wanted, was his request.

"Be happy and live your life your way," were his exact words.

But now he is pushing again. I put down my tea and get up to go. My uncle opens his mouth to say something but changes his mind and closes his mouth. He lets me leave.

We say our goodbyes. My uncle tells me that James and Francis will be there when he gets the chance. He said 'sorry' once again.

I hug and kiss him goodbye.

It took less time to pull into my driveway than it took to drive to my uncle's.

I realised I should have left the car at my uncle's, and I should have walked home because this was another gift from him, but the thought quickly vanishes from my mind when I look next door to Eric's house.

I get out of the car to breathe, breathe with deep breaths. I cut across our lawns, and I stand staring at Eric's screen door, and I repeat, I can do this. I raise my hand and knock on his door. I stand and wait. I hear footsteps, then the sound of the lock turned on the screen door.

It opened to reveal a woman standing in the doorway; not just any woman; a tall, long-legged and scarcely dressed woman. She radiates hostility and power, and I cannot help but feel intimidated by her. I am starting to feel a little depressed and a little upset. Of course, he would have a beautiful girlfriend. I shouldn't have knocked.

"Can I help you?" her voice oozed venom, and it was all directed at me.

"I was wondering if Eric was here," I asked.

"Why do you want to know?" she replied.

That's a bit rude. She could be just a little bit polite, I thought. I won't tell her anything, not with that attitude.

"You're that dull creature from next door, aren't you?" she said.

White-hot anger surged in me. I wanted to rip her throat out. How dare she call me a dull creature? I was a forceful person back home, but here I so wanted to act calm. I suppose that calmness resembles meekness but calling me a dull creature is going too far. How quickly I could reach out and tear out her throat. "Well, are you going to answer me?"

No, I am not, you nasty piece of… stop that, was what I wanted to say. But I don't stoop to that level.

"I just wanted to thank Eric for his help last week; that was all," I replied.

"Were you hoping that he felt something for you? Well, forget it, Eric is mine. I suggest that you just stay the hell away from him, or I may have to get nasty, and you don't want that because I will make your life a living hell. Do I make myself clear? Just stay away from him," she said as she slammed the door in my face. I stood there for a minute, just staring at the door. Then it hit me again; of course, he has a girlfriend. I take a deep breath in and let it out. I walk back home with my back as tall and as straight as I can without falling to pieces. I just didn't think that his girl would be so nasty. 'You could be polite while telling me that you're his girl' were my thoughts.

I open my door and see how sterile my house is. She may have one thing right. I was dull. I had no life in my home, nothing that screamed that I lived here. I will be grateful when my uncle sends over James and Francis. But for now, there is one place I can breathe life into, and that's my back garden.

4

Layla

Changing into my gardening clothes, I'm ready to attack the jungle. The back garden is so overgrown that I don't know where to start. I stare out to the left, in the back corner. There is a big old oak tree, and the base is covered with overgrown grass and weeds. In the right corner of the yard is a small tool shed, and that too is overgrown and strangled with weeds and shrubs.

The backyard is also covered in bricks, edging, rocks, and other bits of debris scattered all over the place, including the patio where I am standing. I can't tell if there were once garden beds here amongst the heavily infested overgrown weeds. I was a little surprised that the backyard looked like this as there was a mowed front yard.

I had to work out which was the best way to attack this? I guess I could always use the wheelbarrow for any plants that I manage to find that I want to keep and replant. I can always pile the weeds and rubbish up near the tool shed. I can keep what edging, bricks, and rocks I can salvage and reuse. I am pleased with my thoughts, and I just throw myself into work with my yard.

I was in the yard for a good couple of hours before time got away, and it was into the night. Now I sit on the concrete patio with a cup of tea, looking out over the partially weeded forest that is still my backyard. I have visions of what I can do with it. The answer is simple; I want peace, and I want beauty.

Over the next week, I had pulled every weed and bit of debris out. I saved what plants survived the strangling. I mowed where I could, and it finally started to look like a bit of a yard instead of an overgrown weeded jungle. I hadn't finished the garden beds yet. I was exhausted, but that is the next thing on the list.

In that same week, James came around with a large truck and put large indoor plants and ferns throughout the house. My generous uncle gave me several of his Tanya Loviz originals and several cast-iron self-standing roses. My house was starting to look like a home, although it still lacked something.

Francis came in and took measurements and said he would be back. When he did come back, he came back with a vengeance. Francis was like a hurricane. He moved me out of the master bedroom and into the next most significant room. Apart from not having an ensuite or the extra-large walk-in wardrobe Francis made my new bedroom look cosy and perfect.

Francis said, "Bedrooms were for sleeping in; the rest of the house and the world is for your life."

He grabbed my arm and dragged me into my new sewing room, which used to be my master bedroom. It looked perfect, a truly remarkable transformation. I have the latest sewing machine, the most expensive threads, needles and fabric. Everything and anything that you could think of is in here. I had nothing like this back home.

It's been nearly a month since I moved in. I spent most of the mornings and afternoons in the backyard, creating flower beds and making a peaceful place to relax.

I have put a beautiful two-seater wooden bench under the oak tree and have placed an archway in the centre of the yard. It's starting to become covered in vines, right behind the arch; I've put a fountain.

I've made a pathway around the fountain through to the archway onto the patio. I also managed to find the clothesline. I found it attached to the right side of the house, which is a good place for it as I won't have any of my clothes messing up my garden view. But today, I felt that I had neglected the front yard. Yes, I mowed the grass, but I haven't done anything else, and the weeds were starting to creep into it. Today, I shall venture out the front and make it just as lovely as my backyard.

5

Eric

Another day and I still haven't had a chance to talk to her. Yes, I have seen her, and yes, I have wanted to go over there. Every opportunity I get, I see her, but her boyfriend's four hundred-thousand-dollar car is sitting in the driveway. I would have Gareth over, but worst of all, Becca would grace me with her presence. I knew why she was coming over; she was trying to stop me from seeing Layla, and it was working,

Today is no different, but at least it's Gareth and not Becca. Gareth and I got a bit messy last night, so he crashed in one of my spare rooms. He keeps a stash of clothes here for times like that, but now he is downstairs waiting for me to get ready so that we can have lunch with his dad.

"Yo, E-man, does that new chick have long brown hair and a tight ass?" he yelled from the bottom of the stairs. Oh crap, I bet Layla is out the front, she has spent the past month in her backyard, and now she must be in the front yard working. I don't want him going over there because he will grab her ass for sure.

I race downstairs, only wrapped in a towel, but I am too late. Gareth is already out the door and across the yard. I am also stunned to move as I watch him move closer to her. She is leaning over her garden, pulling out weeds. That's when he put his hands on her, but what I saw next had me running out the door. As soon as his hand had touched her in one quick blinding move, she had grabbed his hand and flipped him. He

30

had landed hard. I could hear the thump. In that same motion, she sat astride him with a pair of pruning shears up against his throat. I ran across the yards shouting, "Layla, stop!" but she wasn't listening.

"What gives you the right to touch me?" she said in a cold as ice voice.

"Layla!" I yelled. She heard me this time, and when she turned to look at me, her eyes are a piercing grey-blue.

"That's my friend Gareth; he meant no harm by it."

Layla breathed in and closed her eyes. She let the breath out and opened her eyes. They seemed to have gone back to her ordinary storm over the ocean colour. She looked down at Gareth and noticed that the shears were starting to draw blood. Layla dropped them and jumped off Gareth standing, staring at his neck. "I'm so sorry," she said as she held out her hand to Gareth, but he just pushed her hand away.

"Ya already kicked my ass. I don't need to be humiliated any further than I already am," he said with a sly grin. He got up, brushed himself down, and held out his hand to Layla. "I'm Gareth," he said.

She took a tentative step forward. "Layla," she said as she shook his hand.

When they broke apart, Gareth walked back to the house. As he passed me, he put his hand on my shoulder. He looked down at me, looked back at my face, raised an eyebrow, laughed, and then walked back to the house. On his way back, he waved over his shoulder, saying, "See ya next time Lala."

I don't think she had heard him because her eyes are raking up and down my body, stopping several times at my towel then staying at my chest. I wish she wouldn't look at me like that. She affects me in ways I don't understand. I want to go over to her and put my arms around her. I watch as she turns that lovely shade of pink that I like so much. I think it has something to do with the fact that I'm only wearing a towel, but I start to get nervous with her storm-coloured eyes on me.

"I…I…should…." Crap, how does Layla do this to me? "I should go." I can't think straight around her, so I just turn and walk away.

As I walk into my house, Gareth has his feet up on the coffee table, reading a magazine, acting as if he just didn't get flipped onto his back by a girl. I am thankful that he has put a cloth on his bleeding neck; I don't want his blood all over my lounge.

"I like her; she's feisty," he said.

I stare at him; he just keeps on reading his mag. I need a shower. Gareth looks at me, then at the towel wrapped around my waist, and laughs.

I race upstairs and throw my towel onto the bed, and I take another shower. All the while, I was thinking of Layla and nothing else. Her hair, the way she would smile, the way she would talk to her plants in the backyard. I would stand on my balcony, and I would watch her. She would sing as she attacked that jungle of a yard; I did get freaked out one day when Layla was digging up weeds.

I saw a snake moving towards her. I was about to call out to her when she turned towards it and said hello. She picked it up, moved it to the other side of the yard, and went back to the weeding. I would watch her every chance I could get. All I wanted was to be with her, not understanding why, so I kept watching, hoping that I would work it out.

My bathroom door opens, and Gareth is standing in the doorway. This guy has no boundaries.

"Ya girl is super-hot, man, and she is in the backyard," he blurted out.

I turn the shower off, quickly get out and wrap a towel around me. I rushed out to the second storey balcony off my bedroom, I stood and searched Layla's yard, but she wasn't there.

"E-man, you got it bad," he said as he shakes his head and puts his hand on my shoulder.

"We gotta get going, so hurry up, or I am leaving your sorry ass here, and I'll call Becca and tell her that you want her," he said.

Damn, I hate him sometimes. He walks out of my room.

"I'll be down in ten," I shout back at him.

As I move back into my room, a shimmer caught my eye; I look over at Layla's backyard. I see her walking in her yard carrying a silver cup of sorts in her hands. That's a little strange, I thought. She walks along the path and heads straight for the fountain, where she pours in the contents. She leaves the cup by the fountain, then makes her way towards the oak tree. Layla sits on the wooden bench seat and leans her head back. She would be looking at me if her eyes weren't closed.

I wanted to go down there just to be near her. I would walk up to her, pull her up and into my arms, run my fingers through her hair, kiss those perfect lips, that beautiful neck. I would then run my hands down her back. I had to stop myself there, or I would have to go back for a third shower. I went back inside and put on some silk boxers, jeans, and a button shirt. We were going to Gareth's dads for lunch. This man never stood on ceremony and wouldn't care if you turned up in Ugg boots and a pair of boxers. I head downstairs, and I see Gareth is sitting on the lounge with his feet up on the coffee table reading a magazine.

"About time," he said as he throws the magazine on the table and makes his way out the door. I quickly check the house, giving Layla's home

a quick look as I get into Gareth's car.

It is after eleven when Gareth drops me off; he wasn't staying tonight. He had to go over to his restaurant/ nightclub, 'The Cavern'; apparently, there is an emergency in the kitchen, and he had to go. That is fine, I thought, as I wanted to be alone tonight in any case. I make my way upstairs. I was planning on just going to bed, but I could hear a faint voice, so I go out onto the balcony and see Layla sitting on her seat under the tree. She appears to be talking to herself.

Layla

I like him, but I don't know what to do about it. I have never felt this way, she was saying. There is a pause in her conversation as if someone is answering her.

My heart won't stop trying to escape my chest, and I don't know how to breathe. I don't like feeling this way; it's troubling. I wonder if she has an earpiece and on the phone.

I can't be in love. Why does my heart feel broken? She covers her face with her hands. I thought being in love and feeling this way is every girl's dream. Well, I'm not going to stand here and listen to her talk about another man? But one can only dream that she is talking about me and that she loves me.

I move back inside with that thought swirling around in my head as I make my way to my bed. Before nightfall, my last thoughts are of Layla charging into my room, telling me that she loves me, of her crawling into bed next to me, and spending the night making love to her.

6

Layla

Most of my day was spent gardening in the yard. I moved into my sewing room, but the day's events wouldn't let me sleep. I was still sewing the gown my uncle wanted me to make. But none of this did anything for my inability to sleep or for my wandering thoughts. I couldn't get Eric out of my mind, and I felt terrible for what I had done to his friend.

I spent most of my time thinking about how I had attacked him, how Eric came over in just a towel. I couldn't stop staring. I did enjoy staring at his well-toned body. All I wanted to do was run my hands up and down his chest. I want to drag him inside, but then I would remember the tall blonde.

That was when I went into the backyard. I went and sat under the oak tree, and I tried not to think about Eric, but it didn't work. All I could think about was the countless times I had climbed the tree and hid amongst the branches just watching him.

I would watch him working out in his outdoor gym or when he mowed his yard. I even watched him while he was on his balcony after he got out of the shower. He was wearing nothing but a towel. That towel is my favourite thing in his house, apart from him, of course. When I saw him on his balcony, there was more than one occasion where I saw his tall, leggy blonde girlfriend wrap her arms around him. I would turn away and jump out of the tree and leave him to his girlfriend.

Depressed, I would go into my sewing room and make alterations to the gown. That is where I am now. I am trying to focus on my masquerade gown, but it isn't working. I need to clear my head. I need to go outside. Once again, I leave it on the table and make my way out of the room. My phone rings as I pass by it. My phone is another present from my uncle, and it was my uncle on the phone. I notice the microwave tells me it's after eleven at night.

"Hello, Uncle," I said.

"Hello, my darling, how are you?" he asked.

I venture outside and sit down under the oak tree.

"Okay, I guess… It's just…." I muttered.

'How can I tell him all about Eric? I can't, and I don't want him to know, at least not just yet?' were my thoughts.

"Is it about a boy? Please, my child, you can tell me anything. I will not judge you, nor will I get upset with you," he said inquiringly.

It's nice to hear that he wants to listen, but I don't feel right about it. I have never been able to tell anyone anything in all my life, and now that I have a chance to, I can't.

"It is about a boy. I like him, and I don't know what to do about it. I have never felt this way," I explained.

"What way, my darling?" he replied.

At least he hasn't asked for his name, were my thoughts.

"My heart won't stop trying to escape my chest, and I don't know how to breathe. I don't like feeling this way; it's troubling," I said in a troubled voice.

I could almost hear the smirk on his face.

"It sounds as if you are in love," he said.

'No! No, I can't be. I don't want to be.' My thoughts were confused; I didn't know what I should be feeling.

I bury my face in my hands and mumble into the phone. "No, Uncle. I can't be; he has a girlfriend. He doesn't want me the way I want him. I doubt he sees me the way I see him. I can't be in love."

"It's okay, darling. I am sure it will all work out; he will like you. How could he not? You are a beautiful person, my darling," he said.

"You only say that because you're my uncle," I said while weeping.

"Not true … well mostly true, has it made you smile?" he said in good faith.

"A little, thank you, Uncle. Goodnight, Uncle," I said.

"Goodnight, my darling," he said.

I hung up and decided to go to bed. I crawled into bed and replayed the day's events in my head. I couldn't get past the vision of Eric in his towel at this moment; a pleasant heat flooded my body. I started to drift off. Images began to flash behind my eyelids of Eric in his towel coming into my room and pulling me out of bed, walking me to the shower. The shower was already running; steam was already engulfing the bathroom. There was a sweet scent surrounding us; Eric pulled me into the shower with him. I was still fully clothed, and he had nothing on but his towel. He pulled me into his embrace and started to kiss me. The image began to fade as the darkness took me.

I woke the following day wishing Eric was lying next to me. I was the only one in my bed. I went to roll over and go back to sleep, but I thought better of it. I have to get up and finish my gown, I haven't got too much longer to go before the big event, and I need supplies, so I best be getting on.

7

Eric

It's been a couple of weeks since the incident with Gareth and Layla, and I still haven't had a chance to talk with her, though I never miss the opportunity to watch her in her yard. One morning last week, she was out in her backyard when I stepped out onto my balcony. She must have heard me because Layla looked at me and smiled. I smiled and waved at her, and she turned that beautiful shade of pink I like so much.

The day of one of many charity events that happen in Skyhaven is here. Once again, I don't plan on going. I am so bored with them. Nothing exciting happens at any of the. I haven't seen her for the past couple of days; she must be locked away indoors with Mr four hundred-thousand-dollar car. How I want it to be me, so I am in no mood to go anywhere.

Beep beep. There goes another message on my phone. I have been getting these all morning—beep beep.

And quite frequently, I better check it.

Gareth: 'E-man ya coming?'

Eric: 'Nope.'

Becca: 'I hope you are coming.

Eric: 'Nope again.'

Becca: 'You can pick me up at 8 pm.

Eric: 'No way in hell.'

Gareth: 'Dude y aren't ya texting back?

Eric: 'Ignoring you all.'

Gareth: 'It's her, isn't it?

Eric: 'So, what.'

Gareth: 'Come out and party with me.

Eric: 'Nope, Becca's going.'

Becca: 'Please come; I can't wait for you to see the dress I picked out just for you.

Eric: 'Nope, and you don't wear dresses; you wear bandanas and call it a dress.'

Gareth: 'E-man gotta come. I will keep Becca at bay for you so that you can try and relax.'

Gareth: 'E-man! I will come over and beat the snot out of you and dress you in your tux all bloody to boot.'

All the messages now are from Becca as I told Gareth that I was coming for a few hours and saying nothing to psycho Becca that I would be there. I didn't need her crap, not tonight.

I went downstairs at lunchtime and saw Layla receive a box of flowers. I wish I could spoil her. I would give her anything.

I was going into the kitchen to make myself something to eat. When I sat back down with my steak sandwich, I saw a limo pulling out of her driveway, I took one look at my lunch, and I threw it away.

Around eight o'clock, I got dressed in my tux and got ready to leave. I had sent a text to Gareth earlier to let him know not to send his car because I found Becca in it the last time he did. I could make a quick getaway if I had my car, were my thoughts.

At 9:15 pm, I pulled up out of the front of the Stanhope Convention Centre. A valet came and took my car, and I showed my invitation at the door. I had received my invite about a month ago, which I had ignored. You didn't need to RSVP to this event; you just needed to turn up. This one is the 'Annual Stanhope Masquerade Ball', which raises money for the 'Make A Wish Foundation'. I put my black mask on and walked inside. The lobby was alive with so many people.

Some are just skiting about how expensive their clothes are, while others are looking at the items you could bid on in the silent auction. I chose to go the other option, and I will drop a cheque in the well. I just witnessed about three people donate bundles of money in the well, and one of them was Lloyd Peters, one of the billionaire playboys of Skyhaven and a friend. He notices me and walks up to me.

"Good evening Eric, are you alone tonight?" Lloyd said as we shake hands.

"Evening, Lloyd. Yeah, I am alone, I didn't want to come, but I got dragged here by Gareth. What about you?" I said.

"Yeah, same here. I was hoping to spend the night elsewhere but ordered to be here tonight," he said. We start to laugh. We were both pressured into coming tonight. Oh well, I can't do much about that now, were my thoughts. He clasps a hand on my shoulder before saying goodbye and making his way over to David Beacon, another one of Skyhaven's rich playboys and again a friend.

I walked through the doors that led into the main auditorium. There's a sea of men dressed in black tuxedos and a rainbow of colours for the women's clothes. There are waiters with trays of drinks and finger foods; it's never a sit-down meal for this event, always a buffet. The tables and chairs are against the walls to leave maximum room for dancing. I was after the flight of stairs that lead to the second storey balconies, which is where Gareth is going to be, in his private booth, which looks over the orchestra pit. This year they have forgone the orchestra and gone for the rock band. This year they managed to get the brothers' FAN,' Flare and Nova, the only rock band to make it out of Skyhaven, not to mention the best band in Skyhaven.

Beep. Beep.

Gareth: 'Dude upstairs, usual spot when you get here.'

Taking the stairs that lead off to the room's left-hand side, I pass a couple of couples making out on the stairs and in the hallways. I walk to the far box, and I reach the one with the drape closed and a rope across the front saying 'reserved' and standing on guard is one of the bouncers of 'The Cavern'. I nod as I step over the rope. Walking through the curtain and in the front row with his feet up on the rail is Gareth. For once, he isn't reading a magazine. This time he is playing with his phone. Nothing phases Gareth, the only time he lets his Irish temper go is at his restaurant/nightclub.

"E-man, so glad you could make it." He didn't even bother to turn around; he must have told his bodyguard not to let anyone in but me. I sit down next to him, but I don't put my feet up.

"Who are you texting?" I asked.

"Becca. She wants to know if you have turned up yet." I just can't get away from her.

"What have you told her?" I asked.

"That ya backed out last minute and went to The Cavern, but I don't think she believes me," Gareth replied.

No surprise there, I don't know why she wants me so badly, were my thoughts.

"You talked to your girl yet?" Gareth asked.

I just rolled my eyes at him. I didn't want to talk about it.

"Yeah, well, tonight, E-man, you are going to drink and get

ya freak on, with some random to take your mind off Lala," Gareth said.

He didn't look up once from his phone. There is no way that I am going to do that; he knows me better than that. I don't do one-night stands.

"Shit! You have been here what… five minutes, and she has already seen you." Gareth said.

"It's all cool. I just sent a message to Phil. He will stop her for now, but you are going to have to go downstairs and pick out your random so that you can hide in the crowd. Let's pick you a girl," Gareth said.

I shake my head—what a shitty night. I knew I should have just stayed home. Gareth stands up and looks over the balcony and into the crowd.

"Found her!" I leap to my feet, thinking he is talking about Layla when I realise that she wouldn't be here, but then again, maybe she is here with Mr 'four hundred-thousand-dollar car', but he is referring to the one-night stand, but I don't do that. I look out over the crowd, and I see to whom he is pointing in an instant.

The girl that Gareth was pointing out was not Layla, but a girl standing in the doorway looking around lost, not sure of where to go. Her long dress hugs her nicely. It's the kind of dress that leaves everything to the imagination, and you would love to take her out of it. It's blue and has purple and green through it, but what makes her stand out is her dress, mask, and hair covered in lace, ribbons, and flowers. You can almost smell her sweet scent up here.

I take a closer look at her and notice that the mask is attached to her hair. If you take off her mask, it will cause her hair to cascade down her back. She is looking around the room. She looks down at herself then looks at the other women in the room. I can see her face go red as if she has become self-conscious about her appearance, almost like she has too much fabric. But I liked that about a woman. I am not too fond of the idea of a female dressing in small extra tight, and barely-there clothes – like what Becca wears. I would enjoy making my way through the layers of clothes to find her beautiful curves underneath.

"Look, man, you only need to blend into the crowd, that's all, and if she rejects you, you can head over to the Cavern and drown your sorrows. I'll do my best at keeping Becca away." Gareth said.

Yeah, right, she will find me. She always does, I was thinking.

Fine, I don't want to, but I will keep him happy, and if he can keep Becca out of my hair, I will be satisfied. We both leave the balcony. I move off towards the main doors while Gareth goes to find Becca. As I make my way closer to the girl, I can hear her say 'Thank you, but no,' and 'Please excuse me.' Her voice is sweet and very familiar. I was about to reach her when she pushed past someone saying, 'Thank you, but no.' She wasn't paying attention, and she runs straight into me; she almost falls backwards. I manage to grab onto her and keep her from falling. I pull her into me, grasping a tight hold on her. I stare into her face. I can see glitter around her grey eyes, her storm over the ocean eyes, Layla's eyes.

"Layla?" I questioned.

She looks at me, studies me momentarily, a smile spreads across her face, and she then melts into the tight hold I have on her.

"Hello, Eric," she said.

How sweet the sound of my name on her lips is. I once again couldn't think straight. I said the first thing that popped into my head.

"Dance with me," I asked.

What I wanted to say was, my god, you're beautiful. But no,

I asked her to dance with me instead, not that it's a bad thing. A thought then momentarily occurred to me, 'her boyfriend'. He must be around here somewhere, but one dance wouldn't hurt, would it?

"What about your girlfriend?" Layla questioned.

What an odd thing to say. I don't have a girlfriend. I don't know why she would think that. Becca! She thinks my girlfriend is Becca. Time to make her a little bit happy.

"No girlfriend," I replied.

A huge smile spread across her face, and then her hands gripped tighter to me.

"Would your boyfriend mind if I stole you for one dance?" I questioned.

Confusion swept across her face.

"What boyfriend?" she replied.

What does she mean by that? I have seen him and his four hundred-thousand-dollar car.

"The young man with the Bentley, the one I always see in your driveway," I replied.

She started to laugh. It would have been nice to hear her laugh all the time, but not this; it feels very mocking.

"That's my car," she said.

"What?" I said curiously.

"My uncle thought I might need a car, so he sent over his personal assistant James to drop the car off. James had his boyfriend, Francis, come pick him up."

God, don't I feel like a jackass, and now there is one way to move forward.

"Dance with me." I again asked.

8

Layla

My heart leapt out of my chest. "Of course, I will." Eric smiled at me. I was glad that he is still holding me because I swear that I go weak at the knees every time he smiles. Eric moves his arm around my waist and guides me to the middle of the dance floor.

There is a rock band playing up on the stage, and they are playing a mix of music. We stepped out onto the dance floor when they switched to a slow song, and he kept his arms around me. I hope he can't feel how hard and fast my heart is beating.

"You look amazing, Layla," I said with a smile.

I could feel myself going pink, and I thought I looked out of place.

"You don't look too bad yourself," I said.

Groan… why did I say that, but Eric laughed and tried to draw me even closer to him; he leaned in close to my ear.

"I'm glad you don't have a boyfriend. Perhaps we can spend some time together. What do you think?" Eric said.

I think my heart stopped before it started to race, and I began to gasp for breath. Eric wanted me, but before I could say anything, somebody ripped Eric from my arms.

"What do you think you are doing with her?" It was that tall blonde who I always saw at his place. There wasn't much to her dress; it looks as if she has one mask covering her eyes, one

45

covering her breast and one her hips, not to mention I didn't like the way she said 'her'. Eric stood in front of me to guard me.

"Listen here, Becca, I don't know what goes on in that head of yours, but we are not together, and we will never be together. If you don't give up this pursuit, I will ensure that all business ties are severed," Eric explained.

She stood tall and fierce-looking. The people around us were starting to stare at us. He held out his hand for me. As I reached for his hand, she grabbed it.

"Is this about that dull creature next door?" Becca snarled.

Rage, cold-hearted rage filled me, I stepped around Eric and stood in front of her, and I slapped her across the face. I would have punched her, but that would have been unladylike, so I settled for the slap. Everyone stopped, the music included. I could sense the vibes with everyone staring at us.

"If you so much as call me a dull creature again, I will pull one of those chopsticks out of your hair and stab you with it. Now, if you don't mind, I would like to continue with my dance," I said in an abrupt tone.

I looked around and noticed that everyone has their mouths open and their phones out, but when I looked at Eric, he had a grin on his face. He steps up next to me and pulls me in close.

"Let's get out of here," Eric said.

We walk through the staring crowd and out to the lobby. Eric releases the hold on me but takes my hand. We step up to the valet. He hands over his ticket as we waited impatiently for his car.

He said, "You didn't have to slap her, although she did deserve it."

He turns and faces me, his eyes fixed on mine. They are full of warmth and desire. They appeared full of what could only be described as love. I can almost hear my heart screaming yes and my head screaming no at me. Do I dare to hope that it is love that I see and feel coming from him, or am I just wishfully hoping he feels the same?

"You do know that I would have defended your honour," Eric said.

"I have no doubts about that. It's just that was the second time Becca has called me a dull creature, and that was two times too many." I explained.

"When was the first time?" Eric asked.

Eric's car turned up, he opened the door for me, I got in, but I felt like I was sitting on the ground. It was unusually low but had very comfy seats. Eric took his mask off, threw it over to the back seat, and got his iPod going; its volume is down. You could only hear it.

"When was the first time?" He asks me again.

I told him about the day I came over with the invite for dinner, apologising for my behaviour and how she answered the door. He pulled out into the traffic and tore off down the road.

"You can cook," he asked.

I couldn't tell if it meant to be a statement or a question.

"Do you think I can't cook?" I replied.

"Most girls that I know can't cook," he said.

I'm a little upset by that comment. Eric should know by now that I am not like the girls he knows.

"I am not most girls," I tell him.

"You most definitely are not," he said.

I couldn't help but laugh. I like the smile on Eric's face as he spoke. His smile is warm, and his face is all soft and goofy looking. He reaches over with his hand and holds mine, giving it a little squeeze.

Beep Beep. Beep Beep. Beep Beep. Beep Beep. Eric's phone

is going nuts.

"Is that her?" I asked.

"It will be most likely Gareth, not Becca," he replied.

He saw my face when he mentioned Gareth's name. Eric explained that he is his friend and, more to the point, the friend I flipped on his back and nicked his throat with my shears. Not that I want to remember much of that, apart from Eric coming over in nothing but a towel. And that is one image I can't get out of my head, not that I want to.

"I am sorry about that," I replied.

"Don't be. Gareth can be a little sleazy on occasions and a womaniser, but he is a good guy," Eric said.

He gave my hand a slight squeeze.

"Where are we going?" I asked. Noticing we were going in the opposite direction to home.

"Our evening got interrupted, and I would like to dance with you some more, but more importantly, have you eaten yet?"

"No, I haven't eaten," I replied.

I looked down at myself, and I felt at my face with my free hand. I'm too overdressed to go to dinner.

Eric looks handsome, though.

"See, all you did was take your mask off, and now you can go anywhere and fit in. I can't, and I am well and truly overdressed," I explained.

"Not for where we are going, you're not. I said it before, and I will repeat it. I think you look amazing. I saw lots of men in that place, staring at you. I know I was, and I still would be if I didn't have to drive," he said.

I felt my body rise in temperature, and I have no doubts I was as red as I felt hot.

"Can you take your mask off?" Eric asked.

"I can, but it's holding everything together. If I take it off, my hair and flowers come with it, and your car will be full of flowers, not to mention the glitter," I explained.

"That's fine because then the car will smell like you," he replied.

Two very corny lines in just as many minutes, and I don't care. I like it. I start to tug and pull and loosen my mask without causing the least amount of damage to my hair.

"You still haven't told me where we are going," I said.

"We are almost there," he said.

It seemed like that was all I was going to get from him. We have been in the car for about fifteen minutes, maybe less. Eric drove fast; then we pulled up in front of a two-storey building. Eric gets out of the driver's seat. He makes his way around to my side of the car and opens the door. I still haven't gotten the mask off yet. I try to rush, but as I do, a large amount of glitter and flowers fall all over the floor of his car.

"Don't rush me," I say.

It takes another full three minutes to get the mask off, and with half my hair and flowers still intact, Eric holds his hand out for me. I take it as he helps me out of the car. I look around and see a young man in black and red waiting for Eric's keys. After I am out of the vehicle, Eric hands his keys over to the young man.

We are standing on the sidewalk staring at a large industrial building that reads, 'The Cavern'. A large square area sits around the front doors, and there is an area roped off for VIPs. There are two lines of people, one on the left-hand side of the wall and one running along the right side. Eric walks straight to the ropes. He speaks to the bouncer, who lets us walk straight in.

"Evening Greg." He says to the bouncer who lets us through.

"Eric, you are looking sharp tonight," Greg commented.

He sees me, and his mouth drops open, "Good evening Miss," Greg said. I don't say much, but I give him a big smile.

We step through the main doors, and it is massive inside; the ground floor is an enormous lobby. There is a huge bar that takes up all the back walls. Behind the bar, through a small window, you can see the kitchen staff running around. The whole floor is covered in lounges, tables, chairs and plants, not to mention many people. More double doors, and we see wait staff serving food and drinks. The wait staff disappear behind a wall just in front of the double doors. I will hazard a guess that there are sets of stairs that lead to the top floor. To the very left of me, just inside the entrance, there are two men behind a rope dressed in black, and this is the VIP Lounge, only a certain number of people allowed in.

Eric still has a hold of my hand. He leads me towards the man on the right-hand side of me. We walk up to him, and he then pulls the rope aside.

"Hello, Brett," Eric said.

"Hey Eric, it's all ready. Gareth called in your reservation," Brett said.

Eric nods at Brett. We start to walk up a set of stairs with all earthy brown colours with the roof and part of the walls covered in fairy lights.

"What's going on?" I asked.

"Not yet," Eric replied.

When we reach the top, the floor just opens into a magical setting. Earthy colours and fairy lights continue all along the walls and roof. Amongst the earthy browns are greens, there are plants dotted all around the room. Amongst the plants are small tables. The plants create a sense of peace, intimacy and privacy. The most prominent tables seat six, and there isn't too many of them.

A waiter stands behind the bar on the right side of the wall. Around the right back corner, there is a DJ and a dance floor there too. Eric leads me towards a young blonde woman who is standing behind a podium.

"Hello, Eric, I have your table waiting for you," she said.

"Thank you, Cathy. How is your husband?"

Eric replied.

"He is well, thank you, "Cathy replied.

Cathy grabs the menus and shows us to our table, a lovely setting hidden away in the corner where some plants sit near the table. This 12-seater table appears to be important; it is cordoned off with a plaque that says private. She unhooks the rope and gestures for us to a seat. Eric guides me to the booth part of the seating. I sit down, and he sits next to me, and as he did, I could feel my skin turning pink as my blood warms up from flushing.

Cathy hands over the menus. Eric ordered a bottle of wine, some garlic bread and bruschetta and told her not to hurry back for the rest of the order.

We sit in silence. Eric is just sitting, staring at me. I could feel myself start to get a bit self-conscience. I can feel my heart racing, and I feel my body getting hot and, no doubt, turning red. I began to bite my bottom lip. I can't stand this silence at the moment. I just want to hear him speak.

"Mm, are you going to tell me how we just bypassed the normal routine to be sitting here in this charming setting?" I asked.

"Gareth," he replied.

"Gareth? Care to elaborate on that," I said curiously.

Just then, Cathy came back with our wine; she poured our glasses and left. Eric is the first to try the wine.

"Not as good as your family's wine, but not bad perhaps?" he said with a smile.

I take a sip of mine, and he is right; it's sweet but not the same as the family wine, but then again, I am a little biased. It doesn't taste as strong, but it is lovely.

"Gareth owns this place," Eric said.

I was stunned. The man I flipped onto his back and nicked with my shears owns this place.

"All of it?" I ask, and Eric laughs.

"Yes, all of it, and we are currently sitting in a four-star restaurant. You are more than fine with the way you are dressed, flowers and all. Now, as you saw when we walked in, there are two lines outside and two bouncers inside," he said.

I nod. Just then, our bread turns up. I take a piece of the garlic bread and bite into it. The bread breaks apart, the bottom is crunchy, and the top has a light toasting. The garlic butter is deliciously rich and creamy.

"The line with the bouncer to the left deal with nightclub patrons. The nightclub is downstairs in the basement—the line and the bouncer on the right deal with the restaurant. The people in the main part have either finished dancing or finished their meal, and they are having a drink before they leave or waiting for takeaway. Gareth takes great pride in this place." Eric explained.

"Why isn't he here working?" I realised the answer just after the question left my lips.

"He is at the fundraiser we just left." That I knew, his phone kept going off in the car when we left.

"Each year, he holds a fundraiser for the Make A Wish foundation, and it gets bigger each year. He used to hold it here, but it got too big, so he moved it to the convention centre."

We sat and talked for hours. Eric had ordered our meals and dessert and the meal was excellent. Our conversation began on how he and Gareth became friends. Then spoke about his life and his work as a personal trainer; he skipped out communication around his family. I told him I moved out here to my uncle's. I told him about the forest surrounding the family winery and how I liked to spend my time there when I could, which was almost not at all. I, too, skipped over my family.

But as the night went on, we moved closer together. I am sitting right next to him with our legs are touching. He has a hold of my hand and is drawing small circles with his thumb. I stare into those striking blue eyes. His other hand reached up and cupped my face. He starts to lean over to kiss me.

'Ahem. No!' My mind screams at me, and I don't argue with it. I think every part of me screamed no. However, it didn't bother Eric. He stayed leaning in towards me, waiting for me to reciprocate.

'Ahem, NO!' This time the voice inside my head reacts a little louder. Eric sighs and then looks at the person behind us, not releasing me from his grasp.

"Yes?" he asked.

"We are closing up," Cathy said.

I was too busy looking at Eric to pay her any attention.

"And?" he replied with his voice sharp and rude. He didn't need to be rude, were my thoughts.

"Eric!" I snapped at him. Whatever hostile emotions he was holding onto were gone when he looked at my face. He then turned back towards Cathy.

"I am sorry, I didn't mean to sound rude," he replied.

We settled our bill, and he held my hand the entire time, only letting go when he had to. The car trip home was lovely and quiet. He holds my hand all the way home and then pulls into my driveway. Eric gets out and races to my side to let me out. Like a gentleman, he walks me to my door.

"You know you could have parked in your driveway," I said.

"But then, I would not have been a gentleman. And I do have to walk you to your front door," he said.

I smile at him for acting so gentleman-like.

"Would you like to come in?" I ask. Please say yes. Again, I agree with my screaming mind.

"I would love to," Eric replied.

YES! I had to stamp all my emotions down for fear I would jump up and down. He followed me inside, and I stand in the doorway, watching him. He stands in the middle of my lounge room, looking at what I had completed with the house set up since the day he helped me.

I started moving towards the kitchen to put the kettle on. If I didn't, I would still be standing in the doorway staring at Eric.

"Would you like a cup of coffee or tea?" I asked.

"Yes, I would love one," he replied.

I almost jump out of my skin because his voice is now right in my ear.

Eric winds his arms around my waist and presses his body up against mine. My breath catches, my heart starts to race. My mind starts to scream at me, telling me I can't, but my body drowns out everything. He places light kisses on the left side of my neck; my heart starts to beat faster. I can only pray he can't feel it because I think only my ribcage is holding it in.

I lean further into him. I tilt my head back so his lips can find more of my skin. His grip tightens around my hips; one arm tightens around me, his other arm winds its way across my body. He runs his hot, smooth hand over my cleavage, making my body heat up even further. I can hear my ragged breathing.

"I have wanted you since the day you moved in," he said.

His breath is just as ragged as mine. I wonder if the beating of my heart I feel isn't his I can feel. I try to lean further into him, but no matter how hard I try, I can't seem to get close enough. I reach my hands behind me. My right hand reaches for his leg, and I can feel how tight with muscles they are, while my left hand reaches up, and I start to run my fingers in his hair.

I try to pull him closer to me, his kisses becoming more urgent, and his grip on my hips tighten. Several moans escape my lips. My mind is telling me STOP! You need to stop this. My mind's saying this isn't right. You-Need-To-Stop. Though I can hear my mind scream at me, my body is craving more of his touch, more of his lips on my body, and my body screams at me to keep going, just to feel him and finally be free and never look back.

I have never felt as hot; I could feel my body starting to fight with itself; the more urgent we are becoming, my body and heart bellowing for me to continue, not to stop. It yelled for more while my mind screamed and screamed at me. My mind screamed for me to stop, that I couldn't do this, that I didn't know what it would cost me.

Still, my body said it was worth it, but my mind was starting to win out. Eric's right hand left my waist and found the zipper on my dress. He began to release it; the word 'no' must have escaped my lips because he stopped about a quarter of the way down. It was enough to free my breasts from the hug of the dress. Please don't notice my scars are my thoughts. He puts his right hand back on my hip. In contrast, his left hand finds my right breast. I'm now finding it hard to stay upright.

'Layla.' His breath catches on my name. The sound of my name on his lips sends my body into overdrive. Just be free. Freedom is what you have wanted; please just let him make you free, were my thoughts.

'Eric.' My body is yelling at me for more of him, but my brain has finally caught up. It wins out, but before I can act on it, he turns me in his arms, and his mouth descends on mine; I sigh into his.

My resolve has melted away, and I start to kiss him back. My arms wrap around his neck while he grabs a firmer grip on my hips. He tries to pull me closer, but he seems to have the same problem; it's just not close enough, and the kiss intensifies. STOP! My brain is winning out; I don't want to stop, but I had to stop, so I put my hands on his chest. I can feel his heart pounding. I can hear the blood pumping in his body, but still, I gently push on his chest. He responds as I hoped he would, and he breaks the kiss.

"What's the matter?" he asks with his voice is ragged and broken.

How do I tell him? I don't think I can explain the truth. I don't know if he would understand. Maybe he would, but how do I say it? He places his forehead on mine, and I stare into his desire-burning blue eyes. I have no doubts that my eyes are saying the same thing.

"Tell me," he said.

Could I tell him, would he laugh at me? He cups my face with his hands and begins drawing circles with his thumb. I almost lose it and melt back into his embrace.

"I…" Nothing, I can say nothing; heat floods my body for a different reason. I can't do it, and like a small child, I break free of his hold and race to my room and close the door behind me.

I am acting like a child. I tear off my dress and grab a set of PJs, not looking to see if they matched or presentable. I sit on my bed for about a minute, kicking myself. I am acting like a scared child. I am stronger than this. I am a fearless person, but since I left home, I have lost that fearlessness. I am acting like that scared little child that I used to be. In my kitchen is the man I've been dreaming about since the day I moved in.

Now here I am acting like this. I run away out of fear and embarrassment, but how can I face Eric now. Just then, there's a knock on my door. I get up, walk over and open the door. Standing in my doorway is Eric with two cups of tea. He looks at me and smiles. I step aside and walk back to the bed and sit down. I pat the spot next to me for him to sit. He stands in front of me and holds out a cup.

"I didn't know how you like it," he said.

I grab the cup, and he sits down next to me. We sit in awkward silence for a few minutes.

I said, "I'm sorry." That was all I could say, and I couldn't think of anything else to say other than sorry.

"Don't apologise. I think I know why you took off like that, and you don't have to apologise for that; it should be me saying sorry," Eric said.

I'm shocked I don't know why he should be sorry he isn't the one that ran away.

"I am surprised you stayed," I said in a tiny voice. Eric placed a hand on my leg and gave me a gentle squeeze.

"I like you, Layla; you have no idea just how much," he said.

"I think I do, and it's the same way I feel," I said. "And I do have to say sorry for pushing you like that, but this one small thing is not going to stop me from pursuing you," I smirk and take a sip of my tea and almost cough it out my nose.

"Don't like it?" he asked.

"Is the fact that it's coming out my nose, a dead giveaway. I need some more milk and sugar with it." I said. He leans over, looks at the mug, takes it from my hand, gets up, and walks to the door.

"Come on," he said, nodding his head towards the kitchen.

I follow him into the kitchen. I watch as he adds more milk to my tea then he searches for the sugar. I can't help but remember what happened in the kitchen not but five minutes ago, and I blush at the thought.

"A little help here," he said.

It is fun watching him search for the sugar.

"In the bowl behind you," I said.

He turned, picked up the jar and showed me the empty bowl.

"See, its empty," he said.

How strange; I swear I filled it this morning with all I had left until I go shopping. I must have had a confused look on my face because Eric said not to worry. He added honey to it instead. He told me it was still going to taste sweet. I sip at it gingerly. He was right. It is delicious and just about the way I like it.

We sit on the lounge in silence as we drink our tea. It is a sweet, comfortable silence, not the awkward silence of my room, though I didn't like the space between us. So, I scooted closer to Eric so that our legs were touching. He places his hand on my thigh and applies small amounts of pressure, making my temperature rise and causing my heart to flutter. I want him so much, but I don't want him at the same time.

As he runs his hand along my leg, my mind starts to scream at me again, telling me that he needs to know why I can't be with him, but I can't, and I don't know what to do about it. I place my hand on him, and we look at each other. I stare into those incredible blue eyes. I go to say something, but he cuts me off.

"Layla, I don't want to rush this, and I can wait for as long as you want. I was thrilled when you said tonight that you didn't have anyone. It meant that I could have you if you wanted me," he said.

I smiled. Of course, I wanted him.

"We can go as slow as you like," he said.

I finished my tea. I placed it on the table. I grabbed Eric's drink and put it next to mine. I wanted him in more ways than he could ever know. I am scared to act on these feelings. I know I will feel scared and run again. I just wonder how many episodes it will take before he decides that I am not worth it— one way to find out. I tuck my legs up under me, and I face Eric, and I look him in the eyes.

"Can I make you dinner tomorrow night?" I chuckle. I don't think he was expecting that to come out of my mouth.

"As much as I would love for you to make dinner, it can't be tomorrow night. It will have to be next Saturday."

"Why?" I asked.

I think I am pouting; he lightly kisses me on the lips; he runs his thumb over my lips and places another swift kiss on my cheek.

"As much as I want to be here with you, I won't have much time over the coming week to be with you. My father is taking my mother overseas for their wedding anniversary, and I get the job of acting CEO for my mother's business, and the hours are long, and it's every day," he said.

"I think that is so nice about your parents, and I wish my parents were happy and maybe even celebrated their anniversaries. If they were, I might not have left." I said.

I wish I hadn't said that. I move away from Eric and slide further down and into the lounge.

"If they were, you wouldn't be here with me now, like this," he said.

His smile is so sweet and kind; I am glad I am sitting down.

"I know neither of us wants to talk about our families, but I get the feeling that you didn't leave; you ran and ran fast." Eric moves over to me, holds my hand, and places a light kiss on the inside of my wrist. How can he see that I ran? I wonder if he can see that I left a life behind. I breathed in deep and exhaled.

"Yes, I ran. My father showed love and affection to my sisters, but none for me. I wasn't allowed to do much or go anywhere, really," I said.

"Did anyone try to help? What about your mother?" he asked.

"No, I was alone, no one helped, the cage closed in, and the darkness was starting to get a hold. I couldn't see any way to the light, so I ran," I said.

I take a deep breath, and I feel somewhat lighter. There's more to my life, but I can't tell him those things just yet. He places several light kisses on the inside of my wrist. He stands, pulls me into his embrace and hugs me tightly.

"Would you like me to stay?" he asked.

Yes! No! Yes! I am at war again, and once again, the mind wins out.

"I would love for you to…." He can almost hear the 'but' in my voice.

"But not just yet," I said.

"I can accept that," he replied.

He doesn't break the hold on his look at me as he walks me to the door. He looks me straight in the eyes and smiles. I almost fall to the ground. My goodness, he could melt the polar icecaps with that smile. His eyes are full of desire. I have no doubts that mine are the same.

"You can come over anytime you want on Saturday, can come over anytime, really," I said.

Sometimes my mouth runs away from me when I am around Eric. His smile gets even brighter, which I didn't think was possible.

"You don't mind if I leave my car there, do you?" he asked.

Just then, a wicked thought struck me – Mrs Davis – oh how funny.

"No, not at all. You should leave it there all of the week that you are away," I said. A wicked smile plays on my lips.

"Why my sweet Layla do you want me to come and see you every chance I get," he asked.

I am near him now. I go red and try to bury my head in his chest, but he won't let me, he holds my chin up, so I must look him in the eyes.

"Please don't hide," he said.

He leans in and kisses me passionately; my hold on my body almost breaks. I almost go to pull him inside. He breaks the kiss first and darts out the door, leaving me standing in the doorway dumbstruck and wanting more. He darts across the driveway and to the edge of my yard. He then takes a bow.

"Love the PJs," he said as he darted off rather quickly to his house. And I am left in my doorway with my mouth hanging open and turning a lovely shade of red.

I don't remember making my way to bed, but somehow, I did. I was replaying the day, especially the night, in my head. I was enjoying every bit of it, and I would do it all over again. Still, with one change, well, maybe two, I wouldn't run away.

I would have changed my PJs. These are girly, pink shorts with flowers and fairies and a pink singlet with a large fairy. Bloody uncle buying these for me - kind of wish I had picked something else. But my wrong choice in clothes didn't stop the smile or the heat from making me fall asleep into one of the most peaceful nights of sleep I have had in a while. I spent many nights awake wondering about my family and if I could ever have Eric, and now I at least have him.

I wake in the morning to the sound of rain, my flowers will be happy for the extra water. I looked at the clock and noticed that

I had slept in until nine-thirty. I got up and went out to open the front door and all the windows. As I opened the door, the first thing I noticed was that Eric's car was already gone. The second thing was the piece of paper under the door with my name on it.

My Sweet Layla,

I am so glad that we spent time together last night. Otherwise, I would still be sitting here wondering if I could have you and now, I have a chance.

I have left early in the hope that I can see you when I finish work.

Thinking of you. Your Eric.

I nearly broke down. I have never once in my life received a letter like this before. The only notes I got were from my father making demands for my presence. I smiled on my way back to my room. I placed it under my pillow, and I went to take a shower.

My phone was ringing when I got out of the shower. I pick it up without looking at the caller ID.

"Hello, my darling," said my uncle before I could even get a word in.

"Hello, Uncle," I replied.

"What have you planned for the day?" he asked.

"Nothing. Why?" I replied.

"No need to sound so guarded, my darling. I would like you to come over for lunch and nothing more." "Very well, Uncle, I'll be there soon," I said.

"Thank you, darling, bye," he said.

"Bye, Uncle," I replied.

What do you have planned? I ask myself. I get dressed and head over to my uncle's. The quicker I get there, the faster I can get home. I find myself hoping Eric will be home when I get back.

Here I am again, sitting in the library drinking tea and having sandwiches.

"My darling Layla, I hear last night was eventful," said uncle with a smirk on his lips as he goes to take a sip of his tea. Just after arriving, he bumped into a friend and told me to go in by myself. I have no doubts that was his plan all along.

"Am I correct in hearing that you slapped Becca Rankin, as well as leaving with a masked man?" he asked with another smirk.

"Oh my, Uncle, the rumours are running wild, aren't they?" I said.

He laughs his throaty laugh.

"Every man wore a mask," I said.

"I do believe that there was only one sweet-smelling flower that left with a handsome man after slapping a scarcely clad woman," he said.

I shrug my shoulders and keep drinking my tea. Just then, one of the house staff comes in. There were whispers, and then they both excuse themselves and leave me in the library.

Beep Beep.

I look around, wondering from where the noise is coming. I look at my handbag and notice a faint glow in it. I pick it up and realise that it's my phone. Curious, as only my uncle has this number. The screen reads one new message. I open it.

Boy next door. I can't believe it. Eric put his number in my phone as - Boy next door.

The message read; I enjoyed our time together. I would have appreciated you more, but alas, I shall have to wait.

I start to blush, remembering what we were doing in my kitchen, I would have liked more, but I can't, not just yet. I send my reply, 'You are making me blush.' It isn't long before my phone is beeping again.

Boy next door:

'That's a colour I love seeing,' the message read.

I start laughing, and at that point, my uncle comes back in, so I send Eric a reply: @ uncle's, talk soon.

"May I ask what is so funny and whom you are texting?" he said as he sits back down across from me.

I contemplate what I should say to him. I don't want to tell him about Eric just yet. I would like to see where we are going before I tell him. I know he will begin acting overprotective and act as a father, which I don't want. I think I will change the subject off me and turn it back onto him.

"Is everything all right, Uncle, before when you left? What's up?" I said.

"Everything is perfect, and I have a surprise for you, Layla," he said.

Groan, not another one; I have had enough of them. I want him to stop; I don't want any more surprises. He must have noticed my expression, or maybe the internal groan was external because he continued to speak.

"You will enjoy it, it will make your life more fun, but there is a catch to this surprise, "he said.

"Of course, there is," I said as I rolled my eyes at him.

"Come," he said.

We stand up, leave the grandeur of the library and the house. We strolled out the front door, around the side of the house, and we start to head towards the stables. If he thinks giving me a horse is going to make me happy, it won't. I have a horse already, and I had to leave her behind. My horse is one of the things I regret leaving behind.

"Uncle?" I say.

He said nothing, but I can hear a furious horse as we near, I mean intensely fierce. I can hear it thrashing about, kicking at the stable walls, and making much noise. The poor thing sounds like it just wants to be free. If he insists on giving this horse to me, I shall oblige and set it free.

My uncle's stables can easily hold up to ten horses on either side, and the office is vast as well. My uncle likes things to be big or at least spacious; he says he wants legroom. In the middle of the stables, two stable hands are trying to calm down the thrashing horse. As I approach, I get a better look at the beautiful creature.

She is just that, elegant and stunning with her chestnut colour, braided mane and tail. She is tall, so very tall. She spotted me, and in an instant, she calmed right down. I looked at my uncle, who has a massive smile on his face. I can feel tears streaming down my face.

"But how?" How was she here? I asked. I reached up and placed my hand on her nose. I stepped closer and put my forehead on her head, and rubbed her ears.

"I have a friend who owed me a favour, and she managed to smuggle her out of the family stables," he explained.

It was my horse; my beautiful 'Storm Cloud' is here. She is here with me. I never dreamed it would be possible. My uncle gave us a little nudge to move us on, so he could open the gate and let her out. I stepped closer to her and hugged her neck. I heard my uncle clear his throat. I turned to see him holding my very own saddle.

"My saddle too!" I said.

He smiled and held out his arms to me. I rushed forward and grabbed my saddle, if you could call it that. There isn't much to it. It's small and very soft. To ride with it was to ride almost bareback. But Storm Cloud seemed to like it. I had tried a standard saddle, but she bucked until I took it off. I knew I had to make a saddle that was almost non-existent. The other thing she didn't like was the reins; she prefers you to grab hold of her mane. She is a stubborn creature. She would have me ride her bareback all the time. It has been months since I have ridden her; I will use the saddle.

After about an hour of saying hello to her, I commenced putting her saddle on. Storm Cloud and I are ready to go sprinting off into the trees when my uncle told us to wait.

"The catch?" He waited for me to say something, and when I didn't, he continued by saying, "She stays here."

"I sense there is more to it than that." I know my uncle, and I know that there is more to this deal. "There is more. The day you arrived, I noticed that you carried your bow and your arrows," he said.

I stared hard at my uncle, trying to bore through his head to find out what he was doing. He does have an element of slyness and cunning in him.

"And?" What else, I asked.

"There is a charity event coming up shortly, and I would like you to come with me," he said.

"And what does this have to do with me, my horse and my bow and arrows?" I replied.

"A lot. The charity event is an archery tournament held over a weekend. There are several stages, and a few of them requires the use of a horse," he explained.

Ah, and there it is, the reason for my horse to be here. However, my heart does leap with joy at the idea of the tournament, as it sounds fun.

"But I do ask that you come over and train. It has been months since you have ridden or shot your arrow. I already have some of the ground staff organising some targets for you. My darling, shall you and Storm Cloud join me?" he said.

"I shall join you, but Uncle, please tell me what's the deal with these rich charity events?"

"Egos, my darling, and raising money for the charities, of course," he replied.

"Of course," I replied.

"But it's the egos more than anything else; it's all about who can splash about the most money."

"But not my dear Uncle, no big events are showing off your big ego," I said with a smirk.

"No, my darling Layla, I already know how great I am," he replied.

At that, he turned and walked away. I was about to ride off into the sunset as it were when I remembered my phone. I had put my things in the office, so I hopped down and went into the office. I grabbed my phone and sent a message to the boy next door. I got back up on Storm Cloud and rode into the forest that surrounded my uncle's house.

9

Eric

Knock. Knock.

Oh, great. Mrs Lane, my mother's pesky receptionist; I mean, she is good at her job, but I'm going to lose it if she tells me once more how her daughter is single. I had told her several times already today that I am seeing someone; I swear she doesn't hear me. Gareth is standing in the doorway when the door opens, trying to rebuff Mrs Lane and her single daughter offer. I wonder if the girl knows how hard her mother is trying to pimp her out to other men.

"My dear lady, as much as it pains me to tell you, I am now in a relationship with another. I am afraid that I cannot offer my affections towards your beautiful daughter," Gareth said.

He is slick when he wants to be. He kisses the back of Mrs Lane's hand, slides into the office and closes the door behind him. He throws himself down in one of the chairs opposite me and puts his feet up on the desk.

"You are going to have to pay to have the desk buffed if you don't get your boots off," I said to Gareth as he quickly removes his feet and starts to polish the desk. He breathes on it and wipes it over again, and then inspects his work.

"There you go, you fussy bastard," Gareth said.

We both start to laugh at his attempts to hand buff the desk.

Beep Beep.

It's another text from Layla. Well, I hope it is, are my thoughts. The last one said @ Uncle's, talk soon.

"Would that be the sweet flower that you left with last night by any chance?" Gareth asked.

With everything that happened last night and the fact that I haven't stopped today, I haven't had a chance to call Gareth; I guess this is why he is here to find out what happened last night.

"Yes, that would be the sweet flower. And yes, I left with her," I replied.

He's got a very sly smile on his face.

"I drove her home, and I stayed for a little while, then I left, not before putting my number in her cell," I replied. He nodded approvingly.

"Did you sleep with her?" he asked.

I will admit I would have loved to have slept with her, but I am more than happy knowing that I will be able to at some point down the track. Until then, I have her interested in me, and I plan to keep it that way.

"Nah, I didn't, if you must know," I replied.

"There was talk about you and the woman, how much hotter she was after she slapped Becca. You're a lucky son of Bitch," he said.

"Did you see the front page?" Gareth said.

Oh yeah, I saw it. On the front of the social pages is the woman slapping Becca. Yes, this woman was so much hotter after doing that, but she is hot in more ways than that.

"Did she at least get your mind off Lala?"

"Nah, she didn't. She only made it worse. All I think about now is Layla, can't get her out of my head."

"Ah, sorry, E-man, so why didn't she make you forget about her?" he asked.

I know I have a massive grin on my face because I haven't stopped smiling all day.

"Because it was Layla," I replied.

His jaw dropped, and he became speechless.

"That hot piece of ass was Lala?"

"Yes. The girl last night was Layla," I replied.

Before I could say more, he spoke. "But you said that Lala has a guy, the dude with the Bentley."

"It's her car. Her uncle bought it for her. The guy I saw is her uncle's gay personal assistant," I said.

His jaw dropped again. "You must feel like an idiot," he said.

"Gee, thanks, and why am I your friend?" I said, and there is that sly smile again from him.

"Because I am charming, I always tell you the truth, and I'm Irish. What more can I say?" Gareth said.

He is playing the Irish card. His dad was born in Ireland and moved to Skyhaven when he was five. He goes back to Ireland each year to visit family. Gareth has Irish red hair. Well, maybe the temper too, but I have never been on the receiving end of that.

Beep Beep.

I look at my phone, and I notice two messages are waiting for me. I just hope they are both from Girl next door. I laughed at what she must have thought when she read who the text was from this morning.

"You going to read them, or are they too dirty for even the likes of me?" Gareth asked.

I don't like reading or answering my phone when I am at work unless it is essential, but I am in Gareth's company, and I know he won't mind.

Becca:

'I am sorry about last night. Please call me.' She can go to hell for all I care, are my thoughts.

Girl next door:

'Staying at my uncle's, have coffee with me in the morning, please.'

"Anything of interest?" Gareth asked inquisitively.

"One from Becca apologising and asking that I call her, and the second is from Layla," I replied.

"I know who I would be replying to," he said.

As do I, but I think I have something better planned than just coffee.

Gareth checks his phone. He stands up, getting ready to leave.

"Well, E-man, I have other appointments, but I would like for you and Lala to come to the Cavern on Saturday night," he said.

"I can't. I have dinner plans with Layla," I replied. I won't break them, not even for him.

"Okay, that is fine. We will make it Sunday then," he said.

I don't want to, but he is my best mate, and I don't want to reject his kind invitation.

"Fine, yes, sure," I replied.

"Great, I will see you Sunday around nine, now to try and make it out of the office without being mobbed by that receptionist out there," he said.

He walks over to the door, grabs hold of the handle and takes a deep breath. He does a fist pump to psych himself up for leaving the office, not that I can blame him. Mrs Lane has a highly confident, forcible personality. He salutes and opens the door.

"Leaving already, Mr Flannery?" she said.

As he closes the door behind him, I take a moment to reread Layla's message. I do have something more interesting in mind for us. I send her a reply.

10

Layla

By the time I get home, it is nearly midnight; I was going to stay at my uncle's. But I wanted to be back home. Eric sent me a message saying, 'meet me at the fence @ 8 am'. I had told him I would; I thought it was an odd request considering I asked him to come over. I had thoughts of us in the kitchen, but alas, not meant to be.

As I pull into the driveway, I look over at Eric's house and see no lights on. Maybe he has already gone to bed, and how I would like to crawl into bed with him right now. I doubt he'd appreciate that as I smell like a horse.

After my shower, I set the alarm for seven. I could feel sleep creeping in to take hold as soon as I got into bed. As I lay my head down, images of my ride today start to flitter across my eyelids. I fall asleep in a dream with the wind on my face and my hair billowing out behind me, the pounding of Storm Cloud's hooves, the breaking of branches, the spray of water as we went through a stream, the sun leaving and making way for the night. We slowed and listened to the sounds around us as we made our way back to the stables.

Before I knew it, my alarm was going off, my head is foggy, and I can't work out why it would be going off. Then it hit me, of course, coffee with Eric. I leap out of bed. I have a quick shower and get dressed in jeans and a t-shirt. I raced into the kitchen and grabbed the breakfast scrolls I took from my uncle's kitchen just as I left his place.

It is now 8 am as I walk out my back door. I look over towards the oak tree. Just above my seat on the fence, I can see a tray resting on the top. There is a teapot and what looks to be a sugar bowl and milk jug. I walk over; I stand on my seat and look over the fence. The tray is resting on several stacked Besser blocks to keep it balanced. Next to those is a step ladder. I place my plate on the tray.

"Good morning," a voice said.

I look up and see Eric walking towards me dressed in a dark grey business suit. He has a great big smile on his face, and he looks fantastic. I am just glad I am holding onto the bench; it is the only thing keeping me from oozing into a puddle on the ground.

"Good morning Eric, would it not have been easier to come over to my house for coffee?" I said.

He placed two cups on the tray and stood on the step ladder. He looked at me, and his smile faded. He had a look of pain and concern on his face.

"What happened?" I asked.

He reached his hand over and ran his hand light as a feather touch under my left eye across my cheekbone and toward my ear. I am confused as I have no idea what he is saying. I was so eager to see him this morning. I never looked at my reflection.

"You have a huge scratch across your face," he remarked.

I reach my hand up to touch the spot where he is touching. I could feel that my skin is a little rough, but nothing to panic about, it is only a tiny scratch, and it would not leave a scar, so I don't know why he is so concerned.

"It must have happened yesterday at my uncle's when I went for a horse ride. I must have snagged a branch," I said.

His hand cupped my face, and he gently tugged and pulled me closer to him. He leant in closer and kissed me all along the scratch and kissed me on the lips. It was brief. I think I whimpered when he pulled away. He then poured two cups of coffee.

"How domestic, so why not come over to my place?

Why here?" I said. He laughed at my domestic comment. "Because if I were to come over, I wouldn't leave, and I must leave for work soon. I thought that this would be nice, something different. I thought you might like this. You don't?" he said.

"I am enjoying your company, and that is all that matters to me. Seeing that you have to work all week and we won't get much time together until Saturday night, this is just fine and will have to do, I guess," I replied.

"This will just have to do!" he said as he burst out laughing. His laughter is like his smile, I went weak at the knees, and I couldn't help but laugh with him.

When we finished our coffee and scrolls, he took back the tray and told me to wait for him. He strolled back, looking very dashing in the suit as he stood opposite me. He placed his forehead on mine. I can hear the blood pumping in his body. I can feel his heart beating rapidly in his chest with his breath catching every so often. I know my body is doing the same thing.

"I can't wait until Saturday night," he said in a dark, husky voice. As he runs his hands through my hair, my breath is becoming ragged, and my heart is trying to escape my chest. He kisses me long and passionately, then pulls away.

"Until Saturday," he said as he steps down and walks back to his house, never taking his eyes off me.

I start to laugh as he trips a couple of times but doesn't fall over. I stay staring at his home, daydreaming, of course, well after he has left.

The days passed in happy bliss, I would go to my uncle's and ride Storm Cloud, and I would practice my archery. I would text 'Boy next door', and on a rare morning, I would have coffee under the oak tree with the said boy next door, and today is the day. I went food shopping yesterday, and now I shall spend most of the day cooking and getting ready for Eric. I had sent him a message earlier in the day to come over around seven.

I have spent most of the day looking at the clock, and I swear that it stopped moving at around five. I set everything aside while I got dressed in a simple black slip dress. I left my hair down, and I didn't put any makeup on. I had very few flowers in my hair, much less than what I had at the masked ball. I just hope I look pretty enough for him like this.

Right on seven, there is a knock on my door, I tried not to rush over, but every part of me wanted to rush the door and rip it off its hinges. As I got closer to the door, I swear I could smell Eric's scent before I even opened it. He smells of fresh air, earth and soap. I reach for the door, and I close my eyes. I take a deep breath, I hold it, and I let it out slowly, trying to slow down my pounding heart. It was no good. I am flushed and nervous. I open my eyes and the door, and there stands, as bright as a star, dearest Eric, dressed in jeans and a blue button shirt wearing a heart-stopping smile.

"Hi!" Groan. Really, hi, that's all I can say. Oh well, continue with the thrilling openers.

"Please come in," I said. I step aside to let Eric in. He moved faster than I thought possible. In one swift motion, I was in his arms. His lips came down on mine in a heated, passionate kiss. I lace my fingers around his neck, and I move my hands through his soft brown hair. My breathing becomes ragged, and my heart starts pounding. Will I ever get used to this feeling when I am around Eric?

"I've missed you," he says against my lips.

"I've missed you too, but now come, or our dinner will get cold."

He kisses me once more and reluctantly pulls away. I can see the fire of desire in his eyes, he takes a small step back, and his eyes search me up and down; his eyes become more intense more heated. I could tell he wanted to lean in and kiss me again. Still, he didn't. Instead, he reached down to grab a basket, held up his left hand and produced a basket with a bottle of wine, some chocolates, and a DVD.

"I don't know if we will get a chance to watch the movie, but I thought you might enjoy this one," he said.

I take the basket from him, and I hold out my hand, he takes my hand, and I lead him inside, only stopping to close the door.

"So, what's for dinner?" he asks.

I place the basket on the kitchen bench and lead him to the table.

"Just sit down right here," I said.

"So, you're not going to tell me," he asked as he gives me that blinding smile.

"If you really must know; for entrees, we have crusty herb and garlic bread with crisp honey prawns. For our main course, we are having chicken and cashew stir-fry, and for dessert, we have some strawberry ice cream that I made myself."

"You made ice cream?" he said surprisingly.

"Yes, it is no big deal. Now stay seated while I get everything ready," I said.

"Can't I do anything to help?" Eric asks.

"No! Just sit right there," I replied.

"As you wish," he said.

I kiss him on the cheek and bring out the entrées, followed by the main course and dessert.

Our meal was perfect; all the dishes turned out just right, and the conversation flowed.

"That was perfect; this is one amazing surprise. Thank you, Layla. You must have spent some time slaving in the kitchen today to prepare all this. Where did you learn to cook like that? You are indeed one excellent cook," Eric said.

I couldn't help but blush. Back at home, I was always told to take it back and start again. Never had I been told once that I was a good cook.

"Back home," I replied.

He could see the pain in my face and hear the sorrow in my voice as I said those two little words. He stood up and walked to me, and he held out his hands to me. I took them; he then pulled me into him and held me tight.

"Sorry," he said.

How does he know not to talk about my family? When the subject arises, it's quickly squashed. How can he read me so well?

"We should clean up before we watch the movie you brought over. What did you bring?" I said.

We started to clean up the dishes and tidy up.

"For some reason, my hand went to The Lord of the Rings DVD. Have you ever seen it?" I asked.

"No, I haven't. Is it good?" Eric replied.

"Yes, it's good, but it is long." I handed him the DVD and pointed to the TV; he bowed and said, as you wish. I grabbed the chocolates, the wine and two glasses and put them on the coffee table; Eric has the movie in his hands, ready to go. He sits on the lounge and holds his hand out for me. I go and turn the lights out and press play. On return to the lounge, I took Eric's hand, and he gently guides me towards him. I curl up next to him. His right arm wraps around my body and pulls me closer to him, he kisses me on the cheek, and the movie starts to play.

As we watched the movie, I kept getting some strange feelings, several different emotions. I feel so comfy leaning there; it's as if we were made for each other. Eric was sending cold shivers along my body as his hand absently rubs along my arm. Even though I was getting shivers, I felt hot from it, and I wanted to act on it. And the other feeling I was getting was about the movie; I am sure I had heard it before when I was a small child. I can almost hear my uncle's voice telling me this story.

I shake the feelings and go back to the movie, but I can't seem to concentrate on it. Eric's hand leaves my arm. He starts running his fingers through my hair to stroke the lower part of my ear.

I shiver, then heat floods my body. I can't hold on to the feelings of warmth and desire starting to flood my system. I sit up and crawl into Eric's lap. He grasps my hips and slides me further forward. As he runs his hands down my legs, I shudder as his hands touch my bare skin. His hands move back up my legs, hitching my dress further up so it sits on my hips. I close my eyes and lean back, placing my hands on his knees for support. I feel his hands slide up my body, along my breast, up around my neck. He pulls me forward so that our foreheads are touching.

It all feels so perfect. Eric then softly places his lips onto mine. I have never done anything like this, and I thought I wouldn't know what to do, but my body seems to be acting on its own, and my hands find their way to his shirt, and I start to undo the buttons. He then breaks the kiss.

"We don't have to rush if you don't want this," he said in a husky voice. His breathing is beginning to become ragged, and his heartbeat is rapid.

"I know," I said rather breathlessly.

He starts to kiss my neck and makes a path back to my lips and back to my neck. His shirt sits slightly open. I run my hands along his rock-hard stomach. I can feel every muscle as I run my hands up his chest and along his shoulders. I push his shirt down and off his body. I have seen Eric with his shirt off quite a few times, and I have always wanted to reach out and touch him, and now I can, and I did. My hand feels every inch of his bare chest. I can feel his body shudder. I can hear and feel his heart skip beats.

His hands leave a blazing trail along my body as he finds his way to my thighs. He grips them and pulls me forward, and in one smooth motion, he picks me up. I can feel the muscles in his stomach contract. I wound my legs around him; I heard a moan escape his lips.

He took a few steps and turned the movie and the TV off without even dropping me an inch. Just then, his phone rings. He groans, supporting me with one arm, and he digs his phone out of his pocket. I grip my legs tighter. He moans as I do it. Eric looks at the caller id, and he looks crestfallen.

"I have to take this," he said.

I merely nod as he answers the phone and starts to walk backwards.

"Good day to you, Mr Sato." Backs of his legs touch the lounge; he eases his way down and sits close to the edge.

"How can I help you today?" he said.

I don't hear the other side of the conversation.

"I am in a meeting at the moment," he replied.

I laugh at his comment. He smiles and winks at me. I then start to kiss his neck. I feel his body stiffen under me. I know he is trying to keep his breathing under control.

"I'll be at least two or three hours yet," he explained to the caller.

I start to ignore the conversation, and I feel that Mr Sato is not listening and is trying to get Eric out of his current meeting. I try to entice him to follow me and hang up on his caller. I reach behind him and grab his shirt. I untangle myself from him and try to walk away seductively. I can feel his eyes following me.

I keep my back to him as I pull my dress up over my head and drop it on the floor. I reach behind and undo my lacy bra and drop that on the floor. I put Eric's shirt on, but I don't do the buttons up. I look over my shoulder at Eric, and his mouth is open, and his blue eyes are large with want. He drinks in my figure as he tries to tell Mr Sato that he'll call him back as soon as possible.

I walk to my room slowly; I try to move ghostly in the hopes that I look beautiful moving in the darkness. I make it to my doorway when I feel Eric standing at the top of the hallway. I turn, and I can see the sheen of sweat on his chest. I feel the warmth rising in my body. I move swiftly into the room. I must have spooked him a little because I heard him gasp. He comes into my room and faces the bed, I walk up behind him, and I start to wind my arms around his waist as he turns and looks down at me.

"How did you do that?" Eric asked.

I don't answer. I start to force Eric back and push him back onto the bed. I climb on top of him, lean down and press our lips together. One hand caresses my back; the other hand slides across my stomach, breasts, neck, and then into my hair.

My mind and body start to scream again, not now, please, let me have this one moment. I try to plead with myself. Everything quietens for the briefest of moments because I realised that I somehow ended up on my back with my head on my pillows and Eric's body pressed against mine. I can't feel an ounce of his weight, his left hand resting on my neck near my ear, and his thumb is rubbing my ear. I close my eyes and arch into his body. I wish he wouldn't do that for so many reasons.

"Are you sure about this?" he asked like a real gentleman.

No, I wasn't. I want Eric so bad, though; I don't know how to answer. My body is screaming 'yes' while my mind makes my mouth move of its own accord.

"No. But I want you, I want this, but I am afraid, and I think that if I say 'no' to you tonight, I feel I will repeat it the next time we are here in my bed or your bed," I replied.

He kisses me, then smiles. He rolls off me and lays next to me but pulls me in close to him.

"It's okay. I can wait, I am happy that I get to be with you, and if you want to wait, I can wait as well," Eric said as he kisses me again. I can feel the blood pumping in my body; we stay there, kissing for about ten minutes when he breaks away from me.

"I'm going to make a phone call, and I will be back," he said.

He kisses me again and goes out to the lounge room to make his call. I get under the covers, I stare up at the ceiling and think of the first day here to now, and I couldn't be happier. I was never comfortable at home all those years, and I have never been happier until I moved here. I rolled over, and I started to think of how the night could have gone if I had said 'yes'; it brought a smile to my face. Just then, Eric walked back in. I don't know how long I lay there thinking of him.

"What are you smiling at?" he asked with a smile on his face.

Just him is what I think. He is the reason that I am always smiling.

"Come to bed and hold me," I said.

A smile spread; I watched as he unbuttoned his jeans and stripped them down to his black boxers. I drink in his form, and I am thankful he is mine to have whenever I am ready. I scoot out of his way as he crawls into bed next to me. He holds out his arms, and I move into his outstretched arms, we start to kiss, but it doesn't last long.

"Goodnight, my sweet Layla," he whispers to me.

I fall asleep in his arms. I wake up early and notice that the bed is empty. Climbing out of bed, I see that Eric's jeans are still on the floor. Mm… maybe he is in my kitchen naked; I know I love staring at his chest but being able to stare at all of him. Oh, I better stop thinking like that, or my brain will start yelling at me again, and I know it will cause a headache.

I look down and notice I am still wearing his shirt— most of it is buttoned-up. I pad into the kitchen only to find it empty. I walk to my back door, and I see Eric standing with his back to me, near the fountain; his back is just as impressive as his chest. I watch him as he breathes in the fresh morning air. I quietly slid open the door and walk out into the crisp morning air, I know he hears me, but he doesn't turn.

"Good morning, sweet Layla," he said.

I step up next to him, and he laces his fingers through mine.

"I trust you slept well. I know I did." Eric said as he gives my hand a slight squeeze.

"I haven't slept that well in a very long time," I replied. Eric gives me a curious look.

"I don't sleep well at night, I have nightmares, even though I have been here, I still have them, and I can thank my father for that." Now, I can't believe I said that last part.

"You don't have much love for him, do you?" he said.

"No, not much love at all, I guess. But you wouldn't either if you were me and had to grow up with his rule and his law." He tugs my hand and pulls me into his embrace. I look up at him, and I don't feel the cold of his chest against my body. I feel the heat radiating off me.

"Did he …" he asked. He leaves the question hanging; I know what he is referring to.

"No," I say no more, as does Eric, his hands rub up, and down my back, he smiles at me.

"Did you button up your shirt?" I asked. It takes him a few seconds to get my meaning.

"Yes, I did. I wanted to preserve your virtue, and I wanted to do it for my sanity. Do you know how hard it is to look at your naked body and not want to ravage you?" he said. He presses his lips to mine, and a moan escapes my lips, and I can feel Eric's mouth twitch as he pulls back.

"I forgot to mention that Gareth would like us to have dinner with him tonight," he said.

"He does. Why?" I asked, and he laughs.

"I don't know. I guess Gareth just wants to meet you without the garden implements. Is that okay?" he asked.

"Yes, it is fine," I replied.

He kisses the top of my head; he takes my hand and leads me back inside.

"Time for breakfast," he said as she scoots to the kitchen.

"You can cook," I replied, and he laughs at my remark.

"No, I can't, but I can put bread in the toaster, and I make a mean cup of coffee. You go have a shower; I will make you breakfast," Eric said.

I don't say anything; I just smile and go towards the bathroom, leaving him to my kitchen.

11

Eric

Okay, I'm standing there looking at her kitchen, and I have no idea where anything is. Better start doing something; otherwise, she is going to come out and find me looking useless. I hear the shower start, so I press the button on the kettle. Staring into the open space, I feel a cool breeze coming from the cupboard. I walk over and open the door, looking in; there is no evidence of a breeze. Looking around the rest of the house, I notice all the windows and doors are closed. I still don't know where this breeze is coming in.

As I am staring around the lounge room, I hear a noise behind me. I turn and notice a small tin of blueberries has fallen over in front of a packet of pancake mix. I grab both and mix them, I am not sure if it will work, but I can't just stand here in the kitchen with a blank look on my face.

I have the pancakes cooking, and the kettle has boiled. I feel the same cool breeze again, but this time it carries the scent of flowers. I get a strange feeling that tells me I need to pick flowers. This plan is crazy and straightforward. I look at the pancakes, and I work out that I have a few minutes before they burn, so I rush out and pick a few flowers. I come back inside to find a vase and a pair of scissors on the kitchen bench. Where the hell did they come from? This is getting freaky. I trim the flowers and put them in the vase.

I have made the coffee and the pancakes, I have whipped some cream, and I found some maple syrup. I think I have everything, so I set the table, the only thing left to do is get some clothes on.

Walking down the hallway to get my jeans, I see Layla standing in her room, getting dressed, and I can't help but stare. She's dressed in a matching lacy black bra and underwear; my body starts to ache for her. I just want to reach out and pull her to me; she pulls on a pair of jeans and a dark purple blouse. Watching as Layla pulls her hair out from beneath her blouse, I gaze at her neck, and I want to kiss the softness of it. I get a look at her ears; I do a double take. I swear it looked as if her ears pointed; I shake it off. She turns and spots me staring at her, and she turns red, which is a colour I love on her.

"Is brekky ready?" she asked.

I walk into her room and pull her towards me, her body pressed against mine. All I can think of is how I want to feel her body beneath mine, feel every inch of her naked flesh against mine. I want to hear her scream out my name, I press my lips to hers, and all I want to do is lift her and lay her on her bed. I can't, I have to put on some pants, and our breakfast is getting cold. I reluctantly pull out of the embrace.

"Yes, it is ready, but I need to put on my jeans." "You don't have to," she said.

"My, my Layla. I seem to have had a bad influence on you, and I like it," I said.

She smiles and buries her head in my chest.

"Would you like your shirt?" she asked. We both look at her bed, and I see my shirt lying on her pillow. I want her to keep it.

"No, as long as you don't mind me not wearing a shirt to breakfast."

"No, I don't mind," she said and then grabs my jeans and hands them to me, then stands back to watch me. I slide into my jeans.

I can hear her breathing hitch, I smile at the effect that I have on her, and I know she has the same impact on me. No one has held me the way Layla has a hold on me. All that matters is her. I just hope that what I think she feels for me is what I feel for her; everything about her is perfect. I believe we are each other's equal halves. I can't help but always stare at her, and she starts to giggle at me.

"What?" I say.

"You have a goofy look on your face," she replied.

Do I now? I know how to fix those giggles. I take a deep, grumbling breath and give her my most mischievous smile. I take a few menacing steps towards her. I pull myself up to full height and look down into her stormy grey eyes and growl; her fit of giggles stop, and she looks rather sheepish. In a swift motion, I pick her up and throw her over my shoulder and march her back to the dining table; she's squealing at me to put her down.

"Brute, ruffian, knave, masher. Put me down." What was that last name she called me?

"As you wish," I said. I place Layla down on one of the chairs. She tries to smooth her hair down, and her face is flushed from hanging upside down. I sit down opposite her. She looks at the table, and her mouth makes a perfect O as she stares at the table.

"I hope you thanked the flowers." What a strange thing to say; she must have seen my puzzled look because she elaborated.

"When you picked them, I hope you said thank you to the plant for allowing you to pick them."

"No, I had not, but I shall remember next time I pick you flowers." She smiles and nods, pleased with my reply.

"I have a question; what is a masher?" I asked.

She has a fork full of pancakes halfway to her lips, and she lets it sit there as she answers.

"I have been watching looney toons of late, and a little old lady says it as she smacks a big brute over the head with her handbag." She takes a bite of her breakfast. She closes her eyes and smiles; she opens her eyes and says, 'Hillbilly bunny is by far the best episode'.

Our conversation stays with cartoons and our favourite shows and the morning passes quickly. I look at the clock and notice that it is almost eleven o'clock.

"Shit. Sorry. I'm supposed to be in the office already, a meeting for which I will now be late. I cannot cancel the meeting as it was planned for months. I would much rather be here with you than be in that meeting, of course." I said. She gets a sad look on her face.

"Today is the last day, I promise, and then I am all yours," I said. I stand up and move over to her. I put my hands on either side of her head and guide her towards me. "I know we have to go see Gareth, but you will still get to have me," I said and then gave her a brief kiss on the lips.

"I can stay a bit longer and help you clean up, though," I said. Layla tries to shake her head, but I still have a hold on her.

"No, you need to go to your meeting. I'll clean up," Layla said.

She licks her lips, and I must focus, or I won't leave.

"Walk me out," I asked. However, I don't move. I don't want to leave. I am so glad that this is my last day working at my mother's office. She places her right hand on my left hand and gently tugs. I release my hand from her face, and she twines her fingers through mine and leads me towards the front door. We face each other; I wind my free arm around her waist and pull her towards me. I lean down as she stretches up, and our lips meet. I don't want to leave her embrace, but she is the one that pulls away.

"Go! I will be here when you get back," She said as she opens the door for me, and I give her another but albeit brief kiss. As I leave her, I look across the road, seeing Mrs Davis at her letterbox. I give her the most prominent and brightest smile, and I raise my hand.

"Good morning Mrs Davis! How are you this morning?" I said so she could hear me. She turns on her heels and walks back inside. I can hear Layla laughing as I walk home to get dressed for the meeting.

12

Layla

Beep Beep.

It's only been forty minutes since Eric left the house and all I want to do is see him again. When he left my sight, I dreamily went about cleaning and almost finished when I heard my phone go off. I let the water out of the sink and dried my hands. I picked up my phone.

Boy next door:

'Our date with Gareth is at 9 pm. I will be back by 4 pm thinking of you—your Eric.

I sent a reply of 'whatever shall I do until then, your sweet Layla.'

Boy next door:

'I have a few ideas, but they require me.'

Oh my, I can feel myself getting hot, and flashes of our time in my kitchen and on the lounge last night, of us sleeping in the same bed. I best stop thinking like that, or I will be too worked up when he gets here. I send a reply to him: You are making me blush again; you best hurry up. I want you home.

Boy next door:

'As you wish.'

I occupy my time by finishing off one of the dresses that I had started making. It's a simple dress, a blood-red slip dress; it has delicate spider lace over the top of the dress with spun silver through it.

I did not get any more texts from Eric, but it doesn't bother me because the rest of the day has passed quickly. It's already four, and I now hear Eric knock on the door. I put down the dress and go to meet him. I stop just before the main entrance. I can see Eric through the screen door; I can see him fidgeting with the cuffs of his suit. I stand just out of sight, watching him. I don't know why I wasn't rushing to the door, but I was just enjoying staring at him. How is it that this boy brings such a smile to my face, not to mention the weak at the knees part?

"Hello there, Layla. Will you let me in so you can stare at me inside the house? Then I can do the same." He said. How did he know I was watching him?

"It's open any way. You could have come in and found me," I said. He steps inside and shrugs out of his suit jacket, and throws it onto the lounge.

"Would you like coffee?" I ask him as I move towards the kitchen, but Eric doesn't say anything, so I turn to face him. I can see the look in his eyes that he intends to stalk me, and he does just that. Though for some strange reason, I find this fun. I have an urge to scream and laugh at the same time while I slowly run away, hoping that he will catch me. I squeal, and I turn for once, my speed lets me down, or maybe it does it on purpose, but I feel a vice-like grip on my waist.

"Not so fast, my sweet." I hear a deep growl in my ear. It sends my blood pumping through my veins and shivers along my spine.

"Oh, but I was trying ever so hard to get away." My breath is raspy as I try to joke with him, but all I can feel is heat and desire coursing through me.

I could hear his deep laughter in my ear. I leaned back so I could feel his body against mine. "I bet you were," he said. He plants a feather-light kiss on my neck.

"What do you plan on doing now that you have caught me?" I could feel and hear him growl as I asked this.

"Oh, I have quite a few ideas. We could finish watching the movie, that's if you want to, or we could always finish what we started during the movie," Eric said with a cheeky grin on his face.

I mull the idea over in my head, and my mind again is going a little wild. Why is it that he wants me when Eric can have anyone he wants? Don't all males think of sex, so why is he such a gentleman about it with me? Why am I a child about this? It's just sex!

My mind screams so loud at me at that last thought; I fear Eric heard it. It's not just sex for you. It's more than that. You can't be with him; it is forbidden. I try to shut my mind down, but it's not happening. It's still screaming at me; you will lose everything, you will never be allowed to go back, you can't be with him.

"Layla, are you okay?" Eric asked. His voice is starting to sound panicked. I turn in his arms to face him. He is staring at me with a look of pain and worry. I tried to smile but was failing.

"Are you okay? You went slack in my arms and almost hit the floor," he said.

So maybe the scream in my head did more than I thought. I once again try to smile.

"I'm okay, but you are right; we should just watch the movie," I said.

He scoops me up, carries me to the lounge, puts me down, turns the movie on and sits back down next to me. He puts his arm around me and draws me close to him. He starts to draw circles on my arm with his thumb.

"We don't have to see Gareth tonight. I can cancel on him; he won't mind," he said.

"No, we can go; I need to go," I said.

He stops rubbing my arm, and I can feel him looking at me.

"I need to say sorry for hurting him with the pruning shears." I felt him laugh and kiss the top of my head as I said this.

"As you wish," he said.

We sat and watched the movie. Eric's phone went off a few times, but he told me it was just Gareth asking if we would still have dinner with him. I know it wouldn't be her (Becca) not after he told me what kind of person she was. He said he would never again answer her phone calls or reply to any of her texts, and I have no doubts he means it. I know I can trust him.

At around seven o'clock, Eric said we should start to get ready. He kissed me and said he would be back once he had had a shower. I had a shower and was only in my undergarments, and I still had a few touches left to do on my dress to finish it. So I sat in the sewing room, only dressed in my red lacy bra and panties. I concentrated on the dress and didn't hear Eric come into the house, which is a little disconcerting, seeing that I can sense most things happening around me. The only reason I knew he was standing behind me was that I could smell the fresh air, earth and soap. I swear I could also hear his heartbeat stutter. I knew he was looking at my back because I couldn't hear his breath.

But I wondered if he is staring at me as I am nearly naked, or if in this light, he can see the scars on my back, whereas last night in the dark, he might not have been able to see them.

"If you are staring at my almost naked body, I am happy for you to stare, but if it is the scars, I wouldn't worry; it is nothing sinister. I was thrown from my horse when I was little and fell into some shrubs. My rather intelligent horse thought she was helping when grabbing my leg to pull me out, causing the shrubs to dig in deeper. I'm not going to mention what happened when I got home that night. So, you can let that breath out that you seem to be holding." I said as I stood up and slipped into my dress. It's a perfect fit, and it hugs me in all the right places and shows just the right amount of skin.

"Wow, you look great," Eric said with his mouth partially open and a desiring look on his face.

"I'll just grab my shoes and bag," I said, and then I walked up to Eric, kissed him, as well as smile at him. I can feel his arm start to reach for me. I quickly move out of his reach, and I flitted out of the room. Up the hallway, I can hear him growl and fly up the hall towards me. I am stunned at how quickly he can move; he is just as swift and as stealthy as me, and I wonder if Eric's as amazed by the way I move as I am to the way he moves.

13

Eric

I can't believe that she did it again grr…. how does she move so fast, but two can play at that? I am no slouch either; I race out after her. I stop just a few feet from her and stare at her beautiful figure draped in red and black. I would rather stay here and take her out of that dress, leave her in her lacy lingerie, but she wants to go, and I can't say no to her. I doubt I could ever say no to her. All I want is to make her happy.

"Shall we go?" She said as she holds her hand out for me. I take a few steps towards her and pull her towards me.

"Yes, I guess we shouldn't keep Gareth waiting," I said and then kissed her and walked her to my car.

We don't say much on the way to the Cavern, she did tell me she spent most of her day cleaning and doing the dress, which I would love to see her out of again, but damn, it is a beautiful dress on her, and what amazes me is that she made it. My thoughts run back to her sitting in her sewing room wearing nothing but her red lacy underwear. My heart stopped beating when I saw her sitting there, but then I saw her back and all the scars along with it. I don't know how I didn't feel them when I have run my hands along her beautiful back. I place my hand on her leg, and she puts her hand on top of mine.

How does this girl send my world upside down? Since the first day we met, she has been in my head all of the time. I tell her about the very dull meeting I sat in, which I zoned out of several times and the reason as to why I kept zoning out.

We arrived at the Cavern dead on nine. The valet took my car, we went past the ropes and straight to the restaurant.

"Good evening Eric, Miss Dixon," Cathy, the waitress, said.

"Good evening Cathy," I said.

Layla just gave a polite smile and a shy hello; I wonder if she caught the fact that Cathy didn't call her Layla.

"Gareth hasn't arrived yet," Cathy said.

Cathy takes us over to the same table that we sat at last time, but this time when we arrive at the table, there are three place settings with food recently placed on the table.

"Oh, it looks yummy," Layla said.

I help Layla into her seat, and I sit down next to her.

She is about to try some of the food when a waiter comes over to the table. It's Fred, a twenty-one-year-old stick of a boy – I have seen him eat a platoon's worth of food and not put any weight on. As he walks up to the table to take our drink orders, he stops and stares at Layla. I look at her and notice that she is staring just as intently at him as he at her. I see something pass between them, it's only for a moment, but it's there.

Fred recovers and looks at me with a guilty expression on his face. The bastard had better stay away from my girl, or I am going to damage him. Damn, from where is this rage coming?

"Would you like something to drink?" he said as he stares at me with his pencil poised over his book.

"Rum and coke, "I said sternly. He turns to Layla, who is looking rather flushed. "White wine, please," she said. Fred walks away to get our drinks.

"Have you met Fred before?" Damn, I didn't want to sound as

if I was a jealous, angry boyfriend, but that was the way it came out, and in that instant that I said it, I regretted it, but it's what Layla did that made me feel about as low as dirt, the hurt and pain caused with just one sentence.

She blanches and places her hands in her lap, and lowered her gaze to her hands. The colour in her face drains away, I move closer towards her, and I take hold of her hand. She looks at me with tears shining in her eyes; I felt even worse. How could I have hurt her so much?

"Sorry, I…" I stopped speaking because Fred came with our drinks. I was happy when he scurried away after the deadly look I gave him.

"I'm sorry, Layla. I didn't mean to upset you," I said meaningfully.

"No…Yes…" She took a deep breath and tried again. "He knows my father, and my uncle is the only person who knows that I am here. I fear…" She shakes her head as if to clear it, and she was about to speak again when Gareth turned up.

"Am I interrupting a lovers tiff?" he said, seeing the dull look on our faces.

I glared at him, but he didn't notice. He sat down opposite us.

"Or is it that the wine is not so pleasant tonight," he asked.

Layla smiled a little, pulled her hands out of mine and grabbed the napkin and dabbed at her face. I moved back a little. I don't know what to think. Is she upset at me for the way I spoke to her? Or is it that she fears her father that much, she is in hiding from him? And is worried that Fred will tell her father that she is here.

"It's nothing to worry about at the moment," she says. Gareth just nodded at her. "Um… I would also like to apologise for my behaviour some weeks back." Gareth waves his hand absently through the air.

"Think nothing of it, Lala."

"It's Layla." I can see the fire in her eyes, and I know Gareth is about to make her eyes blaze white-hot. I can see it in his face the way he wants to tease her as he leans closer to her.

"Ah yes, it is, but Lala is so much more fun and seeing you did put me on my ass."

"You attacked me."

"I merely came over to introduce myself, and you turned, and my hand touched..."

"You did it on purpose." Gareth clutched a hand to his chest and has a mock look of pain and hurt on his face.

"I am crushed, my dear Lala, that you would think that an Irish gentleman such as myself would go around and grab young ladies."

"Cut the crap. You, sir, are no gentleman." This is getting interesting; I just sit back and watch them accuse and insult each other. I'm a little surprised at Layla; she has never sworn.

"You, my dear, are no lady, not with those killer moves. You could have killed me."

"You should not have touched me." I see this conversation going around in circles.

"Well, you shouldn't have such a nice figure." Layla blushed at that comment. She balked and could not fire back at him. Gareth is right, though, well, kind of right. It's a perfect figure, and I get to have her." "And that lovesick puppy over there should have warned me about you."

Oh great, now I am in the middle of it, and both men are staring at me.

"Well, you raced out of the house before I could say anything, and I had no idea that Layla could move like a ninja, not to mention the fact that I was dressed only in a towel." I looked at Layla, who hadn't lost her pink blush, and I could see that she remembered that day as well. I grab hold of her hand and place a kiss on the inside of her wrist.

"He is never going to call you Layla. He is always going to call you Lala, just as he always calls me E-man. You can't change the man; he's an idiot." She laughed at the last part while I got a "hey" from Gareth.

Dinner was a lot lighter after that, though Layla did say she would stab anyone besides Gareth, who called her Lala. I couldn't blame her; it just didn't sound right. Dessert was about ten minutes away when she excused herself from the table. Gareth watched her leave and continued to watch her to the bathroom just as I did.

"Eric." That can't be right; Gareth never calls me Eric. "Something is not right here."

"What are you talking about?"

"Look, I don't know what it is, but I am just getting this feeling that something isn't right with her or that something is going to happen between you two, and it isn't going to be a good outcome. I think she is hiding something." I know I shouldn't listen when Gareth says he has one of his feelings, but his father has always said he has a strange gift or a sixth sense.

I don't believe he does, but his father says he has it, and he got it from the little people. That is laughable, but then again, he sometimes is correct about his feelings. The thing is this; I know Layla is hiding something. She will tell me when she is ready. I know it has to do with her father and her family; they are why Layla ran away. I don't know the full extent of it. I hope she will tell me when she is ready.

And it's not my place to explain to Gareth that Layla ran. What I don't get is how he knows that she is hiding something.

"I know what she is hiding; well, most of it." His face drops in a stunned expression.

"All right, E-man, I'm just trying to look out for you, that's all."

"I know." Just then, Layla and our dessert turned up and once again, our conversation is light and funny, and Gareth has gone back to normal. We were getting ready to leave when someone brought coffee to us.

"Have a cup before you go." Layla shrugged at Gareth's request, and I said, why not.

"E-man, you are bringing Lala to the next event?" Shit, I forgot about my mum's charity event where I'm to be a judge.

"What event?" asks Layla. "It's cool."

"Shut it, Gareth." He stared at me like I'd gone mental.

"Don't want to spoil it for her." She is starting to look confused.

"Not this weekend coming, the one after on Saturday, there is a charity event that my mother hosts and apart from Gareth's," who happens to be wearing a smug face, "my mother's is the best event on the social calendar. You should come; you would love it." I can see the calculating look on her face like she is trying to work out if she has anything on the weekend. Her face is crestfallen, and at that, so is mine; she has something.

"I can't; my uncle is taking me out that weekend. I will try to get out of it, but I have kind of promised that I would go, and I do owe my uncle." She looked at me with pleading eyes. I know what she means about owing her uncle.

"That's fine, but it won't be as much fun without you." I pulled her towards me, and I kissed her.

"Oh, yak." We pulled apart, and Layla laughed.

We stayed and talked for another half an hour, with Gareth trying to convince us to go downstairs and party longer, but neither Layla nor I were in the mood, that plus I had to get up in a few hours for work. All I wanted to do was get to bed and sleep next to her. I could tell Layla had the same idea about going to bed.

So, we said our goodbyes, and we left.

The drive home is quiet, we don't say much, and I like the silence. It's peaceful, I get the chance to breathe in her floral smell, which still hasn't left my car since the masquerade ball, and I love it. Before I knew it, I was pulling into my driveway.

"I could walk you home, or if you like, you could come in, I know it's late, and you're probably tired."

"Shh, I am tired, and I would like us to go to bed." My heart starts to race. I think I stopped breathing for a second. I help her out of the car and lead her inside. Giving her a quick tour of my house as I lead her straight to my room. She puts her handbag on the chair near the door, takes her shoes off and puts them under the chair, Layla turns towards me, I walk to the tall boy that she is standing next to and pull out one of my shirts.

"Here, to wear to bed." I kiss her, she hands the shirt back, and I give her a questioning look. She proceeds to slip out of her dress and sits it carefully on the chair. I couldn't believe my eyes that she is happy to strip off in front of me. She takes the shirt back and puts it on, then in a few strange moves, she removes her bra from under the shirt and puts it with her dress. She has a worried look on her face, and I'm not sure what that is about, but I take her hand and guide her to the bed. She crawls under the covers. I undress down to my boxers, turn out the lights, and I hop in. She snuggles close to me.

"Good night, my sweet Layla."

"Kiss me," she says in a dreamy voice.

"As you wish."

14

Layla

There were no dreams or nightmares, no endless hours of staring up at the ceiling waiting for sleep to come. All there was, was a peaceful dreamless sleep. I could feel a warm body next to mine. I rolled over to face Eric and noticed that he is already awake and staring at me. I discreetly try to flatten my hair to cover my ears. I don't want him seeing them, so I make it look like I am trying to get rid of my bed hair. I hope that I managed to make it look convincing.

"I'm sorry if my alarm woke you," he said.

"There was an alarm?" he laughed at my rather strange half-asleep spoken sentence.

"What time is it?" I asked.

"About four-thirty," he replied.

What! "Why are you up so early?" I asked.

"I have clients who need me bright and early, especially this one client."

"I thought you only had one week of taking over from your mother." I don't like this idea of him leaving the bed so early.

"It was for a week. I am a personal trainer, and some people can only schedule an appointment before working. But I will have most of the morning off, as well as a break for lunch. I do the arvo shift at the gym."

No wonder I liked looking at his chest so much. "Do you have to leave?"

"Yes, I do; I don't want to. I would rather stay here with you." Eric moved over and kissed me lightly, slid out of bed and went into the ensuite. After about twenty minutes, he came back out dressed in a towel – oh my, how I love seeing him dressed that way – he dug around in his chest of drawers, pulled out some clothes and went back into the bathroom—what a gentleman. Eric came back out wearing gym shorts and a gym shirt. He grabbed a bag out of his walk-in and dropped the bag next to the door. He then came back over to the bed and crawled in.

"Aren't you meant to be going to work?" He starts to kiss me.

"Yes, but I still have a few minutes to spare."

I could have some fun with him, so I pushed him out of bed; though he didn't hit the floor, he managed to roll and land on his feet.

"That's uncalled for," he said.

Oh, he looked so sad, like I just kicked a puppy, but I burst out laughing. I haven't laughed like this in a long time, not since I was little and never with my father, that's for sure. And at the thought of my father, I stopped laughing, and I tried to bury myself in the covers. Eric saw my mood change, hopped back into bed and pulled me into his lap.

"I can stay and cancel my appointment!" he said.

I wasn't sure if he thought I was upset about him going to work or if he knew I was thinking about my father.

"It's okay, go to work."

"Are you sure?"

"Yes, or do I need to push you out of bed again."

He smirked, kissed me again, got out of bed, walked over to the door, picked up his bag and turned to me.

"I'll see you tonight."

I was starting to drift back off to sleep.

"Stay as long as you like, just lock the door on your way out, oh and try not to kill Gareth if he comes over. Have a good day, my sweet Layla."

I can't remember anything else or even him leaving because I started to drift back off to sleep.

15

Eric

I watched as she went back to sleep so quickly. In the dark, I couldn't be sure, but her ear looked pointed. Maybe the moonlight is casting shadows, not to mention the ungodly hour was messing with my head. That's twice now I thought that, and this is one morning that I wish I didn't have to go to work, that I didn't want to leave my bed this early. If it weren't for this one client- David Beacon, I would still be in bed next to my girl. But as he is one of the richest men in Skyhaven, I couldn't refuse the work, not if I wanted to keep my business afloat.

I left home later than I would have liked. Still, I had a good reason, I got to the Beacon estate at around six, half an hour later than I would have liked, I parked the car out the front of the house, I was about to walk up the main stairs when David came running around the corner from his mansion, but David liked the term house.

"Ah, Eric, about time, man, any reason why you are late?"

"Had a late night is all."

"Get laid?"

No, but I did sleep next to the most beautiful girl in the world.

"I could ask you the same thing, but I did have a most enjoyable evening."

"Ah, my issues with the opposite sex are… well, let's say, I'm undecided. But I digress. Are the rumours true, my friend?"

I know where this is going; he's going to ask about Layla and her slapping Becca.

"Can we please just train?" I asked.

"No, not yet; I have to know, are they true?" I sigh internally. I know we are not going to get any training done if I don't answer him.

"If you are referring to the masquerade ball…" he interrupted me.

"I am. I saw the girl you were with, and I saw her slap Becca. Damn hot, man. I also am referring to the rumours that you are now seeing the said girl." Yep, I knew that is where he was going.

"Look, you move your ass, and I may just tell ya her name."

He thinks about it for a minute, then nods, and we both start to run around the perimeter of his estate.

16

Layla

Once again, the days and nights fly by in bliss. I find that I have been able to sleep at night when I sleep next to Eric; he is such a gentleman. I spent my time with Eric when he wasn't working. I spent my free time working on my dresses; they seemed to flow one after another. I would work in my garden too, and it is flourishing. The flowers are smelling even better, and their blooms are lasting longer.

I spent any other free time at my uncle's, where I would ride my horse and practise my archery.

Today is the Thursday before the tournament, and I am to stay at my uncle's to leave Friday. The tournament or archery event is to last the entire weekend. We're to arrive Friday and sign in. Spending the whole weekend, I am not thrilled, but at the same time, I am. I mean, I don't want to be away so long without seeing Eric, but I am happy that I get to ride Storm Cloud. I get to fire my bow. I hope I don't come across as a show-off. Maybe I should hold back a little.

I don't like the idea of not sleeping next to Eric for the next few days. I don't want nightmares. Over the past weeks, I have become accustomed to having his body next to mine. But how do I tell Eric that I don't want to be away from him, that I want to sleep next to him because he chases the dreams away? I will still have trouble sleeping tonight, seeing I can't be next to him. I need him; he has kept the nightmares away.

He should be here for lunch any minute now. I am in my sewing room, playing with one of my dresses on a mannequin, when I heard the door open and close. I heard Eric's footsteps coming down the hallway. I felt his arms wrap around me, and he starts to kiss my neck. The instant his lips touch my neck, my body starts to react in the way only it can when he touches me. He gets my blood pumping and my heart flutter. The more time we spend together, the harder it is for my mind to say 'no' to him. Soon it will be screaming 'yes' just as loud as my body does.

"I have bad news," he whispers in my ear.

"I have bad news as well."

He stops kissing my neck, picks me up and carries me to the bedroom. Not the best place to have a conversation about bad news; he sits on the bed and holds me in his lap. "Ladies first." Deep breath. Here goes nothing.

"You can't spend the night with me tonight. My uncle has invited me to stay at his house so we can leave early Friday. I am sad about not being able to share a bed with you over the next few nights."

He starts to laugh, and he's laughing at the fact that we can't spend the next few nights together, so I punch him in the shoulder. "What was that for?"

"You're laughing at me."

He leans in, kisses me, pulls back and stares into my eyes.

"I am laughing because I was going to say the same thing. My mother's charity event, she wants me to stay so we can finish the last of the to-do list early before anyone gets there."

"I guess we better make the most of the time we have now," he said, giving me a sly smile, and I know what he is thinking.

"Not yet," I whisper to him; his expression doesn't change; he stands up with me still in his arms and throws me onto the bed.

"Oh, I know, doesn't mean I can't still have some fun with you," he said as takes his shirt off and tosses it on the floor.

I squeal with delight and try to get off the bed and out the door, but it doesn't work, and this time he doesn't throw me on the bed; this time, he lays me gently on the bed and lays next to me.

"Now, where was I?" his lips touch mine and my mind went blank.

I don't really remember getting to my uncle's, but I did, and it was later than I thought. It is almost midnight by the time I get there. I walk into the lobby I see my uncle is waiting for me.

"What time do you call this? I expected you here about six hours ago."

Dressed in pyjama bottoms with a plain black t-shirt and novelty slippers, and the worst part is he sounds very much like my father.

"You need your rest, or else you won't be able to compete at one hundred per cent, and I want them to see how brilliant you are with your bow."

He still sounds like my father, and my good mood is fading. I had spent a blissful afternoon and most of the night in Eric's arms.

"You have to go to bed now! We can discuss this later."

Now my good mood is gone. I feel about as low as dirt, and I don't know why my uncle can't see it. Instead, I turn around and start to leave the house. I would rather sleep in the stables with Storm Cloud which is better than sleeping in the house.

"Where do you think you are going?"

I rounded on him. "You are not my father! I left because I was tired of feeling so trapped and depressed about having no life. Yes, I owe you for everything, for taking me in and giving me the house to live in and the car to drive, and the life I have always wanted. Still, when I start living that life, you turn into your older brother and make me feel the same way he did. I won't ever go back to feeling like that, not when I finally feel alive and free. If you must know, I am going to sleep outside in the stables with Storm Cloud."

I turn and walk outside and leave my uncle standing there with his mouth wide open, gaping at me and my outburst.

I reach the stables; I don't bother turning on any lights, the moonlight shines in, and I can see Storm Cloud sleeping. I walk up to her, open the gate, and walk in. As I do, she wakes up, and she starts to thrash about.

"Hush, I've come to stay here." At the sound of my voice, she calms down, looks at me, gives my head a nudge with hers and starts to calm down for me. Storm Cloud has always been an odd horse. I know that a horse will lie down when sick or dying, but not my Storm Cloud. No, she likes to sleep lying down when I am with her. It's the only time that she will lay down, and sometimes I think it is until I fall asleep. When I sit down in the hay, she comes over and lays down next to me. I get in nice and close to her and nestle in next to her head.

I get out my phone and start to text - Boy next door.

"I would rather be in your bed than here with my uncle, who is acting like my father."

Beep Beep.

Boy next door:

'I could be there in a heartbeat.'

He makes my heart stop beating, and it is so uplifting to know he will come and rescue me. I don't think he will like where he must save me from, and Storm Cloud may get antsy.

I send him a reply, 'I would love for you to, but I wouldn't get any sleep, and neither will you. But I will spend my night dreaming of you'.

Beep Beep.

Boy next door:

'And I, you. Good night my sweet Layla.'

I'm starting to feel tired; I snuggle in closer to Storm

Cloud, and before I fall asleep, I sent Eric a text,

'Good night, my Eric xoxo.'

17

Layla

The neighing sound wakes me; I feel groggy and wonder why a horse is in my room. I can feel the fog start to lift. I breathe in, and I smell horse and hay. I remember where I slept, and I now know what has woken me. The sun hasn't come up yet, and Storm Cloud is nudging me. She is already awake and wanting me out of her stable. I can't blame her; she likes her space.

"All right, I'm getting up." I push her nose away and get up. I try to brush myself down as much as I can, but I can't seem to get all the hay out of my hair. I walk back towards the house. I try to tiptoe around the back so I don't run into my uncle or house staff. I have a shower and get dressed in a dress and slippers.

I know what everyone will think when I start to compete in a dress; 'why isn't she wearing a shirt, pants and sturdy shoes?' You would wear that if you were an average person, but I am not normal. I find the dress and the slippers perfect. You would too if you practised in them and wore them all the time at home.

My dress is a deep blue and green, and it hugs my body tightly and is full length, as are the sleeves. Looking at it, you wouldn't think I would be able to move, but I have a full range of movement. I look down at my feet, and you can see my slippers poking out from under the hem, they are silver and very lightweight, and I can feel the ground beneath my feet.

I look at myself in the mirror, I have my brown hair out, and it's cascading down my back. I have bags under my eyes, and I know they are from the nightmares I had last night; even though I was with Storm Cloud, she doesn't keep the dreams away, not as Eric can.

Once dressed, I head down to the kitchen, grab some fruit for Storm Cloud, and head for the stables. My uncle is waiting for me, watching me as I walk towards him. He dressed in a grey suit with a pink shirt, purple tie and a grey waistcoat and has his pocket watch chain hanging from his waistcoat to his jacket. My uncle loves the fashion sense of the 1800s men. He has always said they were very smartly dressing. Today my uncle is proving that he is just that.

He was standing with his hands behind his back, looking dashing, I don't want to face him, not today, not after last night, and I walk past him and straight to my horse.

"Layla, I am sorry about last night. You were correct; I was acting like your father, and for that, I am sorry. It is just that I know what you have been going through. Now that you are now free of it all, I want to keep an eye on you. I fear that too much freedom will go to your head."

I know he loves me and only wants what's best for me, but he doesn't have to act like my father to do it.

"The freedom isn't going to my head, Uncle, and I do have someone who is keeping me grounded."

My uncle has a huge grin on his face, he takes his hands from behind his back, and that's when I notice that he has his cane with him. It is beautiful; it's black with a jewel-encrusted dragons head on it. He leans and starts to bounce on the balls of his feet, almost preening himself like a peacock.

"Yes, Uncle, you keep me grounded, but this time you aren't the reason." He stops bouncing, and his face turns calculating.

"Ah, I knew there was a boy involved, now would that be the

young man you left with at the ball?"

I say nothing; I know my uncle. I know he already knows that the boy I left with and the boy keeping me grounded are the same. I have no doubts that he also knows who, and I am not silly. I know my uncle. He still has his keen sense of intuition about him, it's more of clairvoyant ability, and I don't want to acknowledge his knowledge today, so instead, I feed an apple to Storm Cloud.

I spend the better part of the morning with Storm Cloud, trying to avoid my uncle. I go through my bag that I had brought; it has my toiletries, a couple of dresses and my PJs. My uncle said not to bring too much. He told me that they catered for everything and I only needed to bring a change of clothes. After lunch, we start to load up Storm Cloud. We are in the back of a 4WD, one of many cars owned by my uncle. As I sit looking out the window daydreaming about Eric, I can hear a faint buzzing. I don't pay too much attention to it, only because it's my uncle trying to tell me about the event today. Still, I act like a spoilt child, ignoring him, but I couldn't help it, not today. Maybe he is right; perhaps I am letting this freedom go to my head, especially if I act like a child who holds her breath until she gets what she wants.

"Layla, are you listening to me?"

I turn and face my uncle, "Sorry, Uncle."

"Are you thinking about your young man?"

"Yes, Uncle."

"Is this the same one we were talking about on the phone some weeks back?"

"Yes, Uncle."

"The one we were discussing and the one with whom you left are the same?"

"Yes, Uncle."

"You're not saying much, are you?"

"I'm sorry, Uncle, it's just that he invited me out this weekend, and I had to cancel on him so that I could be here with you." Again, I sound like a whinging child. But my uncle isn't upset by my last comment, and he knows I don't mean it to say the way it's coming across.

"There's something else, isn't there?"

I'm not sure what he is getting at with that question. Maybe he refers to the fact that I am starting to fall for Eric, or perhaps I am worried about sleeping together. He knows what that can do to me and how I will never be able to go back once I have. I know that Eric keeps the dreams away, and I am happy being with him. I go back to looking out the window when we passed a set of massive gates and enter a considerable estate, I am not sure, but this looks bigger than my uncle's place.

"Over there is the main house; you can only just make it out."

I look out his window and notice only a small part of it hiding in amongst some trees. I can also see large stone towers; they look like large stones from here, though it almost looks like the top of a castle.

My uncle points to my side. "Out through those trees is the cross-country trail, that's the second stage, and I have no doubts you will excel at it. Just over there is the main stage or the main arena where most of the weekend activity will be."

I look out my side, and as we weave along the long driveway, I can see a grandstand set up. I can also see small tents surrounding the stadium and a large white main tent.

I can also see what appears to be the main judging area; it almost resembles the area royalty would sit in if this were early 1500. People are setting up targets in the main arena, and I notice one male carrying a target. He has his shirt off, and in the instant that I see him, I can't help but think that he looks like Eric.

The next moment I look, trees obscure my view; we make our way to the stables we pull up behind another car. It seems that we have a bit of a wait on our hands now. We are about the fifth car in line, and the first car is having trouble unloading their horse. I am still not in a great mood. I get out my phone and stare at the screen, and I haven't got a message from Eric yet. Maybe he is busy with his mum's charity event.

I am silently hoping that he is missing me as much as I am missing him. I wonder if he is staring at his phone, wondering the same thing about me. I type out a text letting him know that I miss him, and soon as I hit send, I receive a text message from Eric asking if I miss him.

I burst out laughing and post a reply saying 'yes', and again once I have hit send, I get a text back saying the same thing I sent him. I know my uncle is watching me with an all-knowing smile on his face, but I don't care about his intuition now that I am starting to feel better.

Half an hour later, we are at the front of the line, and we can now unload Storm Cloud. A young man with a clipboard greets us. He marks off my uncle's name and Storm Cloud's from his list and tells us to unload her and put her in stables nine and ten. He asked why we had to have two barns when we were only bringing one horse.

He would see in a minute why I had to have two stables for her. My uncle's stables are large enough for Storm Cloud. His damn intuition had kicked in, and he compensated for her when he built the barns. We get out of the car. I head to the float while my uncle and the driver discuss parking and where to put the belongings.

When I opened the float, Storm Cloud bolted out and straight into the forest. I closed the float and told the driver he could park the car. Everyone was staring at the spot where she had run. It didn't faze me that she ran off as Storm Cloud gets cramped up in that float for a while, and like me, likes her freedom. I just sit by the edge of the forest to wait for her.

Of course, I keep getting stared at, but I don't mind. Some twenty minutes later, I can hear hooves approaching. The next thing I know, I am getting nudged in the back. I stand up and hold my hand on Storm Cloud's mane and guide her towards the stables. The boy that signed us off just stared at her; everyone was just staring at her. I escort her to her barn with my head held high.

"Now be a good girl for me, please." I rub my head against hers. "I will be back later to make sure you're okay, and I will see if I can take you out for a ride then." I walk out of the stable to find my uncle standing there waiting for me.

"I have had our belongings already moved into our tents; care to see where we will be staying the next few nights." He holds his arm out for me, and I take it, and we walk out of the stables and towards a field full of tents and not your traditional tents either; these are very fancy tents.

"It's called glamping," He must have seen the look of 'what' on my face because he continued. "This is a glamorous form of camping; it's all the luxuries of a hotel just outside." My uncle directs me to my tent.

Inside I see a double bed covered with throw pillows and rose petals. There are even beside tables covered in candles.

My bags, saddle and my archery items sitting on a little love seat; there was even a tall boy for my clothes. The tents decorated with fairy lights give off an air of romance. It would be so much better if I were here with Eric.

After unpacking my bag, my uncle grabs me once more and says we will find our hosts for the weekend; he says he wants to introduce me. Still, I have this sneaking suspicion he has an ulterior motive for our little trip here this weekend, and it's not just to show off my archery prowess.

We make our way to the marquee that is sitting just a short distance away from the grandstand. People are scurrying around with tables and chairs. I can see the head chef shouting out orders, left, right and centre.

There are vans full of flowers arriving one after another and campers entering with food supplies. It almost seems a bit of a jumbled mess; it makes you think we aren't supposed to be here today. Still, my uncle said that only competitors are arriving today, and the spectators will be arriving tomorrow.

We stop in front of the marquee.

"Now I know I said we are going to meet our hosts for the weekend, but there is also someone I would like you to meet."

Groan, I know I promised I would do this for him as a thank you for all that he has done for me, but I can't help but feel a little like a slab of meat.

"Don't groan, darling. You will like him."

Him? I look at my uncle. I knew he wanted something else from me but to set me up. He is starting to act like my father, but I can't deny him of this, but I will protest every chance I get. Boy, I sound like a whinging spoilt child. I need to slap myself and start acting like my old self, mentally confident, secure, and fearless. I stand up straight and hold my head high, but my shoulders droop, and all my confidence popped like a bubble. Yep, I can't do it, not right now.

"Please don't look at me like that, darling. Yes, I know you have someone, but that is just one person. Do you have any friends besides him?"

I know he can see that the look on my face says the answer is no. I guess I haven't got to know my neighbours or any of Eric's friends yet. We seem to be in our little world at the moment, and to me, right now, that's all I need. I left all my friends and family behind when I left home; I don't need anyone else but Eric right now.

"Let's see the last event you went to; you slapped someone and left with a masked man."

I smile at the memory of that night, how I found out that Eric was single and how everything just seemed to fall into place, how it was the first night of us being together, only not in that way, of course, not with my mind screaming at me.

My thoughts are broken into when my uncle keeps talking. "Now, if you are to be my date to most of these events when your boy isn't taking you, you will need to meet and greet certain people. You need to schmooze."

"Really, Uncle, schmooze. You know very well that our family doesn't schmooze."

"Yes, I know, but this is Skyhaven and not our home, and here we schmooze. Now shall we meet our host and their son?"

"Fine, but so that you know, I am not happy about it." My uncle laughs at my pouty face, then turns serious.

"Look, Layla darling, I know you have someone, and you won't tell me anything about him. How do I know he is good enough for you? It wouldn't hurt to meet some other people."

"But Uncle, I am happy with whom I have, and I don't want to meet anyone else, and I should think you know the reason why." He gets a sad look on his face and understands.

"Okay, you are correct, but these people are my clients, and I would very much like for you to meet their son."

There is no more discussion because he pulls me forward and encouraged me to walk with him again, not to mention the conversations were going around in circles. I can't believe that he is trying to set me up with some wealthy couple's son. All I want is Eric and no one else, and even that is asking for a lot, but I hold my head high and walk into the marquee.

18

Eric

I enter the marquee from the back, and I throw myself down in one of the chairs; it is now after lunch. I am starting to get hungry. Since about four in the morning, I have been here finishing off the one hundred and one things on the item list someone left me to do. I haven't eaten since I got up this morning. I grab my phone, stare at the screen, and remember what happened earlier today when I texted Layla, and I laugh at the fact that we sent each other texts messages at the same time today.

I haven't had the chance to text her until now. I had the phone ready to text when it is taken from my hands by my mother. My mother and father sit opposite me, and they stare at me.

"Thank you for all your help so far," said my mother.

It's still not done yet, but at least the event doesn't start until tomorrow. I still have time to finish everything. I'm to be a judge at this year's event, and my thoughts turn to Layla with her Uncle. I just wish that Layla was here.

"This year, we have a special guest," my father announced.

I slump in the chair and close my eyes. I try to block everything out and focus on Layla's perfect body in my head. Even doing that sends my body into overdrive. I hear my father clear his throat, and I am reluctantly brought back to my parents and the conversation.

"Aren't they all special guests, mother?" I asked. I am tired from my night without Layla. That my comment comes out slightly sharper than I would have liked, I give my mother an apologetic look.

"As I was saying, our guest is bringing his daughter."

I interrupt my mother. "And what, mother, you want me to show her around, get to know her, maybe sleep with her?"

My parents don't even flinch at my comments or my scathing tone. My father doesn't say much at any time; he keeps quiet and lets my mother do all the talking. I am in no mood to play games with my family, and the socially elite games are tiresome and disgusting. It is one of the reasons I left home to venture out on my own.

"Yes, but you don't have to sleep with her," said my mother, and still, my father just sits regarding my attitude and me.

"I have someone, and I don't know why I have to do this. It's bad enough that I have to spend the weekend without her, but to show this other girl around."

"Yes, you have this girl, but you say nothing about her. All we hear are rumours about you leaving with a girl at the masquerade ball. But this girl is the daughter of a significant client, and I want you to be nice to her." My father stares at me intently before opening his mouth to speak.

"She doesn't know who you are. That is why you are keeping her a secret from everyone, you don't want her life splashed over social media, and you don't want her to know about where you come from."

How does my father do that? I swear it's a sixth sense or something? My mother looks at my father and smiles at him full of warmth and love, but her face is stern when she turns to me.

"Very well, but please at least be nice to this girl today."

"I will be a gentleman, but she's the daughter of some rich couple, so she is probably some stuck up bitch."

"Eric!"

19

Layla

I try to argue my point of not meeting this boy with my uncle. "He is more than likely some upstart snob," but my uncle doesn't seem to be listening to me.

Eric

I don't stop there with my lack of not sleeping next to Layla and the early start of today as I am in no mood. "Let me guess, she has blonde hair, doesn't eat and is plastic. And like most of the spoilt wealthy socialites, they are just that, bitches. Becca is a good example," I say to my parents.

Layla

We are standing in the doorway of the marquee, and my uncle is looking around for someone. Hmmm! I don't want to meet with this person, I am once again acting like a brat, but I don't care right now. "I bet he thinks he is pretty and spends more time on his hair than a girl does," I say to my uncle, and I can hear the snide tone in my voice.

Eric

"Wait, she carries her dog in her handbag." Once I got started throwing insults about this girl I have never met, I can't seem to stop. And I am not caring what my parents are thinking of me right now.

My uncle must have spotted them because we start moving

towards a table at the back of the marquee. "I bet he is dating one girl and has three on the side. Isn't that what all rich playboys do?" I say to my uncle.

"Hang on; she probably spends all her time shopping and on social media." That's one good thing about Layla; she doesn't spend time shopping or being catty on social media. Now I am picturing this girl I am to meet to be similar to Becca.

We are moving closer to a table at the back; I don't want to get closer. I want to turn and run. But once again, the impending doom of meeting this person sends more scathing remarks towards this person.

"Or he is sporty and loves his tanned body just as much as his reflection." I am getting annoyed at my uncle; he knows that I like the boy next door.

"I don't want any more self-absorbed rich girls," I say to my parents.

"I don't want some player, Uncle, and I just want my boy next door."

"I just want my girl next door."

"Ah, here we are." My uncle says with a happy tone.

I look up, and I can see two people facing a young man slumped in a chair. It seems as if he would rather be anywhere else than here. Maybe he was told he is meeting some girl today, and perhaps he is having the same thoughts as me about not wanting to be here. The two people sitting opposite him are exceptionally well-dressed; the man has a black jacket, a blue shirt, has light brown hair, green eyes and a clean-shaven face. He looks familiar, somehow.

The lady is wearing what could be a gold-coloured dress or blouse; she has her strawberry blonde hair in large loose curls. Her eyes are the same colour as Eric's. Thinking about Eric's eyes has me closing mine; I can picture him. I try to shut out the noise and brace myself to meet this boy.

"Ah, there she is, oh my, she is pretty; you should turn around."

I am starting to get annoyed. I don't want to meet this person; I don't care how much money her father has; she won't compare to my Layla. I close my eyes and take a deep breath to try and calm myself and get ready to meet this girl, and that's when it hits me. I smell flowers and a lot of them; my breathing starts to become ragged, and my heart starts to beat erratically.

When I close my eyes and try to calm myself, that's when I hear it; the heartbeat, the breathing—my Eric.

My sweet Layla, I get up slowly. I am afraid to turn around, in case it isn't her that I can smell, and as I look at her, I can see she has the same look on her face that I must have. 'Sweet relief'. I took the few steps it would take to reach her, and I scoop her up in my arms. I kiss her.

20

Layla

Eric's arms are like a vice around me, and his kiss is urgent, and I love it. I am lost in him when I hear my uncle say to Eric's parents, "Oh my, Lillian, I do hope that your boy doesn't greet every girl that way."

I laugh, and it makes Eric break the kiss. He puts his forehead on mine.

"My sweet Layla," he said as he closes his eyes and breathes in deep. He reaches for my hand and leads me to the table to meet his parents. He stands in front of the table, and my uncle has taken a seat next to Eric's mother.

"Layla, this is my mother, Lillian, and my father, Geoffrey. Mother, father, this is Layla."

I reluctantly let go of Eric's hand so I can shake the hands of his parents.

"It's a pleasure to meet you."

Eric pulls a chair out for me, and I sit down.

"If I am to guess correctly, you all know my Uncle Bardrick," they all nod, including Eric. Eric sits next to me, grabs my hand and gives it a slight squeeze under the table.

"I should have guessed that you had money, I mean with your uncle buying you that car and all, but for it to be Bardrick, wow, I did not see that one."

I did a half-smile; I mean, I come from money, but not anymore since I have left home. On leaving home, I had effectively thrown away my old life, including the cash. I became a normal girl with nothing, and I was happy about that, but everything I have now is from my uncle and is on loan. Lillian presses her hand on my uncle's arm.

"I thought she was your daughter, not your niece."

"Oh yes, I consider Layla, my daughter; that's why I always refer to her as my girl." My uncle said as he looks at me and smiles.

"I take it that the conversation of your families never came up," said my uncle.

I give him a stern look; he knows why I haven't talked about our family.

Eric has been so understanding about it as well. I have never pressed him about talking about his family, just as he has never pushed me about mine. I mean, I knew we would both talk about it at some point when we both felt comfortable about it. When I have mentioned anything about my family, no matter how small it might have been, he would just sit and listen and hold me; I am thankful for that.

Eric's father clears his throat. It seems evident that he wants the subject changed.

"Are you competing over the weekend, Layla?"

Before I can answer, my uncle speaks up. "Ah yes, Geoffrey, my good man, I have had her training for the past month."

Eric lifts my hand and lightly places a kiss on my wrist.

"So that's what you have been doing when I have not been with you," he said as he smiles sweetly at me, yep, still weak at the knees.

"Yes, a condition of my uncle's for getting Storm

Cloud out of the family stables."

"I hear that you are quite good." Says Eric's mother.

"It's been a while; even with the practice this past month, I still feel rusty."

Uncle lets out a laugh and proudly puffs out his chest.

"Nonsense, I have seen you. You are as good as always; you have not lost your touch." Uncle faces Eric's parents. "Care to place a wager on it?"

I groan internally, and I can feel Eric squeeze my hand.

Geoffrey gives my Uncle a sly smile. "Sure, why not? What are the stakes?"

Uncle strokes his chin as he thinks about it; I know what he is thinking. He knows I am going to win; he knows my skills will outshine everyone else's. He is just making it look dramatic. Lillian just shakes her head at the two men. Geoffrey smiles and rubs his hands together.

"I have it; should I win, I get your new Aston Martin Vanquish. How does that sound, Bardrick?"

"Good, and should I win, I think I will take that McLaren 650S off your hands. I don't have one of those in my collection."

They are betting with cars, I have said it before, and I will say it again, I don't get these exceptionally wealthy people.

"But to make it fair, I think Layla should have a handicap just to make it more interesting," said Lillian.

"Agreed," said Uncle and Geoffrey at the same time. Eric just looks at me with eyes that say sorry.

"I think Layla should compete dressed as she is and rides bareback; that should make it more sporting," says Lillian.

"Done," Uncle said without hesitation.

"No!" Everyone looks at me.

"Layla?" Uncle gives me a look of what are you doing, hush. "No, Uncle." Eric squeezes my hand. "What's the matter with those conditions? I think that's pretty tough, and I doubt many people could do that." Says Eric.

"That's the thing, Eric I can. I grew up riding bareback and wearing a dress." I will admit that even though I felt so trapped at home, the only time I felt an ounce of freedom was when I was riding Storm Cloud. She hates having a saddle; she only likes to be ridden bareback.

"Bardrick, you sly bastard. The bet is off. I am not losing my car to you when you know very well you are going to win, so instead, a game of poker, I think." Both men start to laugh.

We sit and chat for about half an hour or so, but I start to get fidgety, and I just want to be alone with Eric. He must have had the same idea because he stands and pulls me up with him. He whispers in my ear. "I think we should go." I couldn't agree more.

"Mother, Father, Bardrick." Eric gives a slight nod to each.

"Mr and Mrs Walker, it was a pleasure to meet you," I smile at Eric's parents.

"The pleasure is all ours," says Lillian.

"Uncle." I give him a curt nod, and Eric quickly pulls me away from the table.

"If we were there any longer, someone would have dragged us into doing some work for the event, and right now, all I want is to be alone with you." Eric leads me out of the marquee, and we start to walk towards the grandstand. I can hear the horses when we walk closer to the stadium. I stop walking and pull on Eric's hand.

"Would you like to meet my horse?"

"I would love to." We walk off towards the stables hand in hand.

We don't say a word on our way to the stables, and the silence is pleasant. I keep giving his hand a gentle squeeze to make sure that it was his hand that I am still holding.

"So…" That is all I get out of him. He seems nervous suddenly, and I don't know why I stop up short as he turns to me.

"What is the matter, Eric?"

"The most influential man in Skyhaven is your Uncle."

"Eric Walker, does my uncle intimidate you?" He pulls me into his chest and holds me tight to him.

"Not as much as you do, my sweet Layla," He said into my hair, and I don't know how I do that. I look up at him, and our lips instantly meet. We stand for several minutes kissing; even though we saw each other yesterday, it still feels like we haven't seen each other for weeks.

How does he do this to me? I have never known this to happen, but our passion increases and all I want is him when we start to kiss. But the moment I begin to feel that my mind and body start to go to war. The only thing left to do is break the kiss and learn how to breathe again.

"Come, I want you to meet Storm Cloud." I grab his hand and rush towards the stables.

As we make our way there, I can see a crowd starting to form outside the stables. I can hear one of the horses going crazy; I knew it was my horse. I know that everyone is gawking at her; she hates people staring, and she hates crowds. But when I am with her, she calms down and allows interaction with other people. But she is still very picky about with whom she interacts.

"What are all these people doing here?"

"That would be my horse they are staring at, and that's her making all that noise." We push through the crowd to get to the front of the crush.

"Hey, you don't want to do that; she's wild and dangerous," said the man next to me. I look at him with disdain. I can feel Eric's hand tighten around mine.

"She is mine, and she is a gentle creature." At the sound of my voice, Storm Cloud stopped thrashing about and calmed right down. I moved forward and had to tug on Eric's hand to get him to walk with me. I think he is a little scared of her, and this brings a smile to my lips.

"Don't be a chicken; she won't bite." I reached out my hand to her as we stepped up in front of her, and she nudged my hand. I let go of Eric's hand, hugged her and patted her to keep her calm. I looked over at Eric, who was staring at us.

"What? She's huge!"

"Oh, that. To me, Storm Cloud is just the right colour, size and disposition."

"She's bigger than a Clydesdale. I think she is even bigger than the Shire breed. She's the biggest horse I have ever seen."

"She has always been this way. To me, she is perfect."

"I can see how she dragged you out of the brambles."

I laughed. Yeah, Storm Cloud's size did contribute to dragging me out. I beckoned Eric to come closer. I held my hand out to him as he reached for mine, I grabbed it and pulled him towards Storm Cloud, and I brought his hand up to her nose. "Storm Cloud, this is Eric, Eric, this is Storm Cloud, now I want you to listen to him, okay." In response, she nudges Eric's hand.

"Put your forehead on hers."

"What?" He looks at me with horror; anyone would think he feared horses. I cocked my head at my horse, and he did as I said. I can tell he feels silly about doing this, especially in front of the few people who decided to stare at her. I watch as the two of them stand there, not too sure of each other, but Storm

Cloud gives Eric's head a nudge.

"Now, she might behave for you. And if she does, you will be the only one she does behave for." Layla said.

As he pulled away from Storm Cloud, Eric said, "I'm honoured," he turns his back to my horse and addresses me.

"Now, if you have nothing else to do today, I was wondering if you would like to spend the afternoon with me. I know of this great little spot in the grounds that is rather nice to hide away in."

He turns back to my horse after he said, 'It was nice to meet you'. I think my heart skipped a beat. He is talking to Storm Cloud the way I do. She nudged him once more before she turned to me. I hugged her and told her to stay quiet until I came back for her. I let Eric walk me out and off to his quiet, little spot.

21

Eric

We sit in the hallow where I would always hide when I was small; trees surround us, and the grass we are sitting on is thick and lush. I had sent a message to one of the kitchen staff to organise a basket and bring it out to us. Laying with my head in Layla's lap, she gently runs her fingers through my hair; that simple action is so calming, and I can feel myself wanting to drift off to sleep.

Just as I am about to drift off, I can hear Layla start to sing. It's not a song I have heard of before. I can't tell what language she is singing in, but it doesn't matter. The music is making me drift off to sleep. I feel the wind blow, and with it, it carries the smell of flowers, the scent of Layla.

Opening my eyes, I look up at Layla. She has her eyes closed and is facing towards the breeze. Her hair blows in the breeze, making it flutter out behind her. Small flowers seem to be floating around her. She looks beautiful right now. I don't want to move one inch; I might wake up and find that I was dreaming.

After about ten minutes of watching her, she stops singing, and the breeze dies down, the flowers that were floating around her head and seemed to drop down around us. She looks down at me with a peaceful smile on her face.

"How long were you watching me?"

"For a while."

She starts to blush, and there is that pink colour that I have not seen in a while. I kind of missed it.

The afternoon is moving on quicker than I realized. The sun was beginning to set an orange glow. The setting sun was making that blush of hers more alluring. I sit up, take her in my arms, kiss her and encouraged when hearing her moan my name.

Laying her gently on the ground, how does this one girl send all my emotions wild? All I see and feel is her; her hands work quickly and are nimble as they undo the buttons on my shirt. I am cursing that she is in a long dress today. However, it hugs her nicely, and I can still feel all of her. I know that she still isn't ready for me, but god damn, she better hold on when I finally get to make her mine.

The sun has now gone down, and Layla is lying against my chest, her hand drawing circles on me. God, I love this woman. I have never felt this way before. Is it meant to be this strong and intense? She consumes all my thoughts; I mean, the way I have been acting, especially today, it was almost like a spoilt child demanding my favourite toy back after being taken away.

There are times that I get angry when someone says something negative about her. I just don't understand why I feel this way, but I wouldn't give it up for anything in the world. I am glad I went over to her house to offer to help her move in; it's the best thing I have ever done.

I don't know how long we lay there, but I don't seem to be feeling the cold, and I could stay here all night. I don't want to move, but my mum's charity event starts tomorrow, and Layla is competing, and she will need her sleep.

"Um…" Her fingers stop moving, she rests her chin on my chest and looks at me with a soft, seductive look, but it changes, and now the look on her face tells me she wants to say something, but she doesn't know how to say it.

She tries again. "Can… why is this so hard?" She buries her head in my chest, but I make her look at me. "Tell me, my sweet Layla, what is it you want?"

"Walk me to my tent." I can tell that is not what she wanted to ask, or at least say. I let out a small laugh.

"That's not what you wanted to say, but yes, I shall walk you back to your tent." I gather everything back up and put my shirt back on. I take hold of Layla's hand, and I walk her back to her tent.

Stopping at the front of her tent, I can feel several pairs of eyes on us. Everyone here knows who I am and what my social standings are, but like Layla, I have thrown them out the window, and like Layla, I want the quiet life without the cameras and the fame. All I want is what is in front of me right now.

Layla hasn't let go of my hand; she pulls me into her tent. I put the basket down on the love seat and turn back towards the front of the tent and release the doorway, as it were, and let the canvas drop to block out the rest of the world.

I watch as she extinguishes the candles. My body is screaming at me to claim her as my own finally. I know Layla doesn't want to yet. She stopped me just as I was about to take that final step. Even now, as she blows out the last candle and beckons me to her bed, I can feel our bodies are wanting each other. I can almost hear her body scream out for me.

Mouth open, I watch, captivated as she unzips her dress, and it falls around her feet. I quickly take off my shirt and jeans and watch as she takes off her bra; I feel drawn to her. The next thing I know, she is in my arms and on the bed beneath me. Sometimes my speed astonishes even me.

"Eric…" she moans my name as she digs her nails into my back. I press my body into hers. I want to feel every inch of her; she arches her back, trying to get closer to me. I moan out her name and once again press myself up against her. I run my fingers along her lacy underwear, I pause, waiting to see how she reacts, but when she doesn't stop me, I continue. I slip my hand into her underwear. I can feel the heat coming from her body. I can feel just how hot I am making her.

"Eric…"

"Do you want me to stop?" Please say no, I was thinking.

"No," she said as she throws her head back and arches her body into my hand. I am happy that she finally wants me, but I will not push her too much, nor will I rush this. I plan on making her scream out my name all night long. I slip a finger deep inside of her, and she moans with such intensity.

"Knock, knock." Are you freaking kidding me? Who the…? Layla quickly wriggles out from under me, and I sag into the bed. Layla hurriedly throws her dress back on, goes to the front of the tent, and opens the doorway slightly to see who it is.

"Sorry to disturb you, Layla." Great, it's her uncle.

"No, it's okay." I don't think it's okay, but what am I going to do about it.

I tune out their conversation and lay on the bed, waiting for her to come back to bed.

Layla comes back to bed after about a minute or so.

"Is everything okay?" I ask her. She simply nods and removes her dress before sliding into bed next to me. I know the moment is gone. We won't get the chance again for a while, even though it aggravates me.

I am still very content just to have her here next to me, in our underwear. I can again hear our bodies call to each other to claim the other. Layla apologises for what happened, but as much as I say it's okay, I know, and she knows that it's not. We both still want each other so badly, but I doubt her body or mind can make it back to where we were.

So instead, I am merely content with her being in my arms. I know I chase the dreams away for her, and I know I sleep better with her lying next to me. I feel complete with her lying here, even though I haven't had her yet. I still feel like she is my other half. I can wait, but right now, I have her in my arms, and that thought sends me off to the inky blackness of sleep.

22

Layla

I wake to the early morning light creeping in through the tent, raising my head from Eric's chest to find him staring at me with a sweet smile playing on his lips.

"Good morning, my sweet Layla."

"Good morning," I said, as he runs his fingers through my hair as I look up at his face—thoughts of what happened last night run through my head. When we spent time in the hollow, I was singing while he was lying there listening to me. I was losing myself to the surroundings that were quiet and tranquil. I couldn't help but sing, and as I did, I could feel the wind blow and the stream in the distance. I could feel little flower blossom's dance around my head. Now thinking about it, I didn't know that would happen, not after leaving home.

I was so content with the peace that I lost myself to Eric, we got so close, but my mind didn't tell me to stop. There was no screaming, no sounds of my mind drowning everything else out; it was just Eric and me. My mind screamed at me to stop, and I just didn't want to hear it, but as always, I caved, and we headed back to my tent. Once at the tent, I couldn't hear my mind; my body drowned it out; he asked if I wanted to stop. Without hesitation, I said no; we were so close. I was so close to being free, but my uncle came and knocked on the tent, and the moment ruined. My mind once again screamed at me, louder than I could have possibly imagined.

We lay in bed for several minutes before Eric said that we had to get up and get ready for the day. I am sitting up in bed watching Eric get dressed. I love the fact that he sleeps in nothing but his underwear when we share a bed. I love to run my hands along his chest as we lay together.

"I am sorry that we have to be up early; it's just that I have to do the judging today, and you have to compete." Once dressed, Eric comes and sits on the bed, I feel drawn to him like a magnet, and I lay across his lap.

"What does today entail?" his fingers play with my hair, and he rubs the bottom of my ear, and it sends shivers down my spine. He needs to stop that, and if he keeps going, I will be in big trouble, or at least he is.

"Today is all about the archery and the cross-country competition that starts early and won't finish until this afternoon or perhaps early in the evening. There is the presentation afterwards, and then we have a break.

We'll have a formal dinner and a silent auction. On Sunday, the staff will start to clean up while there is a jousting competition held. All money raised from the bets placed on the jousting go to my mum's charity. So, Sunday is about drinking and betting."

"Do you have to judge the jousting?" I asked.

"No."

Yeah, I get to have Eric all to myself. It must show on my face that we get to spend Sunday together because Eric leans down and whispers in my ear.

"I get to spend all day hidden away with you." Eric moves me off his lap, gets up and walks to the front of the tent. I wrap the sheet around me and follow him.

"You may not see much of me today with me doing the judging, but I will most certainly be watching you."

He pulls me in tight against his chest. One hand is braced up against my lower back, pinning me to him while his other hand is resting against my cheek, and his thumb is lightly rubbing my ear. I wish he wouldn't do that. He has no idea how that affects me.

"My sweet Layla," he whispers against my lips before he starts to kiss me. I'm tempted to take him to bed when I break the kiss and look up at him. He kisses me once more briefly before picking me up and carrying me back to bed.

It's seemed like only another twenty minutes before we even decide to move. The only reason that we must hurry is the fact that one of the staff came over to get Eric, telling him he was running late.

When I leave my tent, I dressed in my usual attire of a full-length dress that hugs my body and a pair of lightweight slippers. If I scrunch up my toes, I can still feel the grass beneath my feet. I have the strap of my quiver on my right shoulder, and the quiver rests on my back so that I can easily access the arrows with my right hand. I carry my bow and my saddle in my left hand. I take no more than a few steps when I see my uncle standing waiting for me with his hands behind his back.

"I have you all signed in." Uncle turns slightly and holds his left arm out for me, I take it with my right arm, and we walk to where they are holding the competition in the central area.

"Does he know?" My uncle gives me a warning look. I hang my head and feel like my father is scolding me; his right hand is still behind his back, and when he sees me hang my head, he stops walking. We face each other, and from behind his back, he produces a small vine wreath with ribbons and flower buds.

"May I?" I turn so my back is to him, and he ties it into my hair.

"It will bring you luck and keep your hair in place." "Thank you, Uncle." I touch it as I turn back around. I can't remember when the last time was. He placed one of his vine wreaths on my head. It must have been before he left. I remember that the first time he gave me one was the day I found Storm Cloud. I smile at the happy memory, not that I had many, but I always had a good day when my uncle gave me one of these.

"It's been a while since I gave you one of these." He said as I smile at him.

"I was thinking the same thing. Maybe this will bring me luck today."

"My dear child, you are a very skilled archer. You don't need luck, but maybe everyone else does." We laugh and talk about every time I wore one of these in past events as we make our way to the arena where I will be competing.

23

Skyhaven Disability Holiday Ranch Annual Archery Tournament 2013

All competitors are to go to the judge's table on the day of the tournament to sign in. There will be six stages in the tournament, with the final two stages on horseback. At the end of each stage, the bottom ten competitors will be eliminated until we are left with either a top ten or five to compete in the last stage. Winners receive a trophy and a plaque that will hang in the Skyhaven Disability Holiday Ranch lobby. All monies raised will help families and carers have a much-needed holiday. Some will also go to supplies to keep the ranch operating for another year.

The stages are as follows:

Stage One:

Three stationary targets per competitor. Each competitor will have ten arrows, ten shots per competitor. There will be no time limit.

Stage Two:

Three stationary targets per competitor. Each competitor will have ten arrows, ten shots per competitor. There is a time limit.

Stage Three:

Three moving targets per competitor. Each competitor will have ten arrows, ten shot per competitor. There will be no time limit.

Stage Four:

Three moving targets per competitor. Each competitor will have ten arrows, ten shots per competitor. There is a time limit.

Stage Five:

Ten stationary targets per competitor. Each competitor will have ten arrows, and ten shots competitor will be on horseback. There will be no time limit.

Stage Six:

Ten moving targets per competitor. Each competitor will have ten arrows, and ten shots competitor will be on horseback. There is a time limit.

During stages five and six, the horse must keep a steady pace. The rider may not slow or stop the horse to enable a clean shot. The winner of the tournament may try his or her luck at the bonus stage Cross country stage:

The course is in a specially designed forest that surrounds part of the grounds. The bonus round is to be on horseback (the horse must keep a steady pace. The rider may not slow or stop the horse to enable a clean shot). There will be a mix of moving and stationary targets, fifty in total. The rider will start with twenty arrows, bring back no less than fifteen, and hit no less than forty targets. Riders must not slow or stop the horse from retrieving the arrows from targets. If the rider manages to complete the course, they will receive a trophy and a cash prize of $10,000.

The day will commence at 9 am and will conclude in the afternoon. The day will finish with a sit-down dinner. There will also be a silent auction where all monies raised will go to the Skyhaven Disability Holiday Ranch. Donations can be left in the wishing well in the dining marquee. All donations are much appreciated.

All competitors must arrive the day before or on the day before 8 am and be ready to compete by 9 am.

If you have any questions, please do not hesitate to call or email me.

Kind regards, and good luck to all competitors.

Lillian Walker

CEO Walker Industries

Chairwoman of Skyhaven Disability Holiday Ranch

I'm sitting in the competitor's area, reading through the rules about today's competition. As well as the events list, there is a massive buffet in the marquee tomorrow during the jousting. Eric did say that tomorrow is drinking and betting on the outcome of the jousts. There seem to be things happening during each of the stages.

I guess it gives people the chance to spend their money and socialise, and not just have to sit all day watching people fire arrows into a lump of wood. Besides, the best part of the day will be when the competitors are on horseback. I remember when I was a little girl watching someone shoot themselves in the foot with an arrow because they couldn't ride and shoot simultaneously. I seem to be having more and more happy memories, not that I had many. All I have ever been able to remember was the bad ones.

Sitting in my little world, I hear an argument, and it brings me out of my trance. There is a crowd standing around the judge's table, and I hear her voice, and I knew my good day was going to go down the toilet.

"She should not be allowed to compete." I know she is talking about me, and I know she will call me a dull creature at some point. If she does, I will stab her with one of my arrows, or maybe I will let loose with a stray arrow.

"And why is that?" I don't recognise the voice; it must be one of the other judges. I get up from my seat, move towards the judge's table and find myself standing behind Becca. I peak around her back, and I see Eric standing behind the judge's table. Next to him is Gareth. Both spot me but don't move or make any indication that they see me. I have a feeling they are hoping that I will attack Becca.

"She is sleeping with one of the judges, and have you seen the size of that horse of hers? It's unnatural; no horse is that big." Oh, I know she will say something she will regret later if she doesn't stop talking. I look at both Eric and Gareth; Eric is ever so slightly shaking his head and looking rather bored, or at least trying to make himself look bored. I can see that, like Gareth, they are almost in a fit of laughter. But the longer I look at Eric, the harder it is for him to keep his face straight. Instead, he has that goofy look on his face which he seems to be doing lately when I stare at him.

"I still don't see the problem. We have the test results from Dr Stevens." I look at my uncle, who has come up behind Eric, and he shakes his head and mouths 'later'.

"She passes all the tests; there is nothing wrong with her," said one of the judges. I couldn't see who it was, but it wasn't the one who spoke before. I could have told them there was nothing wrong with her.

Becca starts to stumble over her words, trying to find something else that will ban me from the tournament.

"But Eric here could be biased towards her, and I want him off the judge's table."

"And why would I do that? I didn't even know Layla was going to be here, and one more thing, her RSVP was received before

I even met her. I don't see why I should have to excuse myself, or do you not know whose charity event this is." She balked at that, but she still came back swinging.

"I still think you should stand down because, after everything we have been through, I have no doubts you are going to punish Michael throughout the tournament, all because I broke up with you." Eric nearly choked, trying to stifle a laugh, as did the other judges and Gareth, but I couldn't see my uncle.

"And because I broke your heart, you went running to that …" don't say it… "dull creature."

She said it, and I was about to jump her when I felt a vice-like grip around my waist. I looked down to see my uncle's arms wrapped tight around me – his bloody intuition - I looked at Eric. He has a worried look on his face, but Gareth has a confused look on his face and probably wondering why my uncle has such a tight grip on me.

I guess Eric was the only one to see the arrow in my hand; that is why he looked so worried. At everyone's gasps and sudden quietness Becca turns and spots me struggling in my uncle's arms.

Eric moves away from the table and comes to stands next to me. My uncle's arms are replaced by Eric's. I watch as Gareth leaves the table as well and stands next to Eric. It takes a few seconds, but I calm right down, and I stop struggling in Eric's arms. He kisses the top of my head. He gently takes the arrow from my hand and hands it to Gareth, who stares at it and puts it back in the quiver, realising what I was going to do.

"Oh, my dear Becca Rankin, green is such a horrid colour on you, now what I know of Mr Walker and my darling niece here..." Says my uncle in a gentle but forceful voice.

"Niece." She pales and looks somewhat scared.

"Yes. My niece. As I said, young Master Walker has never had any affection for you, and I believe that my niece put you in your place some weeks back. If you were scared that my niece was going to win, all you had to do was say so."

"I'm not. I think she is going to get a free pass through every stage." Just then, Lillian turned up.

"What's going on here?" My uncle spoke and summed up in a few sentences what has been going on. Lillian smiles, and it's not a happy smile; it's a devilish smile, a cunning smile. One that says I am the ruler of this land and what I say goes; any who dare to defy me shall pay dearly.

"Oh, I see, and the ruling is simple, Miss Dixon competes with no arguments on the matter."

"But she shouldn't be allowed to compete." Why is she still trying?

"You still wish to argue the point; I shall see that my company has nothing to do with your father's. How does that sound?" She finally decided to stop talking.

"Ah, Lillian. It seems that a few people doubt my Layla, so how about I make it more interesting. I will give you one thousand dollars for every bullseye she makes. Oh, and I have no doubt she will compete in the cross-country stage. So, I will give you an extra one thousand for every bullseye made as well as for every arrow left in her quiver so that could be a guaranteed one hundred and thirty thousand dollars to your charity." The crowd stands stock still; you can almost hear a pin drop.

"She will never make all the shots!" Becca was starting to turn red.

"I have no doubts that she will." Said my uncle proudly.

"Really?" Eric whispered in my ear. I just nodded and shrugged my shoulders.

"Very well, Bardrick. I accept that you are so confident in your niece that she will win every stage, and you will be donating such a large amount of money. Do you agree that she can participate but not win the competition?"

"Agreed. On the condition that Layla's given a chance to compete in the final stage, the cross-country stage without restrictions."

"Agreed." Both my uncle and Lillian shake hands, and they turn to Becca.

"Happy!" says a very sarcastic Lillian. Becca finally realised that she was never going to win the argument, so she stormed away.

Everyone started to walk away, seeing that all the fuss was over. Eric pulled back and looked at me.

"Are you that good of a shot?"

"I have had my bow since I was five and had to practice all day and all night for about three months straight until I could hit every target with a blindfold." I stop there. I will not finish that sentence because I can remember what had happened at the end of that little test, and it is one of the memories that I want to forget.

Eric let go of the grip on me, and he held my hand, and he guided me back towards the judge's table with Gareth following behind us with his jaw almost touching the ground. Eric gives me a quick kiss before letting go of my hand and sitting at the judge's table. I turn to leave and almost run into Gareth.

"Lala," he gave me a wink and walked away from the table. I walk away and head back to the competitor's area to wait to hear my name called.

I find my seat amongst the sea of competitors. I look around the large sitting area and notice that nearly everyone is young. There doesn't seem to be anyone here over thirty or thirty-five. I don't know if I should be worried or not. But it doesn't matter, seeing that I am not competing to win, thanks to Becca, I feel a tap on my shoulder. I turn and find my uncle standing there.

Standing up, he gives me a hug and a kiss on the cheek and wishes me good luck. I sit in my seat, close my eyes and listen to the sounds around me; again, someone taps my shoulder. I look behind me to see a nice-looking red-haired girl; she seems to be about fifteen years old.

"First time?" she asks.

"Yes, it is." She comes and sits next to me.

"I heard what happened, and that sucks," I shrug my shoulders. I can't do much about it.

"This is my second year; everyone here is really tough. I was lucky to make it to the second round last year. I am hoping for at least the fourth stage. I'm Stacey, by the way." She holds her hand out, and I give it a shake.

"Layla."

"That's a pretty name. Well, good luck." I smile at her; then I hear her name called. She jumps up and races to the marshal.

"Layla Dixon." I hear my name called, and I gracefully stand up and go to the marshal. I am placed in front of a target and told to wait until told to fire. I stand with an arrow notched; I have it resting in front of me, just waiting to aim.

"Ready!" I breathe in and out, block all the noises out, and all I see are the targets. All I feel is the slight breeze.

"Aim!" I raise my bow and aim.

"Fire!" Before I fire, I listen to the sounds around me, and I block everything out, all I can hear in the quiet is a single heartbeat, and at its beating rhythm, I calm down. I let loose, and the arrow sails towards the target. The next noise I hear is the thud it makes as it finds its mark in the centre of the target. I let loose with the eight arrows, and each one found its mark as well. My tenth arrow finds its mark in the ninth, and I laugh to myself because all I can think of is my uncle, and I wonder if he will pay extra for a split arrow.

After each round, I would sit on the grass with my bow and

quiver on my lap, waiting for them to call me. I would sit with my eyes closed, listening to the sounds of the arrows being let loose by the other competitors of the thud they make as they hit their mark and of the beating heart I can hear in my ears.

No one comes to sit with me, and I was okay with that. I didn't need anyone breaking my concentration. I just finished Stage Four when the marshals said we would be breaking before starting the final two stages. They told us to have a half-hour break, so I went in search of Eric.

24

Eric

"Layla Dixon!" Great, it's her first round, and she is standing in front of a target wearing a dress. I mean, she looks beautiful but can Layla fire an arrow wearing it. I know she said she has been doing this since she was five, but…

"Ready!" I guess I am about to see. "Aim..." Damn, I want her.

"Fire!" Thud. Holy shit, she made it, and she is already pulling out another arrow. She is so fast. Thud. Damn! Thud, thud. Wow, she is fantastic. Thud! She has already fired five arrows to everyone else's two or three. Thud, her movements are so fluid and effortless. Thud, thud, thud. Thwack. What, the? She split the arrow. I laugh. I wonder if Bardrick must pay extra for the split arrow.

"Wow, she is amazing; did you know she could shoot?" It was one of the judges, a friend of my mother's, who asked me. All I could do was sit there with my mouth open and shake my head at her.

She mesmerises me; I just sit and watch her and no one else. At the end of the fourth stage, there is a break, and I am about to get up to find her when I feel two arms wrap around my neck and I feel a kiss on my ear. I worry a little; then I am hit with the smell of flowers and Layla whispering in my ear. How fast did she move to get here to me so quickly?

"How did I fare?" Struggling to keep my body from jumping

up and taking her to bed. How does she do this to me? I pull her into my lap. I start to kiss her; she tries hard to stifle the giggles, she pulls back.

"Careful people might get jealous or outraged. We don't want another Becca incident".

"Don't care. I want everyone to know that you are mine. We don't have long until you have to continue." I kiss her again.

"Come on, let's get Storm Cloud ready." Our time passes quickly, and before I know it, I walk from the stables and back to the judge's table.

25

Layla

“Layla Dixon!” I walk Storm Cloud up to the starting line to do the last two stages of the tournament. Standing next to her, listening to the marshal telling me that it's not timed and that I must keep a steady pace and must not stop or slow down. Finally, I can start when I am ready.

“Well, my darling Storm Cloud, you ready for this?” She gives me a nudge to let me know that she is, so I mount Storm Cloud, pat her and place my mouth near her ear.

“Let's have some fun on this, my darling.”

My final two stages were just as perfect as the first four, and we hardly break a sweat. There is a break before the presentation ceremony, so I decide to put Storm Cloud in the stables. Two strong arms snake around my waist, and I melt into Eric's embrace.

“Oh, my sweet Layla, you were magnificent.” Eric kisses my neck, and my blood starts to pound in my ears. I moan and tilt my head to the side to give him more access to my neck.

“Eric.” I can't tell if it's a plea for more from him or a request to stop.

“Yes, my Layla.” His hands are tight around me, and his mouth becomes more urgent.

“Eric! Are you in here?” Eric groans against my neck. He lets go of me but takes my hand and pulls me to the front of the stables, and in the doorway is Lillian and my uncle.

"Eric, we need to start the presentation; we need to go." Eric gives me a brief kiss and walks out with his mother. My uncle holds out his arm for me, and I put my arm around him, and he walks me back to the main area.

The main seating area has changed; the target area was now a stage and a podium.

"I know you would have won, darling, if it was not for that horrid Becca, and I have no doubts that she is still going to make a scene." I squeeze my uncle's arm. Eric and Lillian get up on the stage, then Lillian steps up to the podium.

"I would like to thank each competitor today, for, without you, we wouldn't have had such an amazing day. I know there was some um, controversy at the start of the day, and I would like to be standing here saying that our first-place winner was Miss Layla Dixon, due to her outstanding performance, but I cannot." I feel a hand on my left arm and a hand on my right arm. Each hand squeezes my arm, I look to my left and see my uncle, and on my right, I see Gareth.

"You were amazing," Gareth says with a smile.

"Thank you." I focus back on Eric, who is giving Gareth a warning look. I have a feeling Gareth wouldn't try anything with me, not after I had nicked his throat with the pruning shears.

"So, our third-place winner is Billy Sanders." There is a round of applause for a young boy of around fifteen, his face is bright red, and he has the biggest smile on his face. He accepts his award and has his photo taken, and he walks back off stage to await first and second place.

"Our second-place winner is Ms Gina Stevens." She's a rather pretty, brown-haired girl. She has her photo taken and waits with Billy on the side of the podium.

"And our first-place winner is Mr Michael Jacobs." There is resounding applause for this young man. He is a tall, dark-haired man, and as he stands up, hanging off his arm, is Becca. I catch a glimpse of his face; he doesn't seem very happy to have Becca on his arm. He looks even more embarrassed that she is walking up with him and accepting his award with him. They step off the stage and join third and second place. They have their photos taken and asked to wait while Lillian continued with the presentation. "And as I said, I would like to have said our first-place winner is Miss Layla Dixon, but due to certain circumstance." She looks over at Becca, as does everyone else that is there. "I would still like to bring Layla up here to congratulate her on such a wonderful display of talent." I walk up to the stage. Lillian kisses me on the cheek, and Eric gives me a hug and a kiss, but he doesn't let me go as we face the crowd. Lillian continues with her speech.

"Now, each year, our winner can choose to do the cross-country round. As you all know, no one has ever managed to complete the round, though many have tried. Now I had promised a very special guest that Miss Dixon could try her hand at competing for the cross-country trophy. Layla, would you like to give it a try?" Just as I was about to answer Lillian, Becca races up to the stage, dragging Michael with her.

"She can't, and she doesn't have the right to compete; only the winners should be able to compete." I don't think I was the only one to groan. Eric tightened his grip on me as if he knew I would leap from his arms and stab her with Michael's trophy, which indecently happens to be three arrows.

"If you remember this morning, Becca, you are the one that has forced this, you are the one who made me make this agreement, so I think you should step the hell off my stage." Becca holds her head high and goes to leave the stage, taking Michael with her, but he removes his hand from her grasp and tells her to go and sit down.

Lillian asked third and second place if they would like to compete in the cross-country event, and both Billy and Gina declined the offer and Gina adding that she hasn't trained for that part of the event. Michael agreed to it, though, and I told him he could go first and that it wouldn't bother me if I did the course as the sun was setting or if it was pitch black. Eric walked me to the stables to retrieve Storm Cloud.

Eric's parents and my uncle stood with me as we watched Michael do his run. Eric is back at the judge's table. Michael came back with three arrows left in his quiver, and he only hit thirty of the fifty targets. I looked out over to Becca. I could see that she was not happy with his effort. I think he did quite well. I shall have to remember to congratulate him later. I also feel that he will be going home alone tonight, and I don't think he will mind.

"Okay, your turn, good luck." Lillian hugs me, Geoffrey gives me a hug as well as a kiss on the cheek. My uncle hugs me but doesn't say anything as he follows Eric's parents. I stand wondering why Eric's parents are so affectionate towards me, I mean, they only just met me, and they are already treating me like part of the family.

Storm Cloud nudging me in the back interrupts my thoughts.

"Okay, this is our last ride for the day, just like back at home." I laughed a little bit.

"You remember all those times we would sneak out and just ride for hours on end, and we are just going to have some fun, and when we've finished, we can sleep soundly."

"When you are ready to move up to your mark, there will be lights." Said the marshal, I mount Storm Cloud, and we move towards the starting line; the marshal walks with us.

"When you are ready, you can start; there is no time limit." She continues to explain the rules as we walk to the starting line.

"Thank you." The marshal walks over to the judge's table. I can see Eric sitting there, and my heart skips a beat as I stare at him. I can see, he mouths good luck to me. I smile back at him. I lay against Storm Cloud's neck and whisper in her ear.

"Oh, my darling Stormy, it's time to make time slow down, breathe with me, listen to my heartbeat, feel my body, feel the slight movements. We will see all the targets at once and move as the breeze does. Let us show Eric how beautiful we can be together, how graceful and deadly we can be." I give her one last pat and sit upright.

I close my eyes and take a deep breath in and let it out slowly with my eyes still closed. I grab the first arrow and notch it. I raise my bow, I open my eyes, and I let loose with the first arrow, and as soon as Storm Cloud hears the first arrow go, she starts to move. I grab the next arrow and fire at the second target. I grab the third, and it too sinks into the third target. I reach the first target. I rip it out of the board, then use that one to hit the fourth target. I rip the second arrow out and use it to hit the fifth target. I have a small gap before I have to grab the next arrow, so I use the opportunity to fire arrows from my quiver. I repeat the process, never slowing down.

26

Eric

I watch Layla, standing there with my parents and her uncle, Michael has finished his run, and my mum hugs her, my father kisses her. My parents love her. I wonder if her uncle is Bardrick, the most powerful man in all Skyhaven or if it is something else.

Maybe like me, they felt drawn to her like a moth to a flame. "Yo, E-man, what is she doing just standing there?" Gareth finally decides to grace me with his presence. He has been floating around all day chatting up all the girls – he is such a player but never actually plays games with the girls – I wonder if he found anyone.

"Where have you been all day?"

"I have been with your parents, and my dad and I spoke to Lala's uncle. Seriously her uncle is Bardrick. That's huge. I didn't mean to be rude and ignore you all day. I would have chilled with you if you were here, and not to mention that every time you got free time, you looked like you wanted to ditch me and find a quiet spot with Lala." I know he is keeping it subdued because of the company around me, and I am thankful, and I reckon so are the other judges.

"All cool, man, didn't find any girls to talk to?"

"Nah." He pulls up a chair and sits down next to me. I see the marshal walking back towards the table, and Layla looks over at me. And I stop breathing, and my heart stops beating. How is

159

it that she does this to me? "Good luck." I mouth to her, and she smiles at me, and I don't think my body has tried to restart yet. We watch as she just lays rested up against her horse. I wonder what she is doing, and maybe she is talking to her. I wouldn't put it past her to do it. I see her draw out an arrow and notch it.

She manages to hit the first target without even leaving the starting line, and before she has reached the first target, she has fired three arrows. She is quick and is exceptionally graceful. She is smooth and moves effortlessly; I sit mesmerised by her. You can tell that she has spent her life training day after day to get this good, not to mention having so much faith in the horse not to be holding onto her.

"Holy shit, E-man, she is fantastic, she is not even a quarter way through the track, and she is out of arrows. It's freaky; no one can move like that." I was stunned; she is impressive and not a little bit scary with her quick reflexes. Why do I get this feeling that I have seen this before or know how she moves this way? Oddly, I can't seem to put my finger on it or these thoughts?

"It isn't natural, man," says Gareth.

"Maybe she is an elf." Where the hell did that come from? And why would I think something like that? It's that odd feeling that I just can't put my finger on it? We both laugh at my comment, but Gareth gets a strange look over his face.

"Gareth?" He shakes his head and said it was nothing. I shrug my shoulders, and I go back to watching Layla. She and Storm Cloud work so well together, they seem to move as one. I just want this day to be over so I can have her in my arms.

27

Layla

I can see every leaf as it falls to the ground and each arrow as it moves through the air. I can hear the sound as each arrow finds its mark and sinks into the target. I can see and feel time slow down around Storm Cloud and me. Two targets left, all my arrows are back in my quiver, and all I can see are the two targets that remain. In one heartbeat, I sink two arrows into the last targets. I pull them out and put them back in my quiver in the second heartbeat. In the third heartbeat, we cross the finish line.

Storm Cloud and I release the grip we had on each other, and time seems to move in its usual way once again; I lay along her neck. I can hear how her heartbeat is now separate from mine once again.

"Thank you for the lovely ride, my darling Storm Cloud it was fun, and I think you are deserving of the best apples I can find." She throws back her head in response to my promise. I didn't hear or see the crowd that was swarming us.

Then I felt a hand on my leg, and that was when I noticed the crowd and Eric standing with his hands on me, waiting to get me down. I sat up, but I couldn't get down because the crowd started to agitate Storm Cloud. Eric spotted it. He let go of my leg and started to give her a rub on the nose to calm her down.

My heart stuttered and swelled for Eric. I watched as he risked bodily harm to keep her calm for me, and it worked, she calmed down, but I could tell the crowd was still getting to her. I looked around for my uncle, and when he spotted me, I cocked my head to the side to tell him to come over. I slipped down and moved to take Eric's place as my uncle made his way over to us.

"You have to go with Uncle Bardrick, okay." I could tell she didn't want to leave me. It's not like she doesn't like my uncle; it's just that she only trusts me and will only listen to me.

"I have apples and sugar cubes." At my uncle's bribe, she moved away from the crowd and us and followed my uncle.

Eric grabs me and scoops me up in his arms, and kisses me. When we break apart, I am hugged and congratulated by numerous people.

After twenty minutes, I moved away from the crowd and made my way with Eric, holding my hand tightly, over to the marquee. Eric doesn't need to check the seating chart; he told me that we were sitting at the main table. I take my seat, and Eric sits next to me and on my other side is my uncle.

The table starts to fill up, Gareth is sitting with us, but he hasn't arrived yet. Eric's parents join us, and two other men came without partners, David Beacon and Lloyd Peters. David, Lloyd, and Gareth all grew up with Eric. All of them are part of the one per cent and the most eligible bachelors in Skyhaven.

"Lala!" Gareth walks up behind me and puts a hand on my shoulder as he leans in to kiss me on the cheek. I try to contain my rage at his insistence at calling me Lala, but a slight growl escapes. Both Eric and my uncle look at me, but Gareth laughs. He takes his seat next to Eric. An older gentleman that has a resemblance to Gareth sits down next to him.

"Lala, this is my father, Sheamus." He looks at me and smiles, but there is something hidden behind that smile, almost like he knows. I shake the feeling and get on with the evening.

The night passes in a blur, and I was presented with my trophy for completing the cross-country course as everyone waited with bated breath to see if Becca was going to say something about me winning it. But she didn't, prizes were auctioned off, and there was much laughter and dancing. I had a conversation with each of the winners, and I congratulated them on their win.

Michael apologised on Becca's behalf, and I had told him not to worry about it. It was then that I felt arms go around my waist, and Eric informed Michael that he was stealing me from him. I was pulled onto the dance floor by Eric, and we managed to have one dance together before I was taken away by his father for a dance. Then with Sheamus, I even sucked up my pride and am dancing with Gareth.

I will have to admit he is not as bad as one would think. I may have to give him more of a chance, but what amazed me, he could dance. He was ever the gentleman while we danced. As I dance with Gareth, I watched as Eric walked up behind him and tapped him on the shoulder.

"May I have this dance?" I smile and take his hand. He pulls me into him, and we are moving on the dance floor. I melt into his embrace; I could stay here all night, and it feels like all night.

We dance for a couple of songs before I feel his lips at my ear.

"Come, I want to show you something." He dances me to the edge of the dance floor, and then he takes me by the hand and walks me across the grounds; we walk for what feels like ten minutes. Then a giant towering castle comes into view, lit by the glow from the lights in the garden's beds. It's beautiful. All that came out of my mouth was wow, you would swear that King Arthur and his knights of the round table would come riding out to greet you. I stop and stare at the house, if you could even call it that.

"Want a closer look?" I would love to have a look, but I get this feeling that we can't. Then it hits me! So absorbed with today, I had completely forgotten that this is Eric's place, and he grew up here. "Please, I would love to."

"Did you forget that this is my place? Well, my parents place."
How did he know what I thought? Maybe it showed on my face.

"I know it looks like a castle, but I can assure you it is very
modern inside. Come on; I want to show you my room." He
smiles at me, and I start to walk again.

"I can see why your mum holds the archery tournament here.
Your house is beautiful."

"It's a little more than that; the grounds also house the disability
ranch, located on the other side of the property. They ride from
the ranch to the archery arena to practice and then ride back
again." I stare in awe at the house and grounds and what his
mother does for those families in need.

"My mother isn't a flashy person. She doesn't flaunt her money
around, but this house, as she likes to call it, is the only time
that she has flaunted her cash."

I didn't say anything. I wish my father were like that, but no, he
liked to show off the kind of power he could wield and liked to
flaunt what he had. To parade it around, if you will, he would
show everyone my sisters and how perfect they are but not me;
he would never do that for me. He would hide me away, not
acknowledge me.

He would force me to leave his sight and train and train and
train some more, telling me that I was not even close to being
perfect, let alone good. I don't want money, and I don't want
charity from my uncle, but I will take it for now until I can pay
him back. All I want is to live and find my way.

"What is the matter?" I seemed to have stopped walking some
fifty metres away from the entrance, and I must have a strange
look on my face because Eric is looking at me with such concern.

"Oh, it's nothing. Come on; I want to see your room," I try to say with a smile on my face and a wink. Eric moans and picks me up and throws me over his shoulder, and starts towards the house. I couldn't help but squeal and laugh. I love when he throws me over his shoulder.

28

Becca

The DJ's music is starting to annoy me, and I watch as she talks with all the wealthy young men, they hang off her every word. It's disgusting to watch as she talks with Michael. I can't believe he is fawning all over her as well. Why does she have to take everything from me? I am going to make sure that she is out of the picture. Eric takes me back, and as intended, we can be the most prominent power couple in Skyhaven. I watch as she dances with my Eric, I storm over to Michael.

"We have to do something, or at least you have to." I know he knows about whom I am talking.

"Just drop it." How dare he say that to me? He should feel privileged that he is here with me.

"No! I'm not going to."

"Look, I am not going to get involved with your crazy ideas."

"You listen to me, Michael Jacobs. I want her out of the picture."

"Becca, I am not going to listen to this. Eric is a nice guy, and Layla is lovely. I spoke to her during the event, and just then, she is a lovely person. I am not going to help you in any way, shape or form. Were you watching her today? I would be careful if I were you, especially with the way she shoots."

"But!"

"No buts Becca. I'm going to find the guys; you can find your way home." He starts to walk away from me when he stops and comes back to me, just like all men do. "One more thing Becca! Stay - away - from - me." He walks away from me.

"Fine, go! I'll do it myself. I'm not going to let her win."

29

Eric

Ilove the sound of her carefree laugh; I could listen to it all day. We are almost to the door of the house, and I am feeling strange, nervous even, and I don't know why. I put her down facing the door. I hold onto her hand.

"Ready?" She looks at me, closes her eyes and nods at me. I open the doors, and white light floods the main foyer. It felt strange to sleep in my old bedroom Thursday night. I didn't sleep well, and I needed Layla next to me. I found I can't seem to sleep without her next to me. I squeeze her hand and walk her inside.

"Off to the left is the sitting room and off to the right through that door." I point to the second door on the right.

"That door leads to the kitchens. The library's on the second floor, and the wine cellar is through the backdoor to the left."

"So not some draughty castle then?" We both laugh.

"No, but there are heaps of secret passages; I can give you a tour if you would like." I would love for you to say no, please say no, I want to take you to bed.

"I would like to see your room," she says shyly. "As you wish."

I led her to the third storey and was having difficulty walking calmly to my room. All I wanted to do was run up the stairs with her in my arms. We are standing at my bedroom door, and am I feeling like a fifteen-year-old schoolboy sneaking a girl up to his room. Why in the hell do I feel like this? I just hope she doesn't freak out too much when she sees the size of my room.

"All right, brace yourself." I open the door for her. I stand back to let her walk in first. She walks to the middle of my room and turns slowly to soak in everything. I stand in the doorway, watching her. My bedroom is enormous; I would say as big as a small house. There is a giant flat screen on the wall with a game console; I also have a Blu-ray, three-seaters in front of the TV, and on that same wall are DVD's rows and rows of them. Along another wall, I have rows of books.

A set of double glass doors lead to the balcony, and this side of the house looks over towards the archery area. My room is a split level, and if you take the three steps, you reach my very, very large bed. I have a small study near my bed and a huge walk-in robe, and as you can guess, the ensuite is significant as well; it has a sunken spa in it.

What catches Layla's eye is all the plants I have in my room; in every corner and on either side of all my doors, there is a Ficus tree. Hey, what can I say? They look lovely? Standing there watching her, I hope that she isn't intimidated by the size of my room. My parents wanted me to have space lots of space – the only other bedroom that is this size is my parents. Every other bedroom would be considered the same size as a master bedroom in any regular house.

She stands by the balcony doors staring out into my room. She looks beautiful, standing there with her back to the doors with the fireworks going off behind her. I take a few steps in and close the door behind me; I can't keep my eyes off of her. All I see is her and how she was firing her arrows with such deadly accuracy, no wonder she is so swift when I try to chase her. She moves closer to me.

I walk towards her, and we meet in the middle of the bedroom. I reach for her and put my hands on her hips; I pull her towards me and stare into her stormy grey eyes. Leaning down, I kiss her, and in that one kiss, I try to pour everything I feel for her.

She pulls my shirt free and runs her hands along my stomach and up my chest. I tangle my fingers in her hair, and I rub her ear; she moans. Every time I do this, it seems to send her into overdrive. I only do it to hear her moan; it always has the same effect on me. It causes my breathing to become ragged, and I am getting to breaking point the more time I spend with her.

The more I want to feel her beneath me, and I want to hear her cry out my name. I put my right hand on her hip and pull her even closer to me. It wasn't close enough; it's never close enough. My left hand searches the back of her dress for the zipper; as I undo her dress, she rips my shirt open, sending buttons all over my room. I run my hands along her shoulders and push her dress down. Her hands find the button on my pants, I pull us apart, and I stare into her flushed face into her bright, eager eyes.

"Are you sure?" she responds by unzipping my pants. I kick my shoes off. I also take off my socks. I start to kiss her again, place my hands on her perfectly rounded arse, and pull her forward. I lift her as she wraps her legs around my waist; I leave her dress and my clothes in the middle of the floor and walk her to my bed, never breaking the kiss.

We gracefully fall on the bed, and I'm lying above her, keeping my weight off her; I pull back and stare at her almost naked body. I will never tire of looking at her. She has shown me countless times that she is not embarrassed to be naked in front of me. For someone so innocent to be so carefree and comfortable with me, I am beyond speechless. I put most of my weight on my left side to run my right hand along her body. I watch as she closes her eyes and arches her body into my hand; I can feel her heart beating under my hand.

"I'll go slowly," I whisper to her. I start to kiss her again, my hand slides around to her back, and I undo her bra. As I take off her bra, I kiss each shoulder, and I kiss a trail from her mouth to the navel and back again. "Eric." She cries. I run my hand along her stomach to the waistband of her underwear.

"Eric." She pleads.

"Is this okay?"

"It's just…." I know what she is referring to; I'm not going to push her. "Do you want me to stop?" I stare into her eyes, my fingers playing at the edge of her lacy underwear; she arches her body in response to my touch.

"No! Not at all." She says to me; I smile at her.

"It's just…" she didn't get to finish her sentence, for there was a loud bang almost like an explosion, and I don't mean the fireworks that were going on outside or in here. We both sat up and looked out the window. "Storm Cloud!" Layla bolted out of bed, and like lightning, she was across the room, dress on and out the door. I grabbed my pants and followed her out.

30

Layla

I didn't want to leave Eric's bed. I didn't want to leave knowing what was just about to happen what couldn't happen, but I had heard Storm Cloud call out to me, which is strange. As I raced down the stairs, I hear people screaming and yelling. I can also hear horses bolting; as soon as I cleared the doors of Eric's house, I shouted for Storm Cloud. I ran towards the stables; I was at the marquee when Storm Cloud ran straight at me. She stopped dead in front of me and nudged me in the head a little bit rougher than usual, and my uncle was not that far behind her.

"What happened, Uncle?"

"The horses broke loose; there was an explosion in the stables, the horses were spooked and have taken off. You will need to get them." I jumped on Storm Cloud's back.

"Very well, Uncle, lead the way, girl, go find them." She took off towards the forest surrounding the estate.

"Round them up, girl, tell them to come home."

We were out for about half an hour, and we had managed to round up all the horses. We were ushering them back towards the marquee. As we near, I can see a few people setting up portable yards for the horses.

I can see Gareth, his father and Eric's father and my uncle helping, and then I spotted Eric; he was lifting one of the fences. I can see his muscles contract and pop out from his naked chest, and the sweat sheen off him. He spots me and smiles; they haven't put up much lighting, so he can't see the blush spreading over my body. I slowly guide the horses towards the yard.

We pushed the horses into the yard, followed by Storm Cloud, I jumped down, and I run straight for Eric; he held me in his arms.

"That was amazing. How did you do that?" Eric stared into my eyes with wonder.

"Years of trust and she is a big girl." He laughs into my hair and kisses the top of my head.

"So, she is a bully?" I laugh into his chest, and I breathe in deep his smell of sweat, earth, air and soap, my favourite scent.

"Do you know what happened?" I didn't get an answer, and a crowd started to form around me. I don't like the crowds swarming me; I grab a tighter hold onto Eric, he kisses my hair.

"It's all right. I'll take you inside." Eric let go and was about to take me back inside when Lillian came over to us, hugged me, and told Eric to wait. "If I could have your attention." Everyone quietened down to listen to Lillian.

"I would like to thank Layla for returning all horses to us. We do not know what caused the explosion in the stables, which caused it to catch alight, but we will find out how this happened and find the person responsible. I would also like to keep all horses here, I have called the vet, and he will be here in the morning to check all the horses, and I will pay any vet bills that may arise. I will also have your horse brought home to you."

"I would also like to apologise for cancelling tomorrow's jousting event, considering what has happened; I think it's for the best. If you have any more questions, I would like you to follow me to the marquee." Lillian squeezed Eric's arm, and she kissed me on the cheek. As she left, the crowd followed, and only a few people remain. Gareth and his father gave both of us a nod and walked away. Uncle smiled at me and left, as well. Geoffrey walked up to us.

"That was utterly amazing. Thank you, Layla." He looks his son up and down, and a smile spreads across his face. "Aren't you cold, son?" I look at Eric and his bare chest. I doubt he is cold under my heated stare; Geoffrey notices as well.

"I guess not." his smile broadens, then he turns and walks away. I look up at Eric.

31

Eric

I stare into Layla's eye's I could stare at her all night, but I would instead do that as she lies next to me.

"Would you like me to drive you home, or would you like to stay the night?" I know that whatever she says, I will be sleeping next to her. There are no doubts about that.

"We would have to go back inside and get your keys and your shirt, so I think we should stay, and I am feeling tired. Today has been very trying, and I would love to just go to bed next to you."

"As you wish." She smiles up at me, I take her hand, and I walk her back to my room.

"Go have a shower, and I will meet you in bed. Leave your clothes by the door, and I will have them cleaned for you." I walked into my walk-in and found one of only a few shirts that I leave here, I place it on the bed, and I pick up her clothes, and I walk down to the kitchen area and see one of the girls and ask if they could please have Layla's clothes cleaned so that she could wear them in the morning.

The girls in the kitchen asked what had happened. I tell them before making my way back up to my room. I must have been longer than I thought because Layla was already in bed and fast asleep, only it wasn't a peaceful sleep. I could see pain and anguish on her face. She was tossing and turning in bed. I don't bother having a shower; I just strip down and crawl into bed next to Layla. I move closer to her and pull her to me. She relaxes in my arms and falls into a deeper sleep. It doesn't take long for me to fall asleep either; I was glad that I could spend the night next to her.

32

Layla

I woke the next day relatively early, the sun was only starting to rise, and there is a light snoring in my ear. I must have moved because the snoring stopped, and the arm around me tightened.

"Did I wake you?" I ask.

"Not at all, my sweet Layla." I love those three words. I also love the other three words. I don't know if he will say the other three words, and I don't know if I would either. But I know I feel them and hope he feels them as well. I roll over to face the boy that has captured my heart.

His eyes are still closed, but there is a faint smile playing around the edges of his mouth. Hooking my leg over his hip, I run my hands over his stomach and up to his chest; he takes a sharp intake of breath. He grabs my thigh and pulls it higher and closer to his body; he runs his hand along my bare leg. My body starts to burn for him. For once, my body and my head aren't screaming at one another. Instead, my mind warns me again about what I would be giving up and says if you must.

"We really should get up; otherwise, my mother or the house staff will be coming in demanding that we eat before we help with the aftermath of last night." I didn't want to move from his arms or his bed. I start to smile; I can't leave this bed. I have no clothes; they are still in the tent or the back of my uncle's car by now, so I guess that means we should stay in bed. I wish he hadn't given me a t-shirt to wear to bed. I would be undoing buttons to tempt him to stay here with me. "What is with that look?"

"Oh, I just thought that I wish I had a button shirt on," a devilish smile plays on his face. I reach my hand up and touch his face and feel his stubble. I like it.

"And that I am just going to have to stay in bed for I do not have any clean clothes."

"We could stay in bed. I have no objections to that, but I did have your clothes washed last night; they should be by the door. Also, don't you have clean clothes in your tent?" I start to kiss him and run my hands through his hair.

"Thank you," I say against his lips. He pulls back from me; he holds my face in his hands and stares at me intently.

"Do you have nightmares?" Why is he asking me this now? "I'm sorry, I am ruining our morning. I was just worried about you last night that is all." I start to kiss him to drop the subject, and it works. He doesn't need to know about my nightmares, not yet, at least.

Eric pulls the shirt up over my head; his burning eyes stare at my naked body. I flush under his heated gaze. Knock Knock.

"Go away!" he shouts. "No one's in here." I laugh, but that doesn't stop the door from being opened and a person from barging in here.

"It's time to get up, and I need your help." It's Lillian; she strolls in and sits down on the bed. She has my clothes from yesterday, a bra and panties included. Well, that's just embarrassing, but even more embarrassing is the fact that she doesn't seem to care that we are a tangled mess of naked limbs. Eric untangles himself and pulls the covers over me more to hide me from her, but she isn't even paying attention. "Um… Mother!" She is off in her little world; she wasn't listening because she starts to speak.

"I'm going to cut ties with Rankin. I honestly don't understand how she thought she was going to break you two up with trying to burn the stables down." At the mention of Becca's name, well, her surname, we both sat up, I kept the covers covering my body, but Eric let the sheets fall to just above his hip line. I want to run my hand over his bare tanned, ripped chest. I had to shake my head and clear my thoughts on such things. I shouldn't be thinking about those things while his mother is sitting right there.

"I checked the footage from last night; from what you can see, Becca unlocked all of the stable doors to the horses, all but Storm Cloud's; she chained hers shut. The last time you catch her in the video, she is walking into the office. She must have let the gas out of one of the gas bottles or some such thing because the office went up first; then the fire and an explosion had caused the horses to bolt."

"I just do not understand her logic." I think I do, she's twisted, and I have no doubts she was trying to send Eric into her arms in some twisted way. "It's strange," says Lillian. I shift and clear my throat. Both Lillian and Eric look at me.

"Not really, for us, yes, it's strange; but for her, I don't think it is. I bet she was going on the fact that I love my horse so much that I would risk the fire and race in there to get her out."

"Do you think that is why she locked Storm Cloud in so that you would go in?" Asked Lillian.

"Hoping that I perished, which to her would result in Eric going to her." I look at Eric, and he pulls the blankets and me closer to him. He kisses the top of my head.

"You were not worried about Storm Cloud?" Asked Eric into my hair.

"Never, you have seen her size; she is strong and powerful, and she got out. I don't think Becca knew just how strong she was or of what she is truly capable. "

"That she did," Eric said into my ear; his hand moved along my thigh, giving me a slight squeeze.

"How did she get out?" Eric directed his question at Lillian.

"From the footage that we could salvage, you can see her trying to kick her gate. When it didn't break, she turned and kicked the wall separating hers and the one next to it; it broke, and she left through that. She is a smart one." That she is, Lillian gets up and walks to the door, I hear the door open, but I didn't hear it close.

"I'll give you twenty minutes before I come back with a bucket." I heard the door close. Eric's grip on me tightened. I turned to face him, and his mouth sought out mine. He pulled me down to the bed.

We headed downstairs after about ten minutes of Lillian walking out. He held my hand as we headed for the kitchen. We are sitting at the large wooden table used for prep work, and thirty seconds after sitting down, there are plates of food in front of us. I have a plate full of pancakes and bacon with maple syrup. There is a bowl of cereal with fresh cut bananas and strawberries on top, a large glass of orange juice and a small bowl with yogurt with a drizzle of honey over it.

There is way too much food, but I am hungry after last night's fiasco, so I start on my pancakes with bacon. The first bite is to die for, and it just melts in my mouth. Lillian and Geoffrey walk in and sit down with us as we eat, but they don't eat anything.

"As I said last night, we are cancelling the jousting competition in light of last night's events." Says Lillian.

"So, we are going to pack everything away, are we?" Asked Eric. Lillian and Geoffrey just nod.

"Would you like me to stay and help you today?" Eric looks at me and shakes his head.

"No, I will help you load Storm Cloud, and then I will meet

you at your house this afternoon." Eric leans over and kisses me on the cheek. "I should only need you until lunchtime, I think." Says Lillian.

"But I could help; I want to stay." He puts his fork down and takes my face in his hands.

"You did so much last night, and I am not letting you help today. Besides, I am used to helping, and I will get it done quicker if you aren't here to distract me." He kisses me and turns back to his breakfast. "I could stay and watch you work; that could be fun." He closes his eyes and takes a deep breath, and drops his head to his chest. He lets the breath out with a big sigh. He looks at me with a sly smile, almost like he is planning something but to what it is, I don't know, and I am intrigued.

"As I said, you had helped enough; you deserve a break from helping." I didn't say anything as I was hatching a plan of my own. Lillian and Geoffrey just sat and watched us quietly with smiles on their faces. The rest of breakfast quickly passes as we banter playfully between the four of us.

Taking my time to load Storm Cloud, I asked her to play up every time she got close to the float so that another horse would go in front of us. I was delaying my departure so I could watch Eric work. I watched as he helped with the marquee and the tables and chairs. As the morning dragged on, his shirt came off.

I could see the sheen of the sweat on his bare chest, all he is wearing is a pair of jeans, and he is looking incredible with the sweaty tanned chest and his messed up hair. I wasn't the only one to notice I saw a few girls looking at him. I secretly wanted my bow. I watched as he helped load the horses and put the portable stables away.

He didn't look at me all morning; he must have known I was staring at him after lunch while I was still staring. When nearly finished, he finally looked at me and smiled. I had to grab hold of Storm Cloud to stay upright. I hadn't let her out of my sight all day. He started to walk towards us, and I grabbed even tighter to Storm Cloud. I don't know why I felt so shy, but I can't believe that he still makes me weak in the knees.

"Shouldn't you be at home?" He gives me a quick kiss. "Why are you still here?" He raised a hand and cupped my face. My heart is skipping beats, and my breathing is becoming ragged.

"Storm Cloud refused to leave." My words came out slightly ragged.

"Refused to leave." He gives me a sceptical look, and my heart and my breathing stop.

"Yes… Storm Cloud wouldn't leave." His blue eyes stare into my grey ones, and my mind empties; it goes completely blank. He leans in close, and I can smell sweat mixed in with his air, earth and soap scent. It's a smell that I love; his mouth is next to my ear. It sends shivers of need, desire, and lust to shoot up and down my spine. It takes all my energy to stay upright.

"Are you sure that it wasn't you who refused to leave?" My heart speeds up, but I can hear that Eric's hasn't changed at all, and his breathing is calm. But I hear the burning desire in his voice. How can he do this? He hasn't been able to do it before now.

"Did you think I haven't noticed you were staring at me all day; do you like what you see?" I let out the breath that I didn't even know I was holding, and I can see he is enjoying the way he is teasing me. But I am still curious as to how he is keeping his heart rate down.

"I would be happy for you to stare at more of me, perhaps in private." He grabs my hand and places it on his chest just above his heart. The rhythm doesn't change. I wonder how he is controlling his heartbeat. How is he controlling his emotions? I couldn't help myself. I start to run my hand up and down his chest; it's slick from the sweat, and I can feel the muscle's ripple under my light touch. He puts one hand on my waist and the other hand over mine on his chest and pulls me into him.

"Shall I take you home?" Oh my! I am glad he is holding me, or I might have fallen. My voice had left me, and I couldn't answer, so I just nodded. He stared down into my eyes, burning with heat and desire.

"Come!" How can he put so much meaning into one word? He bends and picks me up and carries me towards the house, leaving Storm Cloud behind. We get partway to the house when I hear a voice calling out to me.

"Ah, there you are, darling." It is my uncle, and great there goes my mood again. Eric stopped walking. I heard him groan, and I can't say as I blame him. My uncle reached us, and he didn't give anything away about me being in Eric's arms.

"Darling, I was getting worried that you hadn't come to find me when Storm Cloud was loaded into the float." Eric put me down but still had a good grip on my hand and kept me close.

"I thought I might come and find you, but I see as to how she isn't ready to go yet. Don't let me keep you." I know what my uncle is up to, and I don't like it.

"No, it's all right; we should load her up and send her home." I look up at Eric with apologetic eyes, and he closes his and nods at me.

For the next hour or so, we got Storm Cloud loaded into the float and our stuff loaded into the back of the car. The day was starting to get away from me, and it's getting on into the late afternoon, so instead of going back to Eric's old bedroom to continue where we left off, I had told my uncle that I would get a lift home with Eric. Eric pulled into his driveway. I leaned over and kissed him and told him I would be over after a shower and change.

I stayed under the hot water longer than I usually do, the water was feeling heavenly, and I didn't want to get out. I had forgotten to grab a towel when I went into the bathroom, so I walked to my room naked and dripping water. I left a trail of wet feet in my wake. But it's what's in my bed that makes me regret not grabbing the towel. There in my bed, wearing nothing but black silk boxer shorts, is Eric; I can see that his shirt and pants are on the desk chair. His mouth hangs open as he drinks in my wet naked figure. I reach over and grab his shirt from the chair and go to put it on.

"Don't put it on." But I don't listen, and I put his shirt on. He teased me all day with not looking at me and teased me by some great fathom by keeping his heart rate steady while he sent mine through the roof, so now it's my turn. I crawl onto the bed and sit astride him; he goes to put his hands on my waist, but I slap them away, and in return, I get a sad puppy dog face. I placed my hands on his chest, and I was about to play when his phone rang.

"You better pick it up." I started to slide away, and he tried to grab hold of me to keep me in place, but I was faster. I picked up his phone. I looked at his caller ID and saw that Gareth was on the other end. I tossed it to him.

"Ya boy wants you." He just stared at me with an open mouth. I just pointed at his phone and walked out of my room.

33

Eric

Ilay there stunned, staring at a vision of pure vixen walking out of the room, leaving me here aching and hanging with a vibrating phone on my chest. I had no idea why I thought to lay on the bed in nothing, but my boxers was a good idea, but Layla walked in naked and wet. Damn, I had dreamed so many times of her naked and coming to me. However, I do get nearly every night to sleep next to her partially nude body.

My phone stops vibrating for a few seconds before it starts back up again. How can Layla tease me like that, and throw the phone at me and just walk away? Grr, frustrating. I don't want to talk to Gareth now, but if I don't answer his phone call, he won't stop ringing, and I am in no mood to talk. I want to chase down my girl.

"This better be life and death, ya Irish bastard." I knew he would know what I meant when I called him that. I only call him an Irish bastard when I am frustrated with him.

"Oh, sorry, man, didn't mean to make ya stop halfway through or were ya already done?" Yep, he knew what I meant.

"What did you want, Gareth?" Eric growled.

"Ouch, not even started," replied Gareth.

"Gareth!"

"Sorry, E-man, but I do need you to cover at The Cavern tonight."

185

"Why can't you get someone else to do it?" I don't feel like going out to his place.

"I don't trust anyone else, and I have to go to Ireland with dad. Look, my aunt is sick, nothing serious, but I need to go. I will be away for about a week or so. I need you to pay wages and invoices. Please, E-man, I will owe you."

"Can't you do all that now?"

"I'm actually on my way to the airport now." I don't want to go, and he is so going to owe me for this. "Take Lala with you, but if you two break anything, you will be paying for it."

"Yeah, all right. But it won't make us even; you will still owe me."

"Deal, thanks, E-man, tell Lala sorry." He hangs up; I get up and put on my jeans. I leave the room in search of my sweet Layla. I can hear her singing as I get closer to the kitchen, I sneak up on her, trying not to get noticed, and I succeed. I catch her dancing to whatever song she was singing. I stood for several minutes watching her before seeing me; she blushes that lovely pink she goes and smiles at me.

"Would you like to go dancing?"

At the Cavern.

"Hey, Greg! I see you got the early shift." I shook hands with the large man.

"I swapped with Sam." He released my hand and looked over at Layla. "Evening, Miss Dixon, you are looking nice this evening."

"Thank you." And damn, she is looking nice, it's a simple pair of jeans with black heels and a black and blue corset looking shirt, and she only has a couple of flowers holding her hair back. It's odd to see her in anything other than a dress, but damn, tonight, she looks hot.

"I hope you are well?" Said Layla.

"I am Miss. Well, have a good evening." As we went inside, I directed Layla towards the nightclub part of the Cavern. You would think that Gareth would have his office on either the ground floor or in the restaurant, but no, he has his office in the nightclub. He had said that there is more trouble on that floor, and at least he could keep his eye on it, and you wouldn't mess with Gareth, not with his size. That and he likes to listen to music when he works.

We make our way through the crowd of dancing bodies to Gareth's office. I unlock the door and turn the lights on. I let Layla walk in, and I close the door behind us. In the centre, facing the large window that looks out over the dance floor, is a large desk. It doesn't hold much; a lamp, trays and a few odds and ends. Along the right wall are filing cabinets and bookshelves. On the left is a lounge, coffee table, and next to that is his bar. He has a few paintings and some plants, and it's a nice quiet room for working.

"It's so quiet." Layla is looking around the room. I watch her as she walks over to the bookcase and tilts her head to the side so she could read the titles of the books. I moved over to one of the pot plants and moved it to the side to reveal the floor safe. I open it up and find a box with my name on it.

"The room is soundproof." I sit down at his desk and open the box. Inside I find his tablet and his cheque book, and an envelope with my name on it. He knew I would say yes to him before he even asked me to cover, slick bastard, hence the note.

E-man

Wages need doing; please put in a bonus for Greg ($200). Don't ask.

Please pay for gas, electricity, cleaners, and Phillips fruit. Open my mail and check if any other bills need paying while I am away.

I owe you.

DON'T have sex on my desk; I have to work there.

"This is going to take a little while. But you can help if you want." As she pulled a book from the shelf, I watched as she walked across the room and sat down in a chair by the desk. She tucks her legs under her and smiles at me.

"I could, but why would I do that? I have a book to read, or I could go upstairs and get something to eat, or maybe I could go onto the dance floor." She opens the book and starts to read; I stare at her. I should not have teased her today. I still don't know how I did it, but I managed to keep my breathing and heart rate regular. All I could think about was teasing her, making her blush and go weak in the knees for me, but now she is teasing me.

"Besides, it would be nice to see you in your element." She says, not looking up from her book. How can she watch if her nose is in the book? "But I don't do this for a living." She shrugs and continues to read her book. If we are going to be here most of the night, I think I should order some food for us. I pick up the phone to order a platter and a bottle of wine; ever since meeting Layla, I have been drinking wine with every meal. Well, most meals, but nothing compares to her family wine. I can't believe that I have become a wine drinker, which I thought I would never become.

I worked for an hour when the music called to her; she didn't want to leave. She said she would stay with me while I worked, but I told her not to. I would still be at least another hour, maybe more, and I didn't want to keep her trapped here in the office. I said I would join her as soon as I finished. I watched as she stayed close to the office, but I could see that she wanted to go further onto the dance floor. It took her about ten minutes to melt into the crowd of dancers, but yet I could still pick her out in the crowd; she moved in perfect sync with the music.

34

Becca

"Evening miss, what can I get you tonight?" I stare at the menu, but nothing on this godforsaken list will satisfy me.

"Nothing on this menu will quench or sate my hunger."

"Maybe I can help; what is it you want?"

"Layla Dixon's head."

"Really! I can help with that." I look up from my menu. I am face to face with a young man.

"How?" I am very intrigued as to how this boy can help me.

"I know her father, and let's say he is very interested to know where she has gone."

"And this helps me how?"

"He has something I want, and am I to guess correctly that she has something you want?"

"Yes, she does, but if you have known about her being here and that her father wants her, why is it that you haven't gone to her father?"

"Because you hold the information that I need, that will help get me what I need from him."

"How long would it take to have her removed?"

"It depends. Could be two days or two weeks."

189

"I like the sound of that. When does your shift end?" "One hour."

"Good, join me when you have finished." This is going to be fun. I am almost jumping for joy, and I feel like I should be patting a cat and laughing maniacally. "I'm Becca."

"Fred."

35

Layla

I have been dancing for about an hour, and I am getting lost in the rhythm of the music. It has been so long since I have felt this kind of freedom. Come to think of it; I don't think I have ever felt this way. I know I was never able to feel this way at any of my sister's celebrations. When I made it, I was never allowed to enjoy the celebration; I was forced elsewhere. Let's not forget that my father never celebrated anything for me, so this freedom was lost.

I never got the chance to dance with Eric at the masquerade ball, but tonight I hope I can. Several people tried to dance with me as I moved with the music, but I just moved away from them. I was going to dance by myself until Eric had finished with Gareth's paperwork.

I have my eyes closed, and I am losing myself to the beat of the music when I feel a pair of arms wind their way around my waist. I feel a hot breath on my neck. I was about to strike out at the person who would dare put their hands on me, but I heard the racing heart the hitched breathing, and of course, was hit with the smell of the air, earth and soap, and I heard my three favourite words.

"My sweet Layla." I melted into Eric's chest, but I kept moving with the music; it took Eric a heartbeat to follow suit and keep rhythm with me. I turned in his arms so I could face him.

"All done then?" he leans down and gives me a quick kiss.

"Yes, all done and locked up; we can go whenever you are ready to leave."

"Not yet; I want to dance a little longer."

"As you wish."

We stayed until around midnight; even though I was having fun, I started to get tired. It has been an exceptionally long and stressful weekend. I think it was beginning to catch up with me. I didn't even know which driveway Eric parked in; all I knew was that I didn't walk into the house; I was carried in and carried to bed. I lay in a soft mattress that smells of Eric, so I must be at his home. I felt the bed depress as Eric got in; I moved closer to him.

"I didn't mean to disturb you." He said in a quiet voice, and he kisses my forehead.

"Thank you for the dance." I didn't hear his reply; the cold darkness of sleep took over.

I woke the next morning to an empty bed with a note on the pillow.

My Sweet Layla,

I am sorry I had to leave you this morning (work), but I will be home as soon as possible.

Your Eric.

I smiled and held the paper close to me. It seems that I can add this to the other notes that Eric has left me when he has had to go to work. I had decided today; I would go over to my uncle's and spend the day with him and my horse. I had some matters I needed to discuss with him and only him.

I was standing in front of my uncle's door with my hand poised and ready to knock. Can I tell my uncle what I want and what

I am going to do? Will he forgive me? I wonder if he is even happy with me, I am a little afraid that he may march me back home. Maybe this was a bad idea. I go to leave when the door opens. "Layla? What is the matter?" He looks me up and down, and I don't know what he sees in me, but his face softens, and he opens the door wider to let me pass.

"Come, we will have tea in the library." I walk inside and wait for him to close the door, I follow him to the library, and we sit down at our usual lounge and wait for the tea to arrive.

We sit, drinking our tea in silence. I know my uncle is waiting for me to start talking, but I don't know how to approach the subject of Eric and me and what I want to leave behind.

"It's about the boy, isn't it?" I know I can't hide anything from him; I hang my head. It's not in shame, though; it's more in defeat that I hang my head. It's just that I can't hide anything from him and his intuitive brain of his.

"Yes."

"What is it that bothers you, my dear?" I look up to see my uncle quietly sipping his tea with his eyes closed, waiting for me to speak.

"I want to stay. I don't want to go back."

"What about your sisters?" I know, and this is why I am here. I mean, if I never go back, I am leaving my little sister to the same fate that I was subjected to and can I do that? If I do that, who isn't to say that my father will come and find me and drag me back, to save both of them. But how do I save them and me? How can I be free without making them trapped? I have only been thinking about Eric and me, without any thought of my sisters. Over the last few days, my mind and body in harmony; thoughts of my sisters have crept into my head. How do I protect them from him?

"You do know that choosing this life may very well cause

war." Yes, I know. It's not like I haven't thought about this; I remember when I left home, all I thought about was being free. I didn't know about the consequences. I didn't consider how this would affect my family. I just wanted freedom, and now, thinking about it, I may have left in haste.

I sit in the library at my uncle's house drinking tea when he was called away for a phone call. My mind goes into overdrive. What do I do? How do I fix this? How do I make this right? How do I keep Eric and the life I want while protecting my sisters and my mother? I put my tea down and curl up on the lounge, close my eyes, and all I can see is the faces of my mother, my sisters and Eric. What do I do to keep everyone safe and keep this freedom I feel? I hear the library open and the footsteps of my uncle walking back in.

"It's going to be hard, and it will be painful, but I need you to be strong. It's all going to work out in the end." I feel my uncle's hand brushes my hair away from my face and over my ears; his hand lightly brushes over my ear. I smile.

"Oh, and the way to a man's heart is through his stomach." I hear him walk out of the room and close the door behind him. I know precisely what my uncle was talking about, and I know what I must do, him and his clairvoyant ways. I should be happy but with his ominous warning. Whatever is going to happen, I must be strong. I will go shopping and make a nice dinner and let Eric know that next Saturday, I will be free.

When I got home, I started to prepare dinner, listening to my iPod. So I don't hear Eric come in, which is odd; maybe I was too focused on cooking or what my uncle had said. I don't know how long he stood there before I finally noticed him.

"Hello, my sweet Layla." I smile and lean over the counter to kiss Eric.

"You need to set the table." He never questions me when I demand that he set the table; Eric does as I ask. Once he sets the table, he sits down and calmly waits for me to finish cooking. He told me about his day, and I told him about my day with my uncle. I got the food on the plates and sat down, and I took a deep breath and steadied myself.

"Um… I have had a thought." He smiles at me. I try to keep calm, but I can't; I'm all jittery. It's hard to try to tell him what I want for us and what I would be giving up to be with him, but at least I will have a week to prepare myself for what I needed to say and do.

"You know how we keep getting interrupted at night." He laughs. "Yeah, I know."

"Well, I thought that maybe on Saturday we could…." I don't say anything, but I can feel my face going red.

"Are you sure?" No, not really, but I want to be with Eric, and the only way that is going to happen is if we sleep together. Eric could see the look on my face and knew that I wasn't ready.

"Yes, I am, but there will be conditions." I look at his face, and he raises an eyebrow at me.

"Conditions?"

"Yeah, just a few; it's okay, nothing too sinister. After dinner, there will be no phones and no answering the door, no inter-ruptions, just us."

"I do like that idea, just the two of us all night long." We smile at each other. "That's it for the conditions?"

"Yes, see nothing sinister." He looks at me like he knows that I wanted to say more, but I couldn't. We finished our dinner in comfortable silence and watched a movie, and like every night, we spend it wrapped up in each other's arms. Though I sleep better in his arms at night, and he chases the nightmares away, this night, I feel dread seeping in as I replay my conversation with my uncle today. I repeat in my head; I will be strong.

36

Eric

It's been a couple of months since she moved in and sent my world upside down. Since the first time I saw her, I have dreamt of being with her, holding her and making love. I have had her almost naked skin pressed against my body as we have slept. But I have never had a chance to have all of her, and tonight I get that chance. She's making me leave my phone at home. Which I am okay with; I swear that every time we are together, my phone rings.

She has also stated that there are to be no interruptions once dinner has started. A night with Layla is all I've ever wanted. But I have wanted to be with her more than just for a night. I want to spend every night and every day with her.

I'm dressed in my second favourite shirt, seeing Layla has my favourite as a nightshirt, and damn, it looks better on her than on me. Pulling on a pair of jeans, Layla said that it isn't a formal dinner even though she is going to all this effort for us, so I didn't have to dress formally.

I don't knock on her door anymore, not since the day she told me not to. I can usually find my sweet Layla in her sewing room which used to be her master bedroom, or I could see her in her stunning garden, sitting on the seat under her oak tree.

Today she was in her kitchen cooking, she has her back to me, and I can see her wearing a long purple backless slip dress. She never wears any shoes, and I see her tiny petite feet poking out from under her dress—images of her in the kitchen, with a child hanging off her leg pop into my head. The thought is enticing, but from where the hell did that thought come?

When she turns, I can see that she is wearing a black apron with red roses, skulls and crossbones all over it. It's rather strange to see that on such a floral girl. I walked up to the counter and just watched her in the kitchen.

"Hello, Eric", she leans over the counter and kisses me.

"My sweet Layla, what is with the apron?" she laughs.

"You don't like it?" The cute little innocent smile on her face as she says this has me wanting her.

"I like it very much, but it's strange to see my floral girl go Goth." Layla went bright red when I called her my floral girl.

"Well, thank you, and I like it too. Come, you can set the table while I finish the rest of dinner."

Ten minutes later, we are about to sit down when there is a knock at the door. I shake my head at her, but she gets up. I don't like the look on her face; she seems to have a glimpse of sheer terror and panic. All the colour drained from her face, and she looks like she will faint or throw up.

I stand up, but she tells me to stay where I am. She goes to open the door, but just before she does, she takes a deep breath and steadies herself. I can see her hands and legs are shaking; she opens the door, and standing in the doorway are several tall blonde people, all dressed in elegant clothes.

"Are you going to invite us in?" Said one of the men with contempt. Layla stood back and put her head down as the first man walked in. He has an air of superiority about him, and his blonde hair is past his shoulders. He also has striking blue eyes, and he is wearing an expensive suit. He regards Layla's house with disdain.

Following him in the house is a woman in a flowing dress; she too has long blonde hair and blue eyes. She walks with grace. Still, she looks rather sad; coming in behind her are two girls; dressed like the older woman. They both have green eyes; neither one is smiling. Behind the girls are two men dressed in costly suits. Again, both men have blonde hair and blue eyes; the older man looks rather bored.

Still, the young man is tall and very well built, and he looks strong, almost like he could break me in half. I think he could even give Gareth a run for his money. He is also the only one that smiled at Layla. They all walked over and stood at the dining table.

I stood up from my seat, and we all just stared at each other. Layla is about to close the door when the bored man spoke.

"Cassius will be here in a minute; come." He is quiet when he speaks; I am surprised that Layla could even hear him. As Layla came back over to us, everyone started to sit down. Layla has a ten-seater dining table, and the superior man sat at the head of the table; the graceful woman sat opposite him at the other end.

On the man's right sat the elder of the two girls, then the younger girl sat down next to her, on the man's left sat the bored man and next to him sat the young man. I heard the door shut. I looked over to see another young man with blonde hair and green eyes came in – Cassius – with him, he carried a bag from the Cavern – takeaway - he put it on the counter and sat next to the young man. I am still standing when Layla comes over and stands next to me.

"Eric." I went to reach for her hand but thought better of it. She held her hand out and gestured toward the man at the head of the table.

"This is my father, Jarlen." Father! I am stunned. She gestured to the graceful woman.

"My mother, Delfina." She worked her way around the table.

"My elder sister Elyse, my younger sister Nokomis, this is Orry and his son, Bayloss and Orry's assistant, Cassius." Holy crap, and then some, her family, the family she ran from, and the family cause the nightmares. What the hell do I do or say, for that matter?

"Father, everyone, this is Eric Walker." No one said anything to Layla; they didn't even nod in my direction or to me. All eyes are on Layla.

"Serve us the meal!" Said her father with not even a please; Layla just nodded at her father. I can see why she ran away in the few minutes of meeting her family. I can see that they have no love for her, but how can that be? She is beautiful and intelligent. I want to hit her father for the way he is treating her. I can feel anger building up inside me; ever since meeting her, I feel protective of her.

All I want is to see her happy and smiling, but I can see the pain and the anguish that this man is inflicting on her just by being in the room; Layla turns to me.

"Please help me set the table for our guests." Her eyes are pleading. I can see her whole world has split open, and the pits of hell are swallowing her, and the worst part is, I have no idea how to help her.

37

Layla

This is a nightmare. No, it is worse than a nightmare. I can wake from a bad dream, but this, this I can't wake from no matter how much I want. At least I have Eric, but I think by the end of the night, I won't. My uncle was talking about how it would be painful and how I had to be strong. How do I do that when my world is crumbling before my eyes?

"How are you holding up?" Eric whispers close to my ear.

"I'm not! But I am glad you are here." We set the table. I motion for Eric to sit on my mother's left while I serve up the food brought from the Cavern along with the meal that I had made for Eric and me. After I have finished serving the food, I sit next to him and my younger sister. No one eats their meal, and everyone is staring at me. Their attention turns to my father, who picks up his fork and takes a mouthful of food. It's a cue for us that we may now begin to eat.

I don't eat, and neither does Eric; it is deathly quiet. I don't like it.

But the silence is broken by Cassius.

"You must be excited about the nuptials?" He aims the question at me. Eric is looking confused, and I cannot explain anything. I was going to talk to him after dinner. Still, now, my world is dying and everything in it. My father is destroying my life again, and I could do nothing to stop it because he found me once; he would find me again. Please, I need this night to be over. For

Eric to stay, but I know that is never going to happen now.

"Nuptials?" Asked Eric. Only my father and Cassius – the slimy weasel – looked at us. Then my father spoke, and I could see my life go up in a blaze of glory. I was about to be razed; I was never going to come back from this, even with my uncle's prediction. I don't see how I can come back from this.

"Yes, nuptials, Layla is to be married to Bayloss. She was engaged to him since the day she was born. Our two families were always to be united. This child ran like a scared animal, like the frightened child that she is. And for her to throw her life away on you and your ilk, I think not."

My father said no more, and as I looked around the table, all eyes are on Eric. I, too, watch him as he stands and walks to the door. I get up to catch him, but he already has the door open and is almost out when I grab his arm to stop him. He pulls out of my hold and turns on me, his face full of pain while his eyes are full of rage.

"You're engaged?" Cold fury is all I can hear in his voice.

"I was going to tell you tonight." He cuts me off before I can say anything else.

"You should have said it the day we met, and I wouldn't have wasted my time on you." My heart ripped in two. I couldn't speak; he leaned in and whispered in my ear.

"I wish I never met you." Then he walked out the door. I stood looking at the door; none of my family came over to me. No one stood up, and I am once again alone, feeling empty, a shell; there is nothing. The one hope, the one chance, and it's all gone wholly and utterly gone, and no tears would come, no emotions, just nothing. How does one feel so vacant? I turn around to face the table, and still, no one looks at me. I walk up to my father.

"Why?" It's all I can say.

"I do not explain myself to anyone, especially to the likes of you. We are leaving. You are coming." He stands up and faces me. I pull back my hand. I am about to slap him across the face when he catches my hand mid-swing.

"You will not lay a hand on me." He pushes my hand back with all the force he has and pushed me to the ground. I was unable to stop myself from falling. I laid in a crumpled mess on the floor.

"Ensure she comes." My father walks out the open door, followed out by everyone else but Bayloss. He doesn't say anything as he picks me up off the floor, holding me in his arms as he walks out the door. I am once more leaving everything behind.

38

Layla

"It's been two weeks. Are you coming out?" My sister Elyse is again trying to get me to open my door, I haven't opened my door to anyone, and I will not open it for anyone. I am back home and have locked myself away in my room, not speaking to anyone. I didn't want to talk to anyone or see anyone. I'm supposed to be married in two years, and now seeing I have returned, my father is ensuring I do not run again. I am to be married in six months.

I sit at my desk writing, trying to pour everything I feel into one letter; papers lay in crumpled heaps around my feet. It takes time to get it right. Still, when I finally finish the letter, I hear a light tapping on my door, then I hear the door opening. I sense my mother walk into my room.

"Layla?" I say nothing to my mother. I simply get up and walk out onto my balcony. My balcony, filled with plants and trees and vines, I sit amongst them, hoping I can disappear into them and melt away from existence.

39

Delfina

Watching as my daughter walks away from me, I don't know what to do with my child, she is so empty and gone, and there is nothing I can do to help her. I don't think she will ever forgive me or anyone else for how we have behaved or how she was treated all these long years. I turn to leave when I notice papers on her desk and all over the floor. I walk over to her desk and on top is an envelope marked "Eric" I open it up and inside is a letter.

My dearest Eric,

I know that you will never see this letter, and I know that there is no real point in writing this, but I need you to know how I feel and want you to know everything I need to explain. I was going to tell you everything, but I never got the chance to. But now is my chance. Please forgive me for what I am about to say.

For the past one hundred and twenty-eight years, I have lived with the knowledge that I was never going to be free. I knew that when I turned one hundred and thirty, my life would no longer be my own. That I would belong to someone else, to someone I did not love, and someone that I would never love.

I've spent the past one hundred and twenty-eight years as an empty shell, knowing no happiness, never knowing what it means to be free. Never knowing what it was to breathe, to feel. I would close my eyes at night, hoping that in the morning, when

I opened my eyes, I would be free out from under the harsh rule of my father. But it never happened, and I woke to feel crushed and empty.

It made me think of my sisters when I woke with this feeling and how free they are. My sister Elyse, raised in my father's image, was groomed to rule the Northern Realms. But, Elyse still had the freedom to do as she pleased, go where she wished, and be with whomever she wanted, as long as she ruled just like our father. My younger sister Nokomis knew no boundaries; she had complete freedom. She knew that she would never rule any realm but her own.

Still, I think that she always feared me, feared that I would leave, and destined to live my life in a cage. Never to taste open air, never listen to the flowers again, never to talk with the world. I believe she would break and die just as I have again and again.

I love my little sister, and I have hated what I have done to her for leaving home. I had subjected her to my father and the ways he had treated me for one hundred and twenty-eight years, but I had to breathe. I had to feel, I had to see, even if it was only for a short time, but I had to.

I was always going to go back to protect my sister. I know she would hate me for a time, but I would have saved her from my father's hatred and disdain. I was going to go back, that was until I met you. I was willing to give up everything. I would have left my family, life, and world, and I would have done it all for you. The choice would have been yours to make, but it was taken away from us. Now the decision has been made, and I will spend the rest of my life with him, not you.

To you, our time together will pass and fade, and all the pain I caused you will hurt, but it too will disappear, as will your memory of me. I do not doubt that you will find what you are looking for, and it's not with me. For me, our time together will never fade and never lessen. I will have all of eternity with the memories of our time together, and I will not have time to mourn what little time we had together, for I am required to marry in six months. But by far, the worst part is that an elf only falls in love just once, and never again, and I am still falling.

I know you have no reason to believe anything that I have written. Please speak to my uncle or Gareth's father or your mother. I am sure they may be able to convince you that what I say is true.

My only wish is that I get to see you one last time. Goodbye, my Eric. I am glad to have been able to breathe around you.

Love always and free falling
Your sweet Layla.

Folding the letter back up and place it back in the envelope, and I stare at the balcony window. How do I save you, my sweet child? How do I make that pain go away? How do I stop you from falling into a pit of despair that you will never come out of again? I hold the letter in my hand. I can almost feel your heart breaking as you wrote this. I will make sure that he gets it, my sweet child.

40

Eric

It's been two weeks since she left. I am standing on my balcony looking out over her yard, and everything is dead. There are no flowers, no birds singing, nothing; even her oak tree is looking sad and wilted. I remember the night her family came to dinner and destroyed everything, including her. I have been quick to anger with her, and I did not give her the chance to explain herself. Then I had become so annoyed that I just stood up and walked away from her. Since then, I have been so angry with her and also with myself.

After I had said those things to her after leaving her house, I got in my car and drove. I didn't know where I was going to; I was just driving. I found myself dialling Gareth's phone number and telling him what happened. He told me to get to the Cavern straight away.

I remember walking down to his office in a daze. As I walked into his office, all I saw was the bottle of rum and the two glasses on the table. I grabbed a drink and threw myself in the chair opposite Gareth. I spilled my guts about everything and how much of an idiot I am. I remember that night so clearly.

"From the sounds of it, E-man, you saved her, even if it was for a small amount of time, and as a result, you got screwed over, which sucks. I know you. You would have gone out and gotten wasted and done something foolish. At least if you are here, you can get as drunk as you like, and I will drive you back to my place."

I couldn't argue with that. When I got in the car, all I wanted was to drive somewhere and get smashed and try to forget the last few months. I have no doubts I would have ended up at Becca's. At the moment, I am glad I called Gareth. I downed the rum, grabbed the bottle and poured myself another glass and downed that one as well.

The third glass of rum I started to nurse; all I could think about was what had just happened. I hear Gareth's voice as I sit there, staring at the golden liquid in my glass.

"You are going to do something for me, however. You are going to go over there and talk to Lala. Once you have dried out, of course."

Right now, I don't want to see her, but she is invading my head. I hate and love her at the same time. I don't know why this is affecting me so much.

I don't know how she has managed to get so buried into my body and soul. I have never acted or felt this way before, and it's unsettling. But I still don't want to see her.

"E-man, I have never seen you this way before, and I'm not talking about being drunk. I'm talking about the way you were with her and her with you. Man, you were happy, and when she needed you, you just ran. You need to see her so you can get the whole picture and then decide if you wanna stay."

I didn't want to do anything. Getting drunk is what I plan on doing right about now. I am going to get completely and utterly smashed.

I don't know how many drinks of rum I had, but I was drunk. Gareth put me in one of his spare rooms and left a bucket next to me – for which I am thankful. But I couldn't sleep, because every time I closed my eyes, I saw her face. I saw the way the light left her eyes, her face, and her world had that had shattered. I saw the pain in her look when I told her that I wished I had never met her. The thought of it makes me sick at what I had done to her, and then I rolled over and threw up.

I remember a few days later when I finally sobered up and calmed down. I had gone over and knocked on her door, and it did that eerie open by itself thing. I walked in; everything was the same as it was the night her family came to dinner. I walked through her house; it was painful; it felt like someone was tugging at my heart.

I hated feeling so weak towards one female, and I hated myself for thinking such things. Noticing that nothing had been touched, the food still sat on the table going rotten, all her clothes, everything was still there. Nothing was missing except for her and my shirt. Other than that, her house and yard are still and dead, and she is never coming back.

After I left her empty house, I went to see her uncle. I think I banged on his door for an hour, and neither he nor his staff came to the door. I went back day after day to get his attention, but no one came to the door. I began to wonder if he went after her. I still don't know why I went there or why I kept going back, but it seemed like that was what I had to do.

At the start of the third week, I was on my balcony staring at her yard, wishing I could see some sign of life from there; I just wanted to see her again. I quickly got over feeling weak about loving her, and all the hatred I felt for her just evaporated. The emotions that are running through me now are screaming at me to get her back. I just want her back, and I would do anything to make it happen. I hear a knock on my front door, and in an instant, my heart skips a beat, and I think it's her, so I race downstairs. I throw open the door only to find Becca standing there.

"Oh, my darling Eric, I heard what happened." She tried to embrace me and get a foothold in the door, but I wouldn't allow either one to happen. No one touches me again, no one but her. I am in no mood to deal with Becca's crap, not when I started thinking that she has had something to do with this.

"What do you want, Becca?" Though I already knew what she wanted, and she can't have me. I don't belong to Becca; I belong to Layla.

"I had heard what had happened, and I thought you might need to talk to someone. I know what it's like to have your heart broken; I just thought I could help." Help, that's funny, bitch! You had something to do with this; I know it.

"Was this another one of your crazy plans to destroy my life?" She stared at me, showing no emotion. I had to give her this one; it worked, but not the way she wanted. I don't want her, and so I slammed the door in her face. I heard a slight sound of protest from her. I have no doubts that this will be all over social media in about thirty seconds. I don't care if she does; no one listens to her anymore, not since the slap in the face. I venture back to my room to wallow and stare at the ever-dying garden of hers.

I have spent the past few weeks trying to forget her in every way possible. Still, it's not working, though I have attempted not to say her name, hoping that I would forget her. I have tried not to envision her, but I keep failing every time I close my eyes.

I look out over her yard and realise I don't want to forget. I just want her back; I need her back. I need her to explain everything to me. So I can understand and tell her that it wasn't just her world that imploded that day. It hurts too much to look out over her yard, so I go and throw myself onto my bed.

God, how can one person affect me in such a way as she did? How is it that she has turned me into this weak person who needs her smile, touch, and smell? I inhale deeply, and I smell flowers and a lot of them. It is her smell. I sit up and inhale; the scent again is still here. I hear the front door rattle, and the smell of flowers is gone. I get up and venture downstairs; when I reach the bottom of the stairs, I see an envelope. I go and pick it up; written in perfect script is my name. I know it's from her, I turn it over with shaky hands, and I pull out pages of heavy parchment. My dearest Eric.

"Open up! Damn it! Bardrick, you elf bastard, open the freaking door NOW! Or I swear I will kick it down." I finally hear footsteps, and the front door opens, and standing in front of me looking worn and empty is Bardrick. I shove the letter in his face and point to the part about her being an elf.

"Is it true?" I can see his eyes looking over the letter.

"Is…It…True?"

"Yes, it is." He pulls back his hair to reveal his pointed ears; it doesn't shock me, however. I think back to all the times I thought I saw pointed ears on her, and I start to believe it more. And what's more, it doesn't seem to freak me out. Somehow I have always known. I always felt like myths were real, and now I know that they are. Now I understand why they always felt real because they are.

"Why? Why is she being made to marry him?" He says nothing, but he steps aside and holds the door open wider for me. I step inside and wait for him to close the door. He starts walking me through his house, and he leads me to the library. We sit down, and he summons one of his house staff to bring us some tea. I am getting agitated with him. Why is he so calm? I just outed him as an elf, and he is acting as if it's just another day.

"I know you have many questions, but you will have to save them. Do you want to know why Layla has to marry him? I will start with that." Just as he is about to start speaking, the door to the library opens, and one of Bardrick's maids walks in carrying a tea tray; she places it on the table and walks back out. Bardrick pours us some tea and hands me a cup. I am sitting here with a steaming cup of tea in my hands, waiting for him to keep talking to tell me why.

"It all began a long time ago, an exceedingly long time ago. One family, a powerful family, a mighty family, ruled the realm. It was not a peaceful rule, and as a result, a great war broke out, and all but one family member survived the onslaught. Our realm splintered into four realms; Eastern, Western, Southern, and Northern Realm."

"The sole survivor of the ruling family took control of the Northern Realm. The Eastern and Western Realms are controlled by the two families that started the war, and the family that stood by the Northern Realm rules the Southern Realm. Are you with me so far?"

Not really; it's all a little too much to take in. But I need to know, so I just nod and take a sip of my tea.

"Now there has been an uneasy peace for a very long time now, small fights would break out between the Northern Realm and the Eastern and Western Realm, but the Southern Realm would come to the aid of the Northern Realm, and the uneasy peace would resume. The Northern Realm is still the strongest family and still rules most of our lands, but we are few, fewer than the others. A deal was made between ours and the Southern Realm." He stopped talking and took a sip of his tea.

"Was she part of the deal?" He looked over the rim of his teacup and stared at me; he put his cup back down.

"Not originally; she wasn't. The deal made well before her time and mine is simply a marriage arrangement between the realms. But throughout the years, only boys were born to both families, and the arranged marriage agreement wouldn't work. That was until my nieces came along and seeing Elyse can't marry Bayloss because they are both firstborn. Both are to rule their respected realms, Layla being second born to the realm, this, in turn, made the agreement of the arranged marriage valid, and she was betrothed to Bayloss the day she was born."

I know she said it in the letter, but I had to know. I had to hear it from someone else.

"Does Layla love him at all?" My heart started to rip apart at the seams. I hadn't said her name in two weeks. It hurt; I can't believe how much I miss her and want her back. Now that I mention her name, all the emotions start back up. I look down at her letter and re-read the last lines over again. I don't seem to notice that Bardrick was speaking at all.

"Layla and Bayloss have no choice in this matter; they have been thrown together. But I know that she has never loved him, nor will she ever; she would not have run away if she did." The thought is comforting. I don't think I could handle it if she were really in love with him, not with the way I feel about her, not with my heart breaking over the fact that I will never see her again and that she is going to marry someone else.

"Our hearts are very much like yours. However, Layla believes that we only fall in love once. It is just not true. Some of us fall in love several times over, just like any normal person. Others will spend a lifetime getting to know one another before realising that they are in love with each other, and then there are the special cases like you and Layla, the ones that fall in love and will never fall out of it. I believe that you call it love at first sight."

"Well, for me and mine, it's more intense; it feels as if your heart has been ripped out. You can't breathe when you are around each other, and the beating heart in your chest is no longer yours. It's theirs, and all you want is to be with them."

"But it's more than that, and I can't put my finger on it. I get angry and frustrated when people say things about Layla, I feel so protective of her, and there are other things."

I see that he is smiling at everything that I am saying.

"Such as?"

"Almost like I knew the reason why she ran and the reason why she wouldn't sleep with me. But there are heaps of smaller things. I can't seem to get any of my emotions in check. I'm all out of balance, and I don't like it. I only felt normal and in one piece when I was with Layla." Bardrick just kept smiling at me.

"Well, the reason she didn't sleep with you is that if she did, she would become normal, a human, a mortal. Everything about her as an elf would disappear, but she was willing to give it up to be with you."

"Pardon?" he puts the empty cup down on the table and leans back in the chair.

"There are a few things I haven't mentioned. There was a time when we could walk between the worlds without consequence; that was until the day my brother and I fought. I left, and after that, he closed and cursed the doorways leading here."

"Any elf that crossed the thresh hold would lose their grace and beauty. They would lose everything but keep their ears, hence the brown hair and grey eyes. That's why she always had her hair covering her ears, but even she still managed to be graceful. They would also lose their abilities of sight and hearing."

"They would also lose their ability to hear flora and fauna. Layla can still talk to the flowers and make them grow and talk to her horse. She can talk to animals, but they can't talk to her, and she can't hear them."

This conversation is seriously getting confusing, and it's starting to give me a headache. I don't respond, but it explains the flowers in Layla's backyard, and that day, she talked to the snake in her yard and her horse. We sit in silence for several minutes before he starts to speak again.

"There are but only two options here." He says with an air of knowing that no matter what he says, I will pick the option he wants.

"Options?"

"Yes, options. Option one – and I hope you don't take it – you do nothing and move on. It's a bad idea, in my opinion, and you will never feel this way again with anyone. It would also mean that you die more on the inside from being apart from her every day. Option two – I suggest you take this option – I help you get Layla back, but it's a big but, you may fail, and you may end up dying, but at least she will know how much you love her. You do love her, don't you?" How could he ask such a thing? Of course, I love her.

"Yes, I do, and there is no question about it, option two." Bardrick jumps up from his chair and claps his hands together.

"Glorious, let's get started." He practically runs out of the room. I get up and chase him out the door.

41

Layla

It's been two months since being dragged back home, and I still haven't left my room or talked to anyone. I still don't know how my father could find me or how he found out. It hurts so much that someone may have given me up. What brings me down into the darkest depths of my mind is that I know Eric is never coming for me. I am lying in bed with his shirt, and I think back to the day I was marched out of my house. I didn't get a chance to grab anything, but somehow when deposited into my room, I found his shirt on my bed, and I haven't let it go. I know that this is the last thing of Eric's that I will ever see and touch.

Then was the letter I wrote to Eric, it was there, and then it was gone. I know my mother saw it, and I hope that she sent it to him and had not shown my father as he would have destroyed it.

There was a light tapping on my door, which brought me out of my train of thought. I hear the door open and close. I hear footfalls, and then my bed moves ever so slightly when someone leans up against it as if they are sitting on the floor resting against my bed. I breathe in, and all I smell is leather, metal and smoke.

"Good day Lord Bayloss." I can almost see the smile on his face.

"So, you do speak!" We both laugh, though there is no humour in it. His laugh is nothing like Eric's, but it was still a nice laugh; you could hear joy even if there were no joy to be had.

"Only to you. Only because I must, well, I will have to in only a few short months." I look over at him, and I can see his head resting against my bed, and I have no desire to reach out and touch him. I have no urges to ask him to my bed. I feel nothing towards him, nothing but love for a brother and nothing more. I will never feel anything other than that. "There is something that has been bothering me for the last couple of months."

"And what is that?"

"How is it that you were able to find me?" I hear him take in a deep breath and then let it out.

"Cassius." What! Orry's assistant. "It seems he has been working for your father all along. Your father wanted a spy within our ranks, so he managed to convince Cassius to join him." I started to feel physically ill. How could someone do that?

"What has happened to him?

"When we got back, I wanted to know how your father knew where you were, and that's when I found out what he was really up to." He fell silent.

"What did you do?" I wasn't too sure I wanted to know the answer to the question.

"I did the only thing I could do. I removed his head from his body, but not before I made him regret his decision for betraying the Southern Realm and joining Jarlen." I am grateful for what he has done on my behalf, but he did not have to do that. I know he is in love with my sister.

"Thank you. You did not have to do that."

"I know, but it was still the right thing to do."

"I know you don't love me; I know that it is Elyse that you love, and you know that I only see you as nothing more than a big brother."

"What are we going to do about it, little sister?" I have thought of nothing else these past two months on what I should do about Eric, Bayloss and my father and family. All I came up with was how to save them and not myself, or at least, how to make them happy. I even thought about telling Bayloss about my theories but thought against it, and now he wants to know.

"One of my thoughts was to banish myself, but that would mean the marriage would go to Nokomis, and I can't do that to her."

"I agree."

"My next thought was that we get married, but we do not touch each other, we wait until both you and Elyse are ruling the realms, and then the discussions can begin on absolving our marriage. You can turn your attention to other matters, maybe try and to work with the Eastern and Western realms, try and come to a new arrangement."

"Yes, but where will this leave you."

"Does it matter? You, Elyse and everyone else will be happy. What happens to me is of little consequence."

"But it will leave you without Eric, and not to mention what this is already doing to you. I doubt you will last; you will waste away and die."

"That is a possibility."

"Why not go after him?"

"Because I can't, I have no doubts he hates me for what I did, and I know he doesn't want to see me, and by the time I get any kind of chance to go after him, it will be too late. He will already be married and had children."

I heard him sigh, for he knew I was right, and we both knew there was nothing either one of us could do about it. It could be another seventy years before Elyse takes the throne, and it could be another one hundred before Bayloss, and I take over the Southern Realm; then it would be too late.

More than that, he knows that I would give up Eric if it would mean making others happy because what is one elf to a mortal, or a mortal to an elf. What is left of my heart is shattered. I let out a shuddering breath, then felt a body next to me holding me. Bayloss had climbed in next to me to comfort me.

"He could still come for you."

"I doubt it; you were there." We didn't say anything else. He just held me and let me cry, I had always said I wouldn't cry in front of anyone, but I am glad it is in front of Bayloss and no one else. Even being held, I can't seem to sleep.

42

Eric

It's been two and a half long months without my sweet Layla. It still hurts to think or say her name, but it is getting easier, especially knowing that I will be going after her. I think back to the day in the library, following Bardrick through the library, along the hallway, up a flight of stairs towards a set of double doors on the second floor. He stood before the doors with a childish grin on his face and said,

"Before we begin, I need you to know that this is not going to be easy, and you may not survive." "I know you already said that," I replied.

"Yes, but I need you to know, you need to understand and that this is your last chance to back out."

"I am not backing out. I will go up against anyone that stands in between me getting to Layla." I didn't know if he was happy or sad about it.

"Bayloss is by far the best warrior of all the realms and is yet to be beaten, and I have fears that my brother will undoubtedly cheat you at every turn. I need you to understand that you may not be coming back with Layla if you make it. You may not be coming back at all, and if you do, you will not be the same as when you left." Explained Bardrick.

"What the hell does that mean?" There is no way I will go through hell and back and not come home without her.

"It's going to be extremely hard for you to win and keep Layla. Are you still up for the challenge?" Asked Bardrick.

Am I going to risk everything for the chance to get her back to risk it all for love? As they say, the answer is plain and simple, HELL, YES. I know I will never feel this way again, and I know she will never forgive me if I don't try to get her back. She will never forgive me for the way I behaved. I will not live the rest of my life, knowing that she will spend the rest of her exceptionally long life hating me for not coming for her. If I must learn how to fight to get her back, I will.

"I will do whatever it takes."

He looks solemnly at me, turns and throws open the doors. Inside is open and bright. Training mats cover what seems like half of the second floor; the training area is massive. The back wall displays weapons of different shapes and sizes – bows, swords, javelins, shields – it looks nasty. The wall on the left is a giant climbing wall, and the wall on the right is full of books and glass cabinets holding goodness knows what, but what was truly unique was the exposed roof. All you can see is the ceiling beams.

I just stand staring at it all, trying to take it in. I look back at Bardrick, and he is holding a white pair of pants and a white shirt in one hand and a sword in the other.

"Here, these are clothes for you to train in, they are light and durable, and this is the sword you will be training with; I don't think I can trust you with a bow," said Bardrick. We laugh, and I remember how apt Layla is with a bow.

"Now, we will start with the basics and move to the training maze," said Bardrick.

"Maze?" I give him a quizzing look.

"If you look at the floor, the marks you see are boards that raise out of the ground; they will help with cover and element of surprise. We will also be using the beams for balance and agility." We both look up at the ceiling. I take a deep breath and try to steady my nerves. It is going to be shit scary; I just know it.

"Plus, I also have a few more surprises install for you." I don't like the sound of that; I don't like the sound of any of it. I don't want to kill anyone to get to Layla, but then again, if it means that I will get Layla back, I will have to, especially if they are trying to kill me to stop me from reaching her.

"You better change."

He pointed to a barely visible door on the right wall; I went and got changed. I stood in front of the mirror and looked at myself; all dressed in white, white yoga pants and a white tunic; both are light and breathable. You wouldn't catch me wearing this to any of my training sessions with my clients. At least I have that on my side.

I know that I am strong and fast and should be able to evade most things. I did manage to sneak up on Layla a few times; that should count as well, shouldn't it? Once dressed, I head out to Bardrick, standing on the mats with two swords; he holds one of the blades out to me.

"Shall we begin?"

"Eric, pay attention!" it was the second time this morning that he has put me on my arse and with the tip of his blade at my throat, and it's the second time he has drawn blood. I knew I was starting to lose focus.

"What is going on in that head of yours? You are strong, stronger than a normal human. You should be able to force me back, and you are quick, quicker than any human I have seen. You are swift; you should be able to avoid my blows. Eric, please, pray tell, what is the matter?"

"It's been two months since you brought me in here to train, and now all I can think about is getting out of here and getting Layla."

"Be that as it may, it's just that you are not ready." I was getting frustrated; I had spent two months running on the beams, playing hide and seek in the maze, and attacking Bardrick with a sword. I just want to get her. Is that so hard for him to understand? I want to hold her in my arms. I want to tell her that I love her, but I can't because I am stuck here training day in, day out, and never good enough for him.

"I need to go to her; the longer I am here, the closer she gets to Bayloss. You said that I will never win, that I will fail and die, but with this training, at least I will last ten minutes instead of one. Please, I am begging you, take me to her." I stand staring at him, the stern façade he is wearing fades away, and all that is left is his love for his niece. He smiles.

"Very well, but you need to change."

Bardrick gave me a new set of clothes to change into; he told me it was battle garb and that it should help against some of the attacks, but not all. I changed into the battle leathers and ran out of the change room. In my mad rush, I forget to pick up my sword. But I spot Bardrick, and he points to my sword. I quickly grab it, sheath it and follow him out to the back of his yard where the forest meets his property line.

We walk for about a hundred metres or so, and he stops at two trees where their low hanging branches form an archway. He pulls out a blade and pricks his finger, and wipes the blood on both trees. The air around me shifts, and I feel a strong breeze trying to push me towards and away from the tree, but I hold firm. Watching as the light starts to shimmer in the archway, strange writings appear all along the trees, and the light turns solid and forms a white door with carvings of trees and animals all over it. Bardrick turns and faces me and says,

"I cannot come with you."

"What?"

"I left before the curse was in place. If I were to come with you and leave before they lift the curse, I would be affected just as Layla was, and I like me just the way I am." It made me remember the day he told me about the curse and how much Layla gave up just to be free of her family, and how much she was willing to give up only to be with me.

I would not have known about any of this, and we would have been living in ignorant bliss. I would like to think I wouldn't have cared because I would have had Layla, and that is all that matters to me, and she will be all that ever matters to me. Going in blind, like a lamb to the slaughter, bringing half a cow with me, I feel like I will not take ten steps before I am cut down and tossed at Layla's feet in pieces.

"Now, Eric." He places his hands on my shoulders and walks me to the doorway.

"This doorway will lead to an isolated area outside of the city, and hopefully, your arrival will be unnoticed. Once you are through the doorway, walk straight, do not veer, and you will find your way to the centre of the city, and that is where you need to be." He gives my shoulder a slight squeeze. He steps aside and holds his hand out, gesturing for me to walk through the door.

"Your sword." I draw my sword and hold it at my side. "If anyone stands in your way, cut them down."

"I know, it's just, I have never killed anyone," Eric replies.

"And you don't have to; tell them if they stand in your way of getting to Layla, you will cut them down." I thought all elves were peaceful and not bloodthirsty like this man before me, and Bardrick must have sensed my hesitation about killing anyone.

"Eric, we are not all peaceful, some are rather cutthroat, and those truly loyal to Jarlen will stand in your way. All the rest should move out of your way; they do not approve of my brother's rule or how he has raised his family. And it would help if you did not get too lost either; your sword will guide you. Now go and save your girl and bring her home."

"As you wish." He burst out laughing. I guess Layla told him how I was always saying it to her. I close my eyes, I take a deep breath, and I open my eyes. I reach for the door handle, and I push the door open to the other side.

I look at the forest around me and again at the doorway, and it hasn't changed. I turn towards Bardrick; he doesn't say anything. He just nods at me, telling me that it's okay and I should keep going. I step through the doorway, and I get a small electrical shock, and I feel as if I am stepping through a wall of water.

Once I have stepped entirely through, the landscape around me shifts and changes. What was once the dark green of Bardrick's forest is now hills and mountains. I turn and look behind me, and I stand face to face with a hillside covered in flowers that form an archway.

Closing my eyes, I listen to everything around me. Taking a deep breath through my nose, and the scent of flowers hits me, Layla's smell. But what is strange about my surroundings is that I hear nothing. There's not a bird, not a tree swaying in the breeze, nothing but my breathing and the blood pumping in my ears.

I must have been standing for far too long because I felt the sword tug at my hand. Bardrick was right about pulling me, and there is no real point in me hanging around here. I do as the sword tells me. I move out of the hills and mountains and head into a dense forest.

My feet are starting to hurt a little. I am still not used to the boots Bardrick has made me wear. They are durable and lightweight, but I haven't broken them in yet, and I can feel a blister starting. I feel like I have been walking for hours, and I have not seen another person or elf.

I have still not heard any sounds of wildlife. I swear this forest is getting thicker, and I see no end in sight. The sword kept me on my path, which is good, but I want out of this forest. I want to be closer to Layla.

After about ten minutes, the light starts to filter in, and the trees begin to part. I finally come out of the forest into vast open fields and rolling hills. I can see what seem to be houses dotted here and there, but I don't think you could call them houses; they appeared to be built into the trees.

The trees are massive; some trees seem to be hollowed out or have grown that way. As I moved closer, I start to see movement, no one comes towards me, but I have noticed that a few of them follow me. They keep a safe distance, never getting too close and never getting too far away as to lose me.

After the fields, I moved into more forest, mountains, and rivers and back to more mountains. I came through one of the mountain passes to a ridge overlooking a crystal city; that's the only way to describe it. In the dead centre is a large white crystal tower. The city spirals out from it; you can see colours reflected in the central tower, there are a few balconies on the tower. One, in particular, catches my eye; I can see part of it from where I am standing. There are flowers and green plants, lots of them – Layla - I was surprised that they are alive.

I thought that maybe she missed me, and she was unable to make them grow. Her flowers at home had all started to wither and die. Still, now I am beginning to feel a sense of doubt. Maybe this wasn't such a good idea. What if the feelings I have for her are not returned? What if she has feelings for him now? What if she thinks I was never coming for her and so she fell in love with another?

Looking out over the rest of the city, it's incredible; I can see water flowing in and out. Part of the city is covered in green, and the city square that surrounds the tower has several statues and fountains around it. It's incredible the way the sun shines on the city. It throws colours everywhere.

It's something out of a dream, and the only thing I don't see is people, and I should at least see one or two in the city. It's as large as Skyhaven, if not bigger. How is it that there are no people and still no wildlife?

Once again, I have stood for too long, and the sword tugs at me. I walk towards the centre of the city and wind my way down the ridge. All I can think of is what am I going to say to her or anyone else? I am just drawing a blank; maybe when I am face to face with her, I will know what to say.

43

Layla

“Layla! You need to wake up.” I can feel a hand shaking me; I feel like I am wading through a swamp.

“Wake! You need to wake Layla something is going on; I hear your father’s guards.” Why? How am I asleep? I haven’t slept in over two months. Why am I sleeping now? It can’t be right, and why isn’t my brain working? “Come on; you need to wake; your father has silenced the city.” Silenced the city? Who is speaking, and why was I asleep? Why can’t I think straight?

“Dammit, child, where are your swords?” Swords? Who is in my room? All right, I need to open my eyes. My eyes adjust to the light; I can hear someone going through my things. I look around and see Bayloss rummaging around my room.

“What are you doing?”

“Looking for a weapon.” How strange; I wish my head would clear. I don’t like this fog. I start to look at Bayloss and notice that he is covered in weapons and not any of mine. Did he go to his room to get them, or did he already have them?

“Why are you covered in weapons?” I hear several footsteps coming up the stairs, and my head starts to clear a little more.

“Why do I hear footsteps, and how long have I been asleep for?” He stops and looks at me.

“You have been asleep for the shortest of times.” Well, that explains the fog in my head. "Your father's guards are coming; for what reason, I don't know. But he has silenced the city; it can't be good if he has done that, now I am looking for a sword for you, or you could have one of mine." He draws one of the swords that is strapped to his back and holds it out to me.

I just simply roll off the bed and hit the floor, and in doing so, I freak Bayloss out a little. I reach under my bed and pull out a box that I have hidden under there. I open the box and grab out one of my swords and my bow; it's not my favourite bow; that bow is still there. I stand up and arm myself, and I go and stand next to Bayloss, who is facing my bedroom door. He also has two swords drawn, we may not love each other, but we will protect one another because we will be married in less than four months.

The door to my chambers bursts open; standing there is my father, and standing beside him is Bayloss' father and at least twenty of my father's guards. My father is a fool if he thinks that his guards can defeat Bayloss and me. I trained with Bayloss and his father, and the Southern Realm is known for its cutthroat and bloodthirsty warriors and stubbornness to die when in battle.

"What is the meaning of this father?" My father says nothing. He just stares at me with that look of contempt; he signals two of his guards to move forward towards us. Bayloss moves forward and stands in front of me, ready to strike. Once again, he proves that he will be a loyal husband to me when we marry, or should I say, should we marry, I will be a loyal wife.

"You will not touch her," says Bayloss in a very threatening tone. Orry steps forward and directs the two guards to stand down, they look towards my father, and he nods his head at them. Orry turns to my father, "I will take care of this, Jarlen, take the guards and go deal with our guest." Guest? What guest? My father turns and leaves with his guards leaving me with Bayloss and his father, but Bayloss doesn't ease his protective stance.

"What is going on, father?"

"Please stand down, son." Bayloss does as he is told and moves to stand beside me, but his sword is still in his hand and ready to strike.

"Who is this guest, Orry?" A broad smile spreads across his face.

"A one, Master Walker."

I freeze, my heart stops beating, and the blood stops flowing. Eric? My Eric! He is here. My heart starts to beat, but there is such a pain in my chest, and the air in my lungs won't allow me to breathe correctly. He came. He came for me, but how, how did he get here? My uncle, it had to be my uncle.

Everything seems to catch up with me. Eric is here for me, my father is on his way to meet him, and I am up here. I'm supposed to be down there stopping my father from getting to him. I run for the door but am stopped. Orry has grabbed me around the waist. I start screaming at him to let me go, but his grip just tightens around me. I can hear Bayloss demanding his father that he let me go.

"Be still, child; this will not help you or Master

Walker. Your father has plans for both of you."

"Then you must let me go."

"I'm sorry, but I can't, so you must be still, and I will explain." I'm still in his arms.

"Explain, father!" Orry releases me, and Bayloss grabs hold of me and holds me tight against him. I have so much love for this man, but he does not belong to me, nor I to him. The love is that of a sister to a brother.

"As soon as your young man stepped into our realm, your father silenced the city; he demanded that none shall interfere with the plan he has devised. He plans on having you stashed at the furthest point of the Northern Realm and leave you trapped there."

"Should you leave the designated area, your young man will be sent home. But I don't believe for a moment – your young man has to come and find you, without any help from anyone. If he does seek help, he will be sent home. If either one opens the gates connecting our worlds, they will be closed for good; not even your uncle will be able to open them."

Is it his lot in life to make me suffer? If I help him, I will lose him. I sag against Bayloss. "There is a way to help him without helping him." "How?" demanded Bayloss. "Flowers."

"My father will know." I just know it, if my father wants to make it so that neither one wins. I can't use my abilities to grow flowers. If my father is watching me, he will surely know. What do I do?

"Trust me, please."

And at that, Orry leads Bayloss and me to our designated holding area where I will wait all eternity for Eric.

<h1 style="text-align:center">44</h1>

<h1 style="text-align:center">Eric</h1>

I finally reach the city centre, and there is no one. I look around and wait a few minutes, but still no one. I turn towards the sound of footsteps marching towards the city centre. Turning towards the sound, I see Jarlen, Layla's father. He's wearing black pants, a white shirt and swords on either side of his hips. Behind him looks like a platoon of soldiers, each dressed in black and covered in armour.

I look around and notice the city square starting to fill up. I was being surrounded and most definitely outnumbered; I guess it's time to start worrying. I know I will not land a single blow, but at least I can go down fighting, and the first person I will be charging at is Jarlen.

Standing facing him, all he does is stand there and smirks at me. Oh yes, I am going to slap that smirk off his face. But I think stabbing him through the heart would be better; that's if I can get close enough.

"Am I correct in guessing that my brother let you in?" I draw my sword closer to me, ready to strike; he and several other elves laugh. I try not to let it bother me.

"Am I also correct in guessing that he taught you how to fight?"

"Yes." That was all I was going to say for now. His facial expression had not changed.

"You do know that, no matter how much you have learnt, it will not help you." Bayloss' father, Orry, walked through the crowd and stood next to Layla's father, and he looked rather bored. The two men spoke quietly to each other, and Jarlen nodded to Orry.

"I know you came for her."

"I have." That smirk and that smug look would not leave his face. I can't wait to beat the crap out of him.

"Shall I tell you about what she has been up to since her return?" I shifted a little, which they both noticed, but Jarlen seemed to like the fact that I was concerned.

"Oh, maybe I should say what they have been up to." That bastard! I took a step toward him, and everyone took two towards me. I stopped, and he laughed. Oh, boy, was I starting to get pissed off at him, I am beginning to see why Layla ran, and I would have too.

"I found Bayloss in her bed when I went to tell her you had arrived." I tried not to show emotion, but I can't say that it didn't hurt a little because it did. I know she doesn't love him, so why does it hurt?

"Oh yes, I found them together only but moments ago." I couldn't hold my tongue any longer.

"I don't believe you; she doesn't love him, never has and never will."

"And you think she is in love with you, a mortal!" I know she is, but I'm not going to say it in front of these people. I want to hear her say it to me.

"Jarlen, I am bored, and I wish to return home. I miss the hills of the Southern Realm. Can we finish this?" As Orry was speaking to Jarlen, he winked at me; I wonder what's happening.

"You are quite right; the faster we get this over with, the faster we can get back to what's important." The crowd started to disappear, and the only people left in the city centre were me,

Jarlen and Orry. Jarlen started walking towards me.

"It's simple if you want her, you can have her. All you have to do is find her." I think my jaw dropped, just find her, and she's mine; that can't be right. There has to be a catch.

"What's the catch?" I say to him; I try to sound intimidating, but I know it is not working, and I know that this catch will be huge. Bardrick said he's going to cheat and make it impossible for me to win her back.

"Well, she isn't in her room, and that is the only hint I shall be giving you and the only one you will be getting. There are two catches to this."

I swear he is laughing at me, and only two catches. I honestly thought there would have been more than that, and I dread what he will say next.

"One, you cannot ask for help from anyone, and two, you have until sunset to get to her."

It's too simple, almost effortless, but I know it's not going to be. I can either guarantee that I find Layla, but I either lose her or my life by some twist of fate, and I can't let that happen. I have to figure out a way to win. Then a thought occurs to me.

"Fine, but when I reach her and I will, I get to leave with her, and the marriage is off, and I am talking about your other daughter, Nokomis. She won't take Layla's place." Jarlen looked at me with surprise. I don't think he realised that I knew about the arranged marriage and what would happen if Layla doesn't marry Bayloss. He then looks towards Orry as if to seek permission on the matter. Orry doesn't say yes or no. He still has the look of boredom on his face.

"You still have to reach her, but while you are wasting your time, I shall think it over, but I wouldn't hold out any hope; as I said, you will have to reach her first. Come, Orry; I have a bottle of wine I think you would like." He turned and walked away, and as he did, all his soldiers/warriors turned and followed him as well or faded into the background. Before Orry turned around, he looked at me, smiled and nodded and left after Jarlen. But as he left, I saw that he ever so discreetly dropped something on the ground. I waited for the square to be empty before I went over.

I reached the spot, and I saw a flower was on the ground – how strange – I bent down, and I picked it up and the instant that I did, I was hit with the overpowering smell of flowers, and it was a lot of flowers – Layla! – It was clear what I had to do. I had to find flowers, or at least try to follow the aroma of flowers.

Orry left me the clue on how to find her. I smiled; I had at least one person on my side. Now all I must do is find the flowers that will lead me to Layla, but I must get to higher ground. I need to find a path to follow. I look around, and I head back the way I came. But the strange thing is, as soon as I started to move back the way I came, the smell faded, and I lost the scent. So it wasn't the flowers I had to follow; it was the smell, easy enough.

"Let's begin."

45

Layla

"I can't just sit here." I try to stand, but once again, Bayloss holds me down.

I am getting frustrated and angry. I was taken to one of my hiding spots, no one but I knew of this place. Well, at least, I thought I was the only one who knew about it. Clearly, Orry and Bayloss knew about it too.

Orry assured me that my father still didn't know about it, and I believe that is true; otherwise, my father would not have put me here. It is easy to access, but he would have put me somewhere even harder to find if he hid me. I don't want to be here trapped; I want to be out there running towards Eric, not here.

This place used to calm me, for I would walk through the dense forest to get to my hallow. It's covered in flowers and soft grass and has a spring in which I occasionally swim. But now I have to sit here, and I stare up at the mountains in front of me, and I can feel the mountains to the back of me closing in. I swear that the cliff to my right is beckoning to me. I think the place is closing in and trying to claim me. The only place that isn't trying to suffocate me is the path to my left, and that is the path that Eric has to find, to get to me, but he has to climb down the cliff first.

"I need to get to him. Please, I can't just sit here." Bayloss places his hands on my shoulders and looks me in the eyes. I can see the pleading look resonating from him.

"If we leave, he will kill him, and I have no doubts that you would avenge your young man." I laugh and nod. He is correct. I would go on a killing spree to get to my father. I would kill all of the Northern Realm if I had to, just to get to him.

"But my father gave us a clue on how to get him here." I must have looked dazed and confused because I didn't think he gave us a clue; he just said 'flowers'. How is that a clue, it's a word, and he told me to trust him, but can I trust him?

"Flowers, how are they the clue?" He looks at me with raised eyebrows.

"You can make them grow." Bayloss is right. I can make them grow, and what has that got to do with anything? I suddenly get an idea.

"You are right, I can, and that is how he is going to find me, and what about my father? He will know." Bayloss gives my shoulders a slight squeeze and backs up as far as possible to provide the space I need to work.

I have always been able to grow flowers ever since I was little. I know of no one else who could do it. Apart from making them grow, I can also strengthen their smell. I know Eric will have to start from the city square, but I have never done anything this big. I don't know if I can get the flowers to hear me with me being so far away, but I have to try.

Knowing my father, he would have set a time limit, but there is one thing my father doesn't know about Eric, and that is he is quick. I have seen how fast he can move. I just hope he uses his speed to find me.

I sit with my legs tucked under me and start by drawing a circle in the earth around me, using my hands, feeling the coolness of the grass, the flowers and the dirt beneath my hands. After drawing my circle, I place my hands on my knees, and I close my eyes. I take a deep breath in, let it out, and take several more, trying to slow my heart rate down, but it is hard knowing that Eric is on his way to me.

Never have I done anything this big before. I inhale deeply and lean my head back. I call to the earth, the seeds, the roots, and to all the life that dwells within her. I call it up to the surface to greet and help me; I start to sing. Lost to the music of my singing and the tune of the earth waking to me, I begin to sway. I call her to me. I can feel her move with me. I start to feel her reach out for Eric, to encase him to pull him down to be one with him and me.

I call to them, to the waking ground and for Eric to come to me. I feel a blossom tree touch him, and in what it takes for a heart to beat, I feel him. I sense everything about him. I feel his emotions, and my heart rate speeds up, as does my breathing, but with that, so does the earth. I feel her tremor beneath me radiate out; I slow down my breathing and heart rate. Once I have calmed down, I can hear his emotions. I can feel that he loves me and wants me to come home to him to be his. I start to cry, and I can sense the earth weep with me. I am here, my love.

46

Eric

I just brushed past a blossom tree, and as I did, I felt her; more than that, I could see her. She is calling to me, and I could see her kneeling on the ground, drawing flowers all around her. I could see hundreds of flowers and vines growing around her. I could almost hear her voice as she called for me, but I feel the ground beneath my feet shake more than that. I knew that it was Layla that she was the one who had caused it. I just hope that Jarlen doesn't feel it.

When I felt her emotions when touching the tree, I hope that she could see, feel and hear my feelings; more to the point, I hope that she can feel how much I love her. That I was on my way and that I was getting closer to her.

With no one to stop me and Layla leading me to her, I know I will be able to get to her in time. At the moment, all I can think of is, thank god I work out. I am also glad that I am quick on my feet and quite swift. Now I am smiling in the knowledge that I will get to her in time.

As I race through the city, run through the fields and head towards the forests and mountains. I touch every plant or tree I pass. I do it so that she can see that I am getting closer. Each time I feel one, I can see her still calling for the plants and calling for me. I try to tell her that I am coming to get her and take her home with me. I reach the end of civilisation and reach the mountains and forests. I start to panic a little, there are many trees, and I can see no path to her. I touch the nearest tree.

"Layla, I can't see a path to you; please help." Under my hand, I feel something move. I remove my hand, and on the tree is a flower; it's the same colour as Layla's eyes, 'storm over the ocean'. I scan the ground and see another flower a few metres in front of that one, and another. I watch a little further ahead, and I can see blue-grey flowers growing. I look around, and I can see the sun moving to set. I estimate that I have about maybe three hours left until sunset. I can't be sure.

I go to pick the flower that had sprouted under my hand; when I hear Layla's voice in my head, 'ask first.' I laugh, and I do as she says; the wind blows, and I swear that I hear the word 'yes'. I picked the flower and said thank you, but a long stem came with it as I chose. I looked at the flower, and all my thoughts turned to Layla. Holding this flower, I could see her; giving me the will to keep myself moving.

I start to run through the trees, following the flowers. A few times, I had to stop and check to make sure I hadn't lost sight of the flowers. I don't know how long I had been going since I first got here, but I started to feel thirsty, and I started to feel hungry. I look around for a stream because I can't trust anything here. I don't know how it will react to my body, but at least with water, I would be okay.

Just then, a small plant grows in front of me and sprouts several berries. I look at the plant, and I hear Layla's voice, 'Eat, please hurry'. I ask the plant, then take some berries. I thank the plant. The handful of berries that I ate filled me, and I'm no longer thirsty, and the bonus gave me the energy I needed. I find the flowers and start running through the forest once again.

As I make my way deeper into the forest, it is getting dense, and it is getting harder to find and follow Layla's flowers. I didn't want to slow down to a jog, but I had to. Now that I have slowed down, I hear Layla's voice, but I don't hear it from the flowers, and I don't hear it from the wind. It is her sweet voice that I hear. So I run faster through the forest towards her voice; it felt like I was running for over an hour before I broke through the trees. I stopped at a cliff's edge.

I look around, and I have mountains to my left and right and the edge of a cliff in the far distance. Down in front of me is a hollow with a spring and soft green grass, flowers and my Layla kneeling on the ground surrounded and covered in flowers. Standing behind her with his hand on the hilt of his sword is Bayloss. His head turns, and he stares up at me; he nods his head at me and relaxes his grip on his sword.

He bends down towards Layla's ear and whispers something in her ear; she stops singing, and the plants that surround her vanish; she stands up and faces me.

She has changed so much since I last saw her. Her long brown hair is now bright blonde and tied back, exposing her beautiful ears. From this distance, I can see that her eye colour has changed from her storm over the ocean to bright green. Even her clothing is different, she is wearing a long light blue dress that hugs her body, and I notice that she has lost weight, but I can still see her with all the changes. She is still the girl with whom I fell in love. Her face brightens as she stares at me; I wonder if she can notice any changes in me, I wonder if she can see that I have become more muscular because of the training I did with her uncle.

I look around for a way to get to her, but I can't see a path or a trail that would lead me to her. There is a spring, but it is too far away for me to jump into, and I cannot be sure of its depth. I wonder why she hasn't made her way to me. I wonder why neither one of them has moved. She must have heard my thoughts.

"We can't leave this spot. You still have to reach me."

"But how do I get to you?" She points to my left side.

"There is a hidden path that leads down here." I turn to my left, and a few flowers grow where the path starts. I race along the route. I reach the bottom. I am standing in front of her but still some twenty metres away from her. I walk towards her; it feels like one of those dreams of walking and never getting anywhere.

I am about three metres away from her, and I can smell her sweet smell, and she still doesn't move towards me. I take the last few steps, and I stand in front of her, and I am still holding the flower I picked. So I hold the flower up for her, her fingers brush the petals, and my world explodes. I hear someone screaming, the world goes black and then nothing.

47

Eric

“**Y**o E-man, what are you doing? Hurry up, man, we still gotta pick up my dad.” I’m standing on my balcony wrapped in a towel, with my hand held out in front of me, palm up like I’m checking to see if it’s raining. I have this strange feeling like I am supposed to be somewhere, I have somewhere important to be, and I can feel a fog in my head. I can sense that I am missing something, but I can’t grab it, it’s there, and then it’s not.

“Eric, ya listening?” I must have been standing longer than I thought because Gareth never calls me Eric.

“Thought I felt rain.” I heard Gareth’s reply of ‘yeah, okay, just hurry’.

I put my hand down at my side. I lean on the railing; I look over my backyard, and at my fence that adjoins the empty house next door is a step ladder and a tray resting up against the fence. Okay, that is the strangest thing I have seen; I don’t remember doing it, more to the point. Why would I do that?

The place next door is empty, and now the fog is back again. I shake my head to clear some of the haziness, but it’s not working.

Looking over at the yard next door, and notice that everything is dead and overgrown. I wish someone would buy that place, I got a head rush, and I had to grab the rail. I have never gotten a head rush before. I have never felt light-headed. The only time I feel

243

like my head is foggy is when I have had a big night drinking, and the last time that had happened was, was… Why can't I remember? I run my hands over my face and try to clear my head; it takes a few minutes before the fog and head rush passes.

I look back over at the yard and see an archway. I do a double-take; I swear that I saw something that looks a lot like blood on it, but that isn't the only thing I notice. There is a single flower on the archway, and it has the most distinctive colouring; it's a blue-grey colour, a storm over the ocean kind of tone. Another head rush hits me, and I am grabbing the railing again. Did I drink that much last night that I can't remember anything? But then I don't remember going out drinking, not even with Gareth. Maybe something is wrong with me, or perhaps I am not getting enough sleep.

Walking into my room, Gareth is lying on my bed reading a magazine. I once again get a head rush, and my vision blurs. I have to grab the doorframe to steady myself. Gareth's image is replaced with a girl's shadowy figure, or at least I think it's a girl. I mean, I can see curves, but I can't see any features. I blink, and the image is gone and replaced again with Gareth staring at me before he resumes his reading. I walk over to my tallboy; I open the top right-hand drawer, and inside is a pair of red heels. I pull out a red dress and red heels, turn to Gareth, and hold them up.

"Red isn't your colour, but it's nice. Does it fit?" I gently put the dress and shoes back in the top drawer. I just couldn't bear to wrinkle it – odd.

"You're an idiot. I don't even know how they got there or even whom it belongs to." I start looking for clothes to wear.

"Becca's?"

"Too much material." Gareth laughs at my answer.

"Another girl then?" he asks. I don't remember having another girl in here that would wear something like that. My hands brush against my shirts in my wardrobe, and I grab the door as I'm hit with another head rush. If this keeps happening, I will have to see a doctor.

"Yo E-man, you all right?" I look over at Gareth and notice that he is sitting up and is watching me he has a concerned look on his face.

"Yeah, I am fine; I just can't find my favourite shirt."

"Just wear something. We gotta go and pick up my dad."

"Why are we picking up your dad?" I can't remember having plans with Sheamus.

"He called last night and asked if we wanted to have lunch with him today, demanded it really. It was quite odd. But hey, it's my dad. He is a bit of an oddball." I can't argue with that, the way he tells his stories of the little people. He is a true Irishman. Still, I love him like a second dad, even if he is a bit eccentric.

I grab a pair of jeans and a shirt, and we head downstairs. Just as we are leaving, I toss my car keys to Gareth; there was no way in hell I would drive with these head rushes happening every five minutes.

I stand in my driveway and stare at the vacant house next door. I can feel the fog come creeping back but push against it. As I do, I see flickers of a shadow. I try again to move past the fog, but nothing happens, and I'm left with a headache. Opening the passenger door, I smell a floral scent, and it's not a bottle smell. It's too strong to be a bottle smell; it's too perfect, too fresh to be a bottle. My breathing starts to race, and my heart beats faster. I feel something I can't name. I don't like feeling this way; it's very disconcerting.

"Are you getting in the car or not?" I pinch the bridge of my nose and try to shake away the feeling, I get in the car and close the door, and once I do, I can no longer smell the flowers.

Our conversation on the way to his dad's place is not exciting. He talks about a few of the girls he is trying to win over but finding it hard as they can see through his façade. But they all love his attention. He keeps telling me that I need to play the field and that I need to find someone. But every time he mentions it, I get a sharp pain in my chest, and I swear I can hear a voice screaming, just not at me, but for me. If this keeps happening, I am going straight to the hospital and get a full workup done. I mean, this has never happened to me before. I am a fit young man. This shit shouldn't be happening, so why is it?

We pull up to Gareth's dad's house, and I watch as his dad walks towards the car. I swear he looks like your typical Irishman; he is a solid man with close-cut salt and pepper hair. He's dressed in jeans and a plain navy buttoned-up shirt. He climbs into the back seat of the car.

"Hello, Mr Flannery." I still can't call him Sheamus even though he has asked me to. He nods in my direction.

"Dad." That is all he ever says in the way of hello to him.

"Gareth, how are you, son?"

Even though he has lived in Skyhaven since he was five, he still has a thick accent. He claims that it is due to his trips that he takes each year back home to Ireland to see his sister. Oh, he also claims that it is due to the little people, and he still tries to convince Gareth and me that they are real, and he tries to tell us the old stories, but we are both stubborn and won't listen.

"I'm fine." Gareth and his dad don't speak, and their conversations are noticeably short, except when it comes to sports, their conversations get loud.

"Eric, my boy, where is your girlfriend? Is she not joining us today?" Okay, I have no idea why he said that I have no girlfriend, Gareth and I look at each other, and he just shrugs his shoulders. I hope he is not referring to Becca because there is no way in hell that I would be with that mentally unstable girl. She has some serious issues. I turn and face him.

"I'm sorry, sir, but I am not sure what you are talking about, and I don't have a girlfriend." He studies my face.

"Humph." He turns his attention to Gareth.

"So, do you know where are we going?" Gareth asks of his father. I have been wondering why his dad wants to take us to lunch. He never does this. It's a fight to get them to have lunch together at the best of times. As I try to remember why his father would invite us out for lunch, all I am met with is fog and a blank memory. I was starting to get a headache. I need just to let it go.

"Gareth, where are you going?" I ask him, and he gives me a puzzled look.

"Not sure, just have this nagging feeling that I have to go this way. I think maybe dad mentioned it last night when we spoke, but I can't remember." I look at Sheamus, and he doesn't seem fazed about where we are going, almost as if he knows precisely why we are going this way.

We turn into a long driveway; I look around and finally have a moment where my head isn't foggy or throbbing. For the first time today, as I try to think about the reason for the fog in my head, I am left with a gaping hole as I try to remember what happened yesterday for me to have this fog, but my mind's blank. But I at least know one thing, I have been here before. It's the estate of the top jeweller in Skyhaven. He is only known as Bardrick; as far as anyone knows, he has no last name. We pull up to his house and park behind my parent's car. Why are my parents here? Stepping out of the car, I stare at the home. I close my eyes and breathe in the air. I get a strange feeling, not like the other times today, there is no fog, no head rushes, and my mind isn't blank. I get the feeling that someone else lives here beside Bardrick, someone I know, or at least, lived here.

My thoughts are interrupted by voices and the sounds of a struggling horse. I opened my eyes, and I look for the sounds. I walk around part of the house before the men and the horse come into view. I can see at least five stable hands trying to calm down the beast of a horse. It has to be bigger than a Clydesdale. I can see them trying to drag the horseback towards the stables, I hear footsteps behind me, but I don't turn. I'm fixated on this horse; there is something about her that is familiar? How do I know she is a mare?

"That's a big horse." I don't know who said it as I didn't notice—focused on the horse and the fact that my feet just started walking towards her on their own. I am only a few metres away from her when I hold my hand up and out towards her.

"Quiet Storm Cloud." How the hell did I know her name?

Maybe I heard one of the stable hands say her name. At the sound of my voice, Storm Cloud stops fighting and walks up to me. My hand is still outstretched, and she nudges my hand with her head, and on instinct, I rest my head against hers.

"Shh... she will be home soon." Who will be home soon?

As I stroke her mane, I get a head rush, and some of the fog in my head clears, and I once again see a shadowy figure sitting on Storm Cloud's back, it's the same one from my room, and I still cannot see who it is. I blink, and she is gone. I try to recall the image, but the fog starts again. I take the reins, and I lead her back to the stables. I walk back to the house to meet up with Gareth and his dad.

Gareth and his dad are standing at the side of the house, Gareth's mouth is slack, but Sheamus has a great big grin on his face and a knowing look in his eyes – what does he know that I don't – I walk up to the door. I knock, and the door opened almost instantly and standing in the doorway is Bardrick. He greets us with a nod and turns, and starts to walk down the hallway; we have no option but to follow. Sheamus is the last in the house, so he closes the door behind him.

We follow him through a set of open doors, and inside is an extensive library and in the middle is a table with tea, and around the table is my mother and father and my cousin, Stell. Strange that she is here. I can see some wooden boxes on the floor next to my mother, but what freaks me out is that there is a terrifying-looking sword on the table. Bardrick motions for us to sit as he goes to the bar and pours himself a drink; turning to Sheamus, he holds up a glass.

"Sheamus?"

"Just a small one, my good man." How do they know each other?

I go and sit next to my mother, and Gareth sits next to me. My cousin is on the other side of my mother, while my father is on the other. Next to him is Sheamus, and in-between Sheamus and Gareth is Bardrick.

For about twenty minutes, everyone is saying their hellos and how are yous, and for the whole time, my blood pressure is starting to rise, and my temper is starting to get the better of me. I seem to be the only one, though; I look at Gareth, staring at my cousin. Great! He appears to have found yet another female to win over, and too bad for him that she is my cousin and is off-limits to him. I have had enough of the secrets that they all seem to be sharing. I need to find out why I am here.

"What's going on?" They all stop talking and stare at me. My mother places her hand on my leg and gives it a gentle squeeze.

"How have you been feeling today? Anything strange been happening, something you can't explain?" How does she know, or is it that she is just guessing by the look on my face?

"Have you seen things?" I turn towards Bardrick. How does he know I have seen things, well, shadowy figures. My dad is the next to speak.

"Have you had any strange feelings?" What the hell is going on with everyone? How do they know what is going on with me? I run my hands through my hair and try to clear my head, but it's not working. The fog is coming back even stronger than before.

"You have to fight it, son. If you don't, you will lose it all, and you will never remember." Remember? Remember what! There is nothing to remember, I just need to have the fog lift, and the head rushes to stop, and I can go back to my life. I am hit with a sharp pain in my chest, and my body screams at me to not forget that I have to remember, but remember what?

"Eric, we need you to remember, it's important. There is more than just your life at stake here." What? Okay. I know little of what is being said, I am getting confused, frustrated, and my head is starting to hurt again.

"Can someone please tell me what is going on? What is it that I have to remember?" My mother bends down and picks up one of the boxes that are on the floor. She held it in her lap and looked at Bardrick.

"Eric, my boy, over the past few months, you have been, well, I shouldn't say because we need you to remember, but it won't take much for that to happen. But there is something you have to understand, we five remember." He gestures towards Sheamus, my parents and my cousin.

"My son would remember if he listened to my stories and believed." Said Sheamus

"Dad, the little people again!"

"You just couldn't listen. All you had to do was listen, and we wouldn't be having this conversation."

"Dad, I am not going to listen to you telling me how I should value our heritage and listen to your stories about leprechauns." The two start to argue but are cut short by Bardrick.

"Not now, Sheamus, Lillian please open the box."

My mother lifts the lid on the wooden box, and inside the box is a bow. Nothing too exciting about that, but as soon as she opened the box, I smelt the same floral smell as when I opened the car door. Again, it brought the same feelings as before. I reach my hand out but stop just before touching it, and I look at my mother; she nods her head at me, encouraging me to continue. I place my hands on it, and nothing happens, no instant images, no fog lifting, just nothing; they all look at me.

"There's nothing." My mum puts that box down and picks up the next one. She opens the box and inside sits the trophy from her charity event. There's nothing special about it; I have seen it before.

"And?"

"Eric, look closely." My mum points to the trophy, and there is a name on the bottom of it, but I can't read it; strangely, the writing is blurry. But I'm not going to tell them that; they will know that something is wrong with me. Though I think they already know that it looks blurry to me and can't see the name on it.

"Pick it up," states Bardrick. Obeying, I lift the trophy out of the box. I run my finger over the name in hopes that I will somehow be able to read it. I closed my eyes and tried to concentrate on it, I got a few flashes of Storm Cloud with the shadowy figures on her back, but that's about it.

"Please, Eric." I hear my mum's plea, but I still get nothing, I run my finger over it once more, and I get the floral smell again. I see the images again; this time, the shadowy figure is replaced by a girl with long brown hair and a bow in her hands.

It wasn't just any bow, a handcrafted bow, a bow that had to have been wielded with deadly accuracy to have won the cross-country trophy. The fog starts to lift, and I am getting a clearer picture of what happened at my mum's charity event.

I can see that I am sitting at the judge's table watching the archery tournament, and every contestant is a blurry figure, all but one girl with long brown hair. I watched as she hit every target, and at the end of the main tournament, she ended up in my arms. Then I was back at the judge's table watching her do the cross country event; I watched as she once again hit every target.

She did it on horseback, and once again, I found that she was in my arms. I was hit with the smell of flowers. Then other images started to flood my head; everything started to clear. I could see us in bed. I could see her wearing my favourite shirt, her walking into her room with nothing on.

I saw the day I walked out on her, and my world exploded. I was hit with everything all at once, causing me to have a massive headache. But what hits me is the images of Bardrick training me and of me going through the gate to find Layla.

Layla! My heart and my breathing stop. How did I forget Layla, and why isn't she here with me?

What had I done wrong? I followed all of Jarlen's instructions, getting to her before the sunset and I did it without any help. So how is it that she isn't here with me? I can feel my world starting to crumble again. I had her; I was no more than a few inches away from her, so how is it that she isn't here? I was struck by lightning; her father found out that she had helped me, that she showed me the way to her. But if he knew that, why wasn't I sent back sooner? Why did he wait until I was within arm's reach of her?

He didn't like the fact that I won, that I beat him. So in return, he sent me back here with my memories of Layla gone, lost. But the question is, how did my parents and Bardrick know? How did they know what happened? But there is one thing I know for sure, and that is that I am going to kill Jarlen.

Layla

I screamed and screamed and screamed again. Eric was just there. I was about to go home to him, and then he was gone. All that was left was the flower he held out to me, now lying lifeless on the ground. I dropped to the ground. I picked the flower up, and as I did, I started screaming again. I felt arms wrap around me, but I don't shrug out of the embrace; I know it's only Bayloss trying to stop me from screaming, and I know he is only trying to calm me down. He does, but as he does, I start to cry.

Once I was all cried out, the anger started, my father had planned this from the start, and he set Eric an impossible task of trying to find me. But he still found me; I may have helped a little.

However, he still managed to find me so, how is it that I am still here and not in Eric's arms, not in his bed. My father must perish for this, and this is the final time that he disrupts my life. For a hundred and twenty-eight years, he has ruled my life. He has made the choices in my life; it has never been my life. Not until I had met Eric. I want that back. I no longer want to be here under his rule, and the only way for that to happen is to stop my father.

"Little sister?" I know him calling me to calm me down, but that will not happen this time. Oh no, this time, I am going to let the fire inside me burn and rage. I will burn everything to the ground if I have to; I can feel the earth beneath me tremor.

I am going to direct all of this rage towards my father, who so richly deserves it.

"Big brother."

"Yes." His grip loosens on me.

"I need a weapon, and we are going after my father." He stands up and walks around to face me. In one hand, he is holding a sword out for me, and his other hand is out for me. I take it; he hauls me up from the ground and hands me the sword.

"What now?" That is an easy question to answer.

"My father has caused me so much pain over the years, and when I finally found what I have been after, he tears it away from me, never again! I am going to get Eric back, and I will go through my father to do it.

"You will hear no arguments from me." I grip the hilt of the sword, and I start the long walk back to the city centre. The sun has gone, and night has truly set in, and there are only our sight and the moonlight to guide us. Bayloss and I walk in silence, and the silence gives me time to think.

I remember the day Eric came knocking on my door and all the days that followed, the first touch, the first kiss. I think about how I was free from my home, free from my father when I fell in love with Eric. I remembered right up until the day he walked out on me. I was smiling and laughing to myself up until then.

I felt the world squeeze my heart and tried to crush me again, but I had to remember that he came for me. That he was here, then he was gone, ripped from me once again, and by my father. That is it, no more. I will go through my father to get Eric back. I stopped thinking about Eric for a moment to look around and gauge how far away we were from the city centre. When I can see that we are almost back, I look over at Bayloss.

"What do you plan on doing once we are face to face with your father?" he asks of me.

"Hadn't thought that far ahead." He laughs. I am so glad that he is in love with Elyse. I don't think I could do any of this if he were in love with me. I wouldn't be able to leave to go after Eric.

"Thank you, and I am sorry."

"For what?"

"For causing the families so much trouble, and for me, leaving and disgracing both of our families." He grabs my arm and forces me to stop and look at him.

"No, you have not caused my father or me any stress, nor have you disgraced us. We are both in love with someone else, and I have no doubts you would have done the same for me."

"Yes, big brother, no doubts."

We start walking again, and we are just about to walk into the city limits when I feel a sharp pain in my leg. I look down to see a dart sticking out of my leg; I pull it out and look at Bayloss; my head starts to swim. My body starts to feel heavy. I can feel my body begin to sway. I can feel myself starting to fall to the ground. Bayloss reaches out for me but stops as I brace myself the best I can for the impact of hitting the ground; I landed on my knees. I fall to the side, and I am lying on my left side. I look over at Bayloss, who has collapsed on one knee.

"Your father." I hear Bayloss say in a groggy voice.

I didn't think anything could bring him down; he is the strongest fighter and the largest elf. Out of the corner of my eye, I can see our fathers' guards coming for us, Bayloss struggles to get up, and he does. Still, he gets up without a weapon, the world tries to blackout, but I fight to stop it. I can do this; I will get up. I wanted to repeat it, but my head is getting dense and foggy.

"Father?" I hear Bayloss say in a distant voice, Orry is here?

Did he have something to do with this, with me being drugged?

"Sorry, son, they're not after you." Bayloss tries his best to stand in front of me, but he is back down on one knee. The world starts to fade to black.

"Take Lady Layla to her room." I don't know who said it; it sounded as if they were underwater. My body loses its fight with the drug, and I fall entirely to the ground, my eyes are closed, and the blackness is almost upon me. I hear noises, and I try to open my eyes, but I can't.

"I'll take her." I feel hands, and then I feel nothing.

Oblivion takes hold.

49

Eric

"**C**an someone please tell me what the hell is going on?" Gareth's voice breaks me from my revere and the anger building up in me over what Jarlen has done to Layla and me. No one says anything to him, so he turns to his father.

"Dad! Please, what is happening?"

"I tried to tell you; I have tried to get you to listen to the stories. I have even tried to get you to come back to Ireland with me, but you just don't want to listen."

"Well, I am paying attention now."

"I think it's best we show him." Sheamus looks at my mum, and I thought he would have asked Bardrick to show Gareth his ears. My mum nods her head at my cousin, Stell. My cousin stands up and starts to shimmer, and her black hair, dark green eyes, and suntanned complexion vanish and standing in front of me is… not sure what.

"You're a tree," Gareth said so eloquently. Well, he was somewhat correct; she looked a little like a tree.

Her skin has a tinge of green and is covered in vines, thick vines around her torso and thighs. In contrast, on her arms, lower legs, neck and up the side of her face, the vines thinned out, her hair is wild and bushy with flowers and vines coming out every which way, and her eyes are a bright violet colour. She is quite beautiful but not even she can compare to Layla

257

to me no one can.

"You're fey, aren't you?" I ask her. She nods at me, so my mum's stories were true, all of them. I wonder if she is the one who blessed my mum. "Are you the fey my mother helped?"

"I am, but she has helped more than just me over the years. She has been blessed by many. Your mother was blessed when she carried you, and because of that, you are blessed with speed and agility." Her voice sounds musical, like the sound you hear when the wind blows through the trees. It's nice; it makes you a little dreamy and want to sit and listen to her talk.

"You're hot!" That's a little uncalled for, but I guess Gareth found his voice, we all stare at Gareth, but he seems only to have eyes for my cousin. I suppose she isn't my cousin, but I couldn't see her as anything else other than my cousin, and I have the urge to protect her from Gareth and his womanising. I feel kind of proud that he is taking it in his stride and not freaking out. But he can stay away from my cousin.

"No! Plain and simple, Gareth. No."

"Are you warning me off E-man because she isn't your cousin? And more to the point, you still haven't told me what is going on here. I still don't get it." I go to speak and try to explain everything when Bardrick interrupts me.

"Gareth, there are some things you are going to have to accept. One: The little people are real, and as you can see, as are the fey, and elves are real as well." He pulls back his hair to reveal his pointed ears, and to Gareth's credit, he just sits there, absorbing it all and still is not freaking out. Maybe deep down, he did listen to his dad's stories and knew they were true.

"Now it's going to take you a little while to remember, but Eric here had been dating my niece, who is an elf." He turns to me and glares at me.

"E-man, you were just giving me flack about telling Stell that she is hot when you have been with an elf, double standards, man." Okay, I can give him that one.

"There are other things you need to know, but they can wait, but what's important is Layla was taken, and Eric went to get her. Consequently, he's had all memories of Layla erased from his mind, including anyone who had met her." I saw Gareth reach for his neck; he touched the spot where she had nicked him with the pruning shears. He got a big smile on his face.

"Lala." That was all he said, for his face went blank. I have a feeling he now remembers everything that had happened with regards to Layla.

"Yo E-man, you are going to have to go and get her. You can't leave her there."

"I know." I couldn't say more; I knew I had to go and get her, but how? I have no doubts that Jarlen had closed the doorways between us so that I can't come back; he erased my memory of her. He probably felt that he was safe from me, so maybe he didn't close the doors. I look around at the faces. Each one of them is looking at me. I can tell that they are wondering if I am going back for her.

"I will go back, and I will bring her home."

My parents look at Bardrick, and their faces change. I can see tears start to well in my mother's eyes; my father puts his arm around my mum. Bardrick looks at my cousin and nods at her; Stell stands and grabs the terrifying-looking sword from the table. I haven't noticed it until now; it's longer than my sword and Layla's bow, which are both quite long. The blade seems to be made from some form of crystal. In some places, it is two inches wide, others only an inch wide. It is most definitely not a straight blade; it has crescent shapes along it and jagged teeth.

Designed for maximum carnage, but also a stunning blade containing veins of silver. The handle is thin, the sword's hilt decorated in vines that extend out over the handle. There is only a small gap between them, where you can grasp the handle. Even then, there's only enough space for a tiny hand. It looked more like a decorative blade than one use for killing.

"This blade was forged by Layla." Okay, I am stunned. I didn't know she could craft weapons, but then again, Layla is an elf.

"It was given to the fey to protect until returning to her; that time is now. This blade wields great power and cannot be used by anyone but her, though she told me that only one other should be able to wield it, and I have no doubts that it is you she was talking about."

"How can you be so sure that Eric is the one to wield it?" Thank you, Gareth; everyone is beating me to ask the questions that I need to ask. Maybe my brain still hasn't caught up with everyone else yet. Stell smiled.

"Because Layla said, only who is to set me free can carry my blade." No one said anything; they all just looked at me, they knew it, and I knew it. I am the only one who can set her free, and I am going to. But wait. What about my parents, and Gareth, aren't they coming with me?

Almost as if they could read my mind, my mum starts to cry, and the faces of my Dad and Sheamus are sad.

"The doors have been closed and sealed. I can open the one here, but it will be a one-way trip. I am sorry I cannot do more." Stell is sad as she delivers the news to me. I can see tears in her eyes.

"You will go by yourself and will walk through the Northern Realm alone. You will save Layla, and you will stay until the realm is stable and you can travel safely between here and there." She states as a tear rolls down her face.

"No! I am going with him." Gareth stands up and tries to stare down my cousin, which is hard to do, seeing she looks like a tree and somewhat threatening holding Layla's sword. Bardrick puts his arm on Gareth and pulls him down again.

"No! No one goes with him. Once he has passed through the gateway, he will be trapped there until freed, and that could take years, and he may never return." Now I know why my mum is crying. It is going to be the last time I see her and my dad.

How are they going to explain my absence from Skyhaven? Why should I care? I am going after Layla; that is all that matters. I stand up and face Stell; my mum stands as well and hugs me.

"I am so proud of you. I love you."

"I love you too, mum." She let go of me and sat back down; my father got up next and hugged me.

"Use what the fey blessed you with, and you shall be victorious." As he sat back down, my mum threw herself at him. I got a simple nod from Sheamus and Bardrick, and I turned to Gareth.

"I ain't saying goodbye, not to you. I will follow you somehow." Love you too, man. Gareth responded.

"You need to change first." Bardrick beckons me to follow him. As we leave the room, I hear my mother's soft sobs, and I start to feel homesick, knowing that I may never return to see my family. I follow Bardrick to the second floor to the training room. There he gives me another set of battle clothes to change into, and we make our way back to the library. I make my way to Stell, who is holding onto the sword.

"Hold out your hands." I did as she asked, and she places the handle over my hands.

"Now, take the blade." How? How do I grab the handle when I can't even fit my hand through the vines to grasp it?

As I move my hand closer to the handle, the vines start to move. I can understand it; as soon as I get a good grip, the hilt starts to encase my hand. The silver vines from the blade begin to siphon from the blade and begin to cover my hand. My arm up to my shoulder is covered in liquid silver; I twirl my wrist, bend my arm and roll my shoulder. I am amazed that even though my whole arm and shoulder are covered in silver, I have a full range of movement.

"That's cool, but how do you take it off." Gareth runs his hands over my shoulder. Strangely, I can feel his hand; he taps on it, but I feel nothing. This is weird.

"Only Layla knows how her blade works. She is the one who crafted it."

"It does not matter, it's time to go, and I need Stell's help to change the archways destination to get you closer to the city."

Bardrick was the first to leave, followed by Stell, my parents, and Sheamus. I walked with Gareth, we all followed Bardrick to the archway. I spent the next half an hour saying my goodbyes while Stell and Bardrick changed the entrance.

"The last doorway led to the very outskirts of the city. I thought if I had done that, your arrival would have gone unnoticed. But I was wrong, and it gave my brother time to set his trap for you." Bardrick's face is apologetic.

"This time, I have helped move the doorway as close as possible. With this, we are hoping that Jarlen won't have time to set any trap for you. But you have to go quickly. I have no doubts that someone has noticed the doorway. We did our best to hide it, but it won't stay hidden for long."

"Good luck. I hope the next time we see each other,

I can walk freely through the Northern Realm."

50

Layla

I can feel soft covers on me and the warmth of the sun hitting my exposed skin. I am having trouble waking up, my head is all foggy, and yesterday's events and last night evade me. I close my eyes tighter and try hard to think of what could make my head so foggy. I roll over, and I roll into a body lying next to me – Eric? – I have my Eric back.

"Eric?"

"I am sorry little sister, but no." I roll back over and curl into a tight ball, and in a rush, I remember what had happened yesterday. I remember that I had Eric, and my father took him away from me. I will never see him again; my father made sure of that. I will spend the rest of my life with Bayloss, a man I do not love. I know my father will punish me even more by allowing me to watch Eric's life unfold without me. I start to cry.

"Your father wants to see us." I don't want to see him. I never want to see him again. I would rather gouge my eyes out. I would be alone for all of eternity than be anywhere near him ever again.

"Your father has moved our wedding forward; he wishes to discuss it with us." Discuss? That is laughable more to the point he will be telling me where and when I am getting married.

"We should get going; we don't want to give him another reason to punish you even more." I feel Bayloss get off the bed, and I can hear his footsteps. They stop at the door, but I don't hear it open. I guess he is just standing waiting for me to get dressed.

Taking my time in getting out of bed and getting ready, and to his incredible honour, Bayloss just stands at the door waiting for me. Once dressed, I walk over to Bayloss, and he holds the door open with one hand and holds out his arm for me. I know he is only offering me his arm to keep me from collapsing into a heap on the floor. I take his arm, and we walk to the main chamber of the tower.

As we step through the large double doors, I still get amazed at just how big this room is; it takes up the entire floor. The place is glass and has five candelabras, one in the dead centre of the room while the other four are spaced evenly around it.

In the centre of the room is a large table that can comfortably seat forty men. The table is moved to the furthest part of the room when it is not in use. '

Opposite the main doors (when the table isn't there) are the main thrones, they are on a raised platform, and there is one each for my parents behind the main thrones and to the left are three smaller ones, one each for me and my sisters I, of course, have a middle seat.

I look around the room, I see my father and Orry arguing over paperwork that's spread out over the main table, my mother sitting on her throne watching my father, and I can see my sisters sitting on their chairs; no one was looking at me. I looked up at Bayloss.

"Thank you for the escort." He nodded at me and walked over to our fathers to either end the argument or join it.

Taking a deep breath and my back straight and head held high, I walk towards my mother. I stand before her and watch as she continues to stare at my father. I can't help but wonder if she feels the same about him as I do or if she loves him, and if she does, she would be the only one who does. She finally looks at me and motions for me to kneel before her. I do as she asks, and my mother leans close to my ear.

"I am sorry for this, my darling child." She kisses me on the cheek and watches her husband as if nothing had happened, as if I was never there.

I stand and walk over to my sister's; they, too, are staring at my father. Neither one looks at me. I take my seat in between them. I place my hands on the armrests; my sisters take one of my hands each and give me a slight squeeze. I hope they know how sorry I am for putting them through so much trouble. I would like to tell them that I would not have left if I knew it would cause this much drama.

I can't believe that through my leaving, I have caused so much heartache on all sides. I don't know what I am going to do. All I can say is I'm glad to have met Eric. I get a strong feeling of Eric. I can feel my heart squeeze; I can almost feel him. I feel my eyes stinging and hot tears sliding down my face, I always promised that I would never cry in front of people, but today I have done it twice, not very gracefully for the wife of the future ruler of the Southern Realm.

My sisters try to hug my arms to their bodies to try and comfort me. I can't believe that through all the drama and the pain of what I have done. They still love me, and the tears flow even faster. Elyse drops my hand, leans forward, and turns her head towards the door as if she is trying to listen.

"Did you hear that?" Nokomis dropped my hand and tried to listen to whatever Elyse was hearing; I couldn't hear anything. I think my head must still be foggy from whatever drug my father poisoned me with last night.

"There! Did you hear it then?" Nokomis and I shake our heads. I look over at my mother. I can see that she is still staring at my father. The men didn't hear whatever Elyse could; she seems to be the only one hearing anything, and that's saying something.

However, Elyse has always kept her talents hidden from the rest of us. I can talk to plants, Nokomis can control the weather, but Elyse never told us what she could do; maybe this is part of it.

"I think it's headed this way." That doesn't sound promising. Just then, the main doors swung open with such force that they almost flew across the room. Everyone stopped what they were doing and stared at the doorway; we are all stunned. No one should have made it to the main chamber undetected, but I know the reason as to why. For standing in the doorway carrying my sword - which had the power to hide one's life force - and covered in blood is my Eric.

"JARLEN!" screams Eric.

51

Eric

I step out of the archway, and I find that I am on the outskirts of the city, Thanks to Bardrick and cousin Stell. I don't have to travel as far to get to Layla. I can see the central tower, and I can see the balcony covered in plants. I can see that some of them are turning brown and dying.

I now know that those plants are in tune with her emotions, and I know that she must be dying or at least depressed without me. I am surprised that any of the plants are still alive. I doubt she was made to forget; I have this feeling that Jarlen would make sure she felt everything and remembered everything. I know how she feels about me. I sensed it when I chased after her; I felt it in the plants she called. I kneel on the grass, pouring everything into the ground to let her sense that I am here, that I am coming for her again and will always come for her.

I look towards the balcony, but the plants remain the same. I could feel the ground shake beneath my hand, but I could not feel Layla when I touched the ground. All I can do now is go and get her.

Walking to the city, it doesn't take too long before I encounter the first lot of guards, at least fifty or sixty men. However, I can't tell if they are Jarlen's men or Orry's or if they belonged to someone else entirely. I don't care; I will cut my way through them if they try to stop me. I am not afraid this time. I know what I want and what I have to do. The guards spot me and block my way into the city. They move around and surround me; I don't know how I will get out of this one, but I sure as hell will try.

"Last time you were here, we sensed your presence but not this time." The voice spoke with authority, but I couldn't tell from where the sound was coming.

"When you last came through, Jarlen silenced the city." Silenced the city?

"Jarlen has immense power, so much so that he can make us bow to his will while he sits in the tower. He ensured that we did not interfere with his plans to destroy you." I stood there, not saying anything. What could I say? I feared that whatever I said would fall on deaf ears, and I'd die where I stand.

I watch as one of the elves in the front part steps forward. The elf has long blonde hair and dressed in black battle leathers. He has a silver breastplate with a crest upon it; maybe it's the Northern Realm's crest. There is a sword in his hand; none of the others has their weapons drawn. I take a few steps towards him. I hold my sword tightly, just waiting for them to strike. Neither one of us speak; we just stare at each other as he gets closer to me. He stops in front of me.

"You are the mortal, Eric Walker. No mortal has ever stepped onto our lands since the doors were closed, and now you have stepped onto our lands twice."

'The last time that you were here, we were asked not to interfere. Jarlen wanted to see what you were capable of, and I guess we all were." That's why I encountered no obstacles on my way to find Layla, but what about now, I wonder?

"But this time, we weren't alerted to you, but we did sense someone open a doorway, but it only lasted the briefest of moments and then it was gone. It seems that you are shielded."

Thank you, Stell and Bardrick.

"As you can tell, no one but those who surround you know that you are here, and that is the way we would like to keep it." Does this mean that I am about to die where I stand, never reaching Layla? Will they dump my torn apart, lifeless body at her feet? I only just see him move, giving me barely enough time to raise my sword and take a swing at him. He ducks under my wayward swing landing his shoulder into my chest, forcing all the air out of my lungs and forcing me to the ground.

"Get up!" I try to get up off the ground, but the air hasn't returned to my lungs, and I find it increasingly difficult to breathe. I am wracked with pain as I suck in a deep breath. It feels as if he has broken more than one of my ribs. I get to my knees and about to rise to my feet when I see him moving towards me. The training I received kicks in as he tries to kick me in the face, and I counter his attack and force him back enough to give me the space I need to rise to my feet.

"So, who are you loyal to?" I wait with bated breath. My question unanswered; instead, he charges me again. I take my stance, and as he swings his blade, I counter his attack, strike back, and force him to stagger backwards a step or two. I can almost see him crack a smile. I advance, striking out at him, though I do not manage to land a blow. We dance around each other. As he tries to attack me, I dance out of his way and counter his attacks. However, I end up defensive while I could run my blade through him and end it quickly. I have never killed anyone before, and it makes me sick to the stomach just thinking about it. I land a blow to his nose with my fist; this forces him back.

"You trained with Bardrick." What has that got to do with anything?

"How do you know Bardrick?"

"Because he is the only person with that fighting style, and I have been up against it before." I am wondering if he is friend or foe

"He, too, broke my nose." There is a slight smile on my face at that news.

"Bardrick is a stone-cold heartless murdering bastard, and one of his styles was to get in nice and close and kill them and watch the light fade from their eyes just inches from his." He straightens his nose. I can hear the sickening grind of cartilage and pop as it is popped back into place. A slight shiver runs along my spine at the sound.

"I wonder if you are as well." He rushes me, and our swords connect, and he steps in close to me. I anticipate his move of wanting to return the favour, which is not going to happen. I force him to back away from me, enough that I manage to land a kick to his upper thigh, making him stumble but not fall to the ground. He comes at me again; we are wasting time with this pointless fighting. What is he trying to prove? While my thoughts are elsewhere, I miss his movement and feel a sharp pain in my leg. There is a cut in the battle leathers, and there is blood flowing from a wound on my thigh. I feel the anger build up in me, and I can feel the sword in my hand sing out for blood to spill. With rage and the feel of the sword drawing me into battle, I run at him and land a kick to his ribs. I am upset that I don't hear the sound of bones breaking. We fight for a few more minutes when he finally stops fighting me. We stand opposite each other within a ring of elves that surround us. I have had enough, and I want to know what is going on with this guy.

"I ask again, who are you loyal to?" I am breathless as I ask this.

"The question is, what will you do if we give you an answer you do not like?" I raise my sword and point it straight at the elf that stands before me. "I will do what I must and if that means I have to take as many of you with me, I will."

I watch as a few of them smirk, I stand my ground, but I ready myself for a fight.

We stand opposite each other, our breathing ragged. I can still feel the pain in my ribs, and the blood flowing down my leg has finally stopped. He is no better; blood on his face from the broken nose holds his right ribs.

"I am Varner. I am loyal to this realm and those who are loyal to it. I will stand with you." I hear I will stand with you from everyone else, and everyone moves to stand behind me. I don't know if I can trust any of them. But right now, I need all the help I can get. Varner walks towards me and stops a few feet away from me.

"Trust no one but the men that stand behind you, and if you cannot remember them, then just remember me." The realisation of the situation is starting to hit home as I am beginning to feel sick at the thought of having to kill another person. Varner comes and stands next to me; as we look over the city that lays before us, we see an army of elves coming towards us.

"It would seem as if Jarlen knows I am here." I hear a snigger from Varner.

"It would seem you are correct." They stop marching at the city's edge and take up their positions while waiting for us to advance. The feeling in my stomach is getting worse. I am trying to keep it together, but it's not working.

"The men before us are loyal to Jarlen." Along with the sick feeling in my stomach, I can feel a smile spread across my face at the thought that if I get through this lot, I am one step closer to Layla.

We move forward as we do, more and more men spill out onto the city centre, and I do not know who is loyal to whom. I guess the only person I can trust is standing next to me - Varner, but even then, who says I can trust him, he may instantly turn on me.

"Kill any who are not me," Varner says to me. I turn and look at the men that are behind me. I try to remember their faces but am finding it difficult.

I turn back around and face the front and the oncoming onslaught.

I will not be brave and say I'm not scared because I am freaking the shit out. I can see the central tower that is my target, I will get there, and I will stop at nothing to get there.

"We will help you get to the central tower; that is where she is going to be." Varner echoes my thoughts. Again, it is hitting home at the idea of killing, and it is making me nauseous to the point of wanting to vomit.

I have never killed another living being, and here I am about to kill elves of all things, and all for a girl. I can feel the sword singing in my hands. I can almost hear the sword crying for their blood.

The first wave rushes us, and on instinct, I take a defensive stance. I have to fight the urge to flee; as much as I want to run away and not look back, I know I can't. I have to move to an offensive stance. I have to meet them head-on; I can't look back. I need to do everything I can to get Layla back. I need her in my arms and my bed. The sword sings for blood, anyone's blood. The feeling is starting to wash over me as well, and I am beginning to feel the effects of bloodlust mixed with the feeling of nausea.

I watch as the first wave comes towards us; we are outnumbered by at least fifty to one. I position for impact; the enemy is almost upon us. The sound is indescribable when we all come together in a clash of swords. I block and strike the first attacker, then I dodge and block another attacker. I strike at them.

I seem to be dancing with several opponents; our swords strike one another. Out of the corner of my eye, I can see bodies dropping to the ground, the earth beneath our feet soaking up the blood that is spilled. Some have died from being gutted by swords, while others died from arrows sticking out from head or torso wounds. I am thankful for my quickness to avoid their attacks, but I am having trouble landing blows or at least, I think I haven't landed anything. When I focus on my opponent, I see blood seeping through cuts in their battle armour.

I quickly look at my blade and see that it has blood all over it. I dodge yet another attack, and as I strike back, I see an opening and thrust my blade deep into the chest of the elf that stands before me. My stomach tries to release bile. I hold down the urge to throw my guts up. I withdraw my blade; as I do, I feel the warmth of blood land on my face. I move quickly to my next adversary. The feeling of bloodlust and adrenalin outweigh the need to release the contents of my stomach. I find the opening land my deathblow, and another elf lays dead before my feet; blood pouring from his body, the light leaving his eyes. My body starts to move of its own accord. My next opponent is faster than the others, and he manages to strike at me. I dodge just enough that his blow is only a glancing blow, yet I feel the blood trickling down my unprotected left arm. I change my stance to counter my open left side. The fight seems to go on and on; there seems to be no end in sight. The bodies keep coming, and they keep falling.

I can feel Varner's presence at my back, and I can hear his sword hitting his opponent's sword.

Wave after wave keeps coming for us, but we fight them back and slowly move towards the central tower, leaving a wake of dead elves behind us. I am focused on the elf that I am fighting, that I do not hear nor see the arrow heading for me. After killing the elf before me, I was hit by an arrow right in my chest. The arrow's force causes me to stumble to the ground rolling into a heap on my right side.

There is pain in my chest, and I can't seem to catch my breath. I grab the arrow shaft with a shaky left hand. I am staring at the arrow sticking out of my chest. I hear Varner call out my name; I look up ever so slightly to see Varner kill his opponent without remorse and is by my side. He rolls me onto my back, the pain in my chest intensifies, and I still can't breathe.

"Varner." My voice cracks and breaks and hurts to get his name out.

"Hold still." He moves my hand from the arrow and cuts open my shirt to reveal that the arrow had not pierced my heart but stuck in my armour. The pain in my chest is from being winded.

"What the!"

"How?" exclaims Varner. I was wondering the same thing. Varner pulls the arrow from my chest and drops it to the ground. Just then, an elf saw an opening to attack us. I pushed Varner out of the way as I quickly get up and run my blade through the would-be attacker. I stood there, sword in his chest, the light going out of his eyes. That's when I noticed that the blade was draining blood from his body into the sword; it started to turn silver—moving up along the blade to the hilt, along my arm and across my body, generating more armour. That's how the arrow didn't pierce my heart. I join the fray. Varner is once again beside me as we fight.

"The sword, it's Layla's, isn't it?" he shouts over the sound of battle.

"Yeah, it is." It feels like an eternity since we started the fight, but we seem to be pushing them back.

"How did you get it?" it's hard to have a conversation while I am trying to fight. Another dead body lies before my feet. My blood-stained clothes from all that I have killed, yet I feel nothing for the loss of life I have caused here today.

"I got it from my cousin." The waves of elves coming after us seem to be retreating, we still are no closer to the tower, but now our path is more apparent. We have a break in the battle and regroup. Varner does a quick headcount of the men that surround us.

"We have lost around fifteen men." I turn to Varner. "I am sorry."

"Don't be. We are warriors, and we knew what we were doing. You are still here, and that's all that matters at the moment. Come, we still have to get you to Layla." I must have stood for about a minute before my body was telling me I needed to move.

I need to keep going. I need to get to the tower. I need to get to Layla. I am here for her, and I am here for the freedom of the realm. If the elf before me wants freedom from Jarlen's rule, I shall spare them, but if they follow him blindly, they shall taste the end of my sword.

As we move closer to the city's centre and closer to the tower, I see a wall of elves blocking my way to the tower; it's at least twenty elves deep. I turn around and look at the elves that have followed me, and behind our small force, I see yet another wall of elves running towards us. I brace myself for the fight that is about to happen and for my impending death. The army behind us does not stop running; they run past us and straight towards the wall of elves that block my path.

"For the freedom of the realms." They scream as they run past, it was only a split second, but I saw that the crest on their breastplates are different from the one Varner has.

"Southern Realm." I hear Varner say, Orry's men. With a smile on my face, I charge into the fray.

I am fighting for only a few minutes with Varner at my side before I break through to the tower's main doors. I don't see anyone in front of me. I take a quick look behind me. The fight is almost over; with Orry's men joining us, we overwhelmed those who stood guard, and now most are surrendering rather than dying.

"Go, you won't encounter much resistance between here and the main tower chambers. I doubt there will be any more bloodshed."

"Thank you, Varner; I could not have done this without you." I place my hand on his shoulder. He puts his hand on my shoulder as well.

"Go! We will stop all from coming this way" He gives me a little shove and moves back out into the crowd.

I have no idea where I am going, but I feel the sword tug at me. I do not resist; I find myself racing up several sets of stairs. I don't encounter anyone. I wonder if they all left the building and were standing out the front to stop me. I reach the main doors, and two guards are standing with their swords drawn. She is just through those doors, and so is her father.

With that thought, I do not hesitate; I kill both of them. Knowing that Layla and her father are just beyond that door, I start to feel love and anger. The anger fuels my desires to kill Jarlen and take what is mine, and with that rage, I kicked in the door, almost kicking them off their hinges.

52

Eric

"JARLEN," I scream out. I start to search the room for Layla and Jarlen; my eyes lock on him, standing with Bayloss and his father at a large table in the middle of the room. My gaze, drawn to a girl with blonde hair, being held up by two other girls, my sweet Layla. I watch her as several emotions flash across her face, shock, awe, relief and then fear. I don't stare too long at her. I must deal with Jarlen.

Turning my attention back to the three men standing stock still, staring at me, I raise my sword. It's covered with the blood of his people and the silver that coats my arms, shoulders and torso. It tells you just how many people I killed to get this much silver armour over me; I point my blade at Jarlen.

"I have come for Layla and your head." The last part was a little dramatic, but I need him to see that I am not leaving without her.

He steps away from the table and starts to head towards me. I don't back down. I can't back down, not after all I have been through, not to mention Varner and the other elves that helped me get here.

"Do you think you can take me with that sword and that armour? I can cut through any armour that any man wears."

"Have you not looked at the sword that I am carrying?" He looks closely at my hand along my arm and my chest. I watch as surprise crosses his face before it's replaced with a stern look.

277

He knows whose sword I wield.

"Yes, I have Layla's sword." I hear a few gasps as everyone looks at the sword I carry. It's hard to tell what kind of weapon I have as it's covered in blood. I look over at Layla, and she is struggling to get out of her sisters embrace. I can hear her saying,' let me go. I need to go to him.'

"And because you carry her weapon, you think that you are going to beat me." He starts to laugh; everyone is watching him. At the sound of their father's laugh, Layla's sisters release her, and she runs towards me. As much as I want to hold her when she reaches me, I grab her and pull her behind me.

"Stay behind me." I feel her body press up against my back.

"I have no idea if I can take you all by myself, but quite a few elves are laying out there that died by my hands. They may have something to say about it." His laughter stopped.

I felt Layla's hand grip my free hand; she squeezes it.

You may be right. I may not defeat you; I doubt I will even land a blow. I am not alone, and I seem to have gathered quite an army of your citizens, as well as the Southern Realm's soldiers. Not to mention, this sword from my cousin, who has offered her loyalty, also my parents and brother." Jarlen starts to laugh again.

"Well, the army, I can wipe out in one swift motion, and I have no doubts that I can take out your family, and then there is just you." Oh, my turn, a sly smile plays on my lips. The blood drains from Jarlen's face; I think he knows that I have just outplayed him.

"Oh, I forgot to mention that my cousin is of the Fey royal court, and my brother Gareth is Irish and has an extended family, so a recount. The Fey and the little people. Let's not forget the small army that stands outside this tower. Still think I can't beat you?"

"You also have the Southern Realm." I watch as Bayloss and

Orry unsheathe swords.

"You would defy me, Orry?"

"Yes, I would." It seems as if Jarlen is defeated, and he knows it. He doesn't seem to be putting up too much of a fight, which is a great pity. I would have liked to have cut him and spilled some of his blood. Layla's mother stands up and walks over to her husband. She stands in front of him and stares at him for a full minute before turning and walking back to her daughters.

"You know you are bringing down the Northern Realm." I was about to speak when Layla let go of my hand and stepped forward.

53

Layla

"This is what is going to happen." I move from behind Eric, and this time I stand in front of him.

"The realm will pass on to me, and Bayloss will rule the Southern Realm with Elyse beside him." I look over at Elyse, and I can see the happiness pouring off her. I can see tears in her eyes, and I look over at Bayloss. He mouths thank you at me; Orry nods at me.

I am thankful that Orry and Bayloss like my idea, but that is not all that needs completing to make our realms live in harmony. My father's face is vicious; I can feel the hate radiating off him.

Why does he feel this way?

Why is it always directed at me?

Have I been that bad of a child over the past one hundred and twenty-eight years?

I have tried to love my father these past years, but I can't. There isn't anything about him that is lovable. I have so much to do to get this realm back to how it was, to get it back to how my great grandfather used to rule, where all four kingdoms were at peace or at least relative peace, and I intend to bring the realms to order. I can't do it with my father around; this is where his rule ends, and mine begins.

"One of the many things I'm going to do as a ruler of the Northern

280

Realm is bring down the barricade you had put in place after your brother left. Also, Eric stays here with me, and the other major course of action is, his family has free passage." I turn and look at Eric.

He smiled at me and took hold of my hand. His touch calms me, but it also fires me up. I turned back to my father, whose facial expression had not changed.

"You're going to let the Fey and the People free reign in my realm."

"IT'S MY REALM! And I will rule it as I see fit." My voice vibrates and echoes off the walls of the main chamber. I watched as my father shrinks back before he rights himself and stands tall, he tries to take a step forward, but Orry and Bayloss stop him.

"I said I would rule as I see fit, but before I send you away from me and our realm, I have a few questions for you, father." He just stared at me like always, never showing me any form of emotion other than hate and displeasure.

"Ask them." And there is still venom in his voice as he speaks to me.

"You have a love for the realm, our people, my mother and my sisters, but I am met with hostility.

Why?"

"Because you are not mine." He says with a straight face.

I have always met with disdain, I couldn't help but feel my heart just drop, and I could feel my life ebb away. Eric squeezed my hand and pulled me towards him until my back was against his chest; I could feel his heart beating against my back. It doesn't bother me that I may be covered in blood either; I can feel his body against mine. It means he is real, he came for me, and that means everything to me. It means that I can stand in front of my father and take the realm from him.

"Oh, I am your father, but the moment that you were born. YOU belonged to them. You were to be a part of the Southern Realm, so you were never mine, but I had to live with you. I had to raise you.

I had to raise you to be one of them to rule against me; I couldn't have it. I couldn't have you leading the second strongest realm. I couldn't have you challenge me."

"Then you should have treated me like your daughter!" That was all I could get out; I couldn't say any more. I was too stunned at the realization that this could have all prevented if he had just treated me like his daughter. I can tell that no one knows what to say. Eric keeps me pressed up against his chest with his arm wrapped around my waist and holding me close to him. I breathe in and stand up straight; as I do, Eric lets go of my waist and allows me to step away from him.

"If you had treated me like your daughter, I would not be standing here now with Eric taking the Northern Realm from you. Our people would not be lying dead out there; this is your fault, father, no one else's." I hear the footsteps behind me. I don't turn around to see who it is.

"Eric?" They address Eric, and I watch as Orry steps closer to my father and nods at me; when I know it's safe to turn my back to my father, I see one of the elite guards standing in the doorway.

"Varner?" Eric addresses the guard at the door, who bows his head towards us.

"The city centre is secured; we have not encountered any more resistance." Before I could say anything to him, Eric answers him.

"Thanks, Varner." He nods and stands in the doorway. I look up at Eric; he just mouths, 'tell you later to me'. I turn my attention back to my father. I am relieved that the bloodshed has stopped and that I can now rebuild the Northern Realm the way it is supposed to be.

"Orry, Bayloss, please escort my father to the cells, and there he will wait to have his powers stripped." "And there shall I stay?" My father questions me.

"No! Once your powers have been removed, you are to be exiled to the barren lands, and that is where you shall stay."

"Not to the human world?" I could have burst out laughing.

"So, you could find a rouge Fey or one of the many numerous other beings to give you back your powers. I think not; if you stay within our world, I know you can't get any power back, no matter whom you go to, and you will not be able to travel through the gateways because I will make sure that you are trapped within our world."

"You would do this to your father?" I let out a laugh. And Eric raised his sword at him.

"You would dare call yourself her father after what you had said about her not being your daughter not but a moment ago. You are a sorry excuse for an Elf," roared Eric at my father. I raise my hand and place it gently on the top of my sword and lower the blade back down again. The room is quiet for a few minutes before I speak. I look towards Orry.

"Orry, if you wouldn't mind." He sheaths his sword and grabs hold of my father's arm, and marches him to the door. I watch as Varner goes with Orry, his sword at the ready. I look towards Bayloss then to my sister Elyse.

"Could you please head downstairs and deal with our people? Let them know that I will address them tomorrow with regards to what will happen with our realm and the other three realms." Bayloss stands in front of me and waits for Elyse to walk to him, my sister grabs my hand and squeezes it, and she plants a kiss on my cheek and gives Eric a slight nod before leaving with Bayloss. My little sister Nokomis walks up to Eric.

"Welcome to the family." She has a great big smile on her face as she says it.

"Sister, can I ask a favour of you," I say to her. I know that our relationship has never been good at times, but I know that she loves me, and I hope to have her support.

"You can ask anything." She doesn't even hesitate to answer me.

"I would like a celebration for Eric and me and Elyse and Bayloss, and I would like it for five days." Her face clouds over briefly before she answers me.

"Make it ten."

"Done!" her smile brightens, and she skips out of the room.

A thought crosses my mind that she intends to invite someone that lives outside the Northern and Southern Realms; a smile plays on my lips. I look at my mother, and I watch as she walks towards me; I want to look away. I know that I have brought her shame for what I have done to my father, but I can't look away. She stops in front of me.

"It was brave of you for what you did, darling I am so proud of you." she turns to Eric.

"You too, my son." She walks out of the room, leaving Eric and me standing there.

54

Layla

It is several minutes before either one of us moves; we are just standing there. I look Eric up and down and see that he is covered in blood from head to toe; he looks a little gruesome. Still, he came here for me, he came back for me, and I love him for that, and now he is all mine. I never have to give him up ever again, and I get to keep him.

Letting out the breath that I seemed to have been holding, I think I have been holding it in most of my life, and now that I am free, my heart and my body feel so light and free. I can feel all my muscles relaxing all at once. I stare at him, and I watch as his face softens and that goofy look creeps across his face, I think he is thinking the same thing as me, and I have no doubts that I have the same goofy look. We gravitate towards each other, but before we are close enough to touch, he stops and holds out his arm to me, the one with the sword attached to it. I have not had a chance to look at him with my sword attached to his arm and covered in blood. My heart beats faster; the room is so quiet; I just know that he can hear it.

"Um, how do I take this off?" I can't help but laugh. I know I shouldn't. I am the one that made the weapon, and I am the only one who knows how to remove it. I hold my hands out to him.

"Just give it to me." He holds it above my hands, but nothing happens. I smile at the thought that he doesn't want to give up the blade. My blade is connected to the heart, mind, and willpower to control it. The only way he could have wielded it was with sheer undying love and a desire to save me. That would have been the only way, but now I think he is afraid that all of this will vanish if he hands it over. I can't say as I blame him. I believe that it's going to disappear.

I lift my hands and touch the blade with my hands. The liquid silver starts to flow back into the swords crystal blade. I watch as it moves across his torso up his left arm across his shoulders, then down his right arm past his wrist over his fingers. I take the now entire sword resting in my hands and sheath it in his belt. He places his hand over mine as it rests on the hilt.

Eric pulls my hand close to his chest; his strong hands massage my small hand. He takes a step closer to me and draws me closer. Our bodies pressed against each other, my heart pounds loudly in my chest or is it his heart that I feel pounding against mine. Before long, his lips have found mine, and heat floods my body. Oh, how I have missed his touch. I have missed the way he makes me weak in the knees. I have missed the smell of his earth, air, and soap. I have missed everything about him.

His kiss became more urgent; our desire for one another is getting to breaking point. If we don't stop now… but for once, my mind goes blank and does not scream at me, and even if it did, I was not going to stop, not when I finally have him here in my arms, not when I can call him mine. I am happy to keep going, we are alone, and I know that my family will not come; I can have him here. It is Eric that breaks the long heated, passionate kiss.

"I need you. I can't hold back anymore." He is breathing hard and fast; his eyes are so full of hunger. I take his hand, walk him out of the room, and I start to climb the stairs that lead to my room. As much as I love the silence and his hand in mine, I need to hear his voice; I need to know that he is still there. I need to know this is not a dream, and I need to hear his voice.

"I bet you have questions?" I say the first thing that comes to mind. I don't know if that was a brilliant thing to say. Sometimes my mouth just opens, and words spew forth. He stops partway up the stairs, I turn and look into his face, and we stand staring at each other.

"I have many questions, but right now, I can't seem to voice any of them." He pulls on my hand, and I trip down the step I am on and stumble into him. Eric holds me close to his chest, gently running the back of his hand against my cheek. I instinctively close my eyes and lean into his touch, and a moan escapes my lips.

"You don't have anything you want to ask me?" The words leave my lips before I have a chance to stop them. But it doesn't matter. I can feel his chest move as he laughs.

"Nothing that can't wait until tomorrow." My brain is working overtime, and it's conflicted with wanting to know what questions he might have. I do and do not want to ask. I try hard to keep my questions to myself, but I can't seem to stop myself from asking; my heart begins to ache at the impending answer.

"Would you have always come for me?" I want to rip my tongue out; why is my head screaming at me for him to answer my questions. I never wanted to think about this question or even ask it ever. I did not want to hear the answer that will accompany it. Every time I thought about this question, all I can recall is the last thing that he said to me as he left the house. I honestly thought that he would never come for me; my heart starts to hurt.

There is pressure on my body; I can feel it crushing me. I don't want to hear his answer, so I bury my face in his chest and try to stop the tears that threaten to spill over. As he holds me tight against him, I think about how I would have gone to him, but I couldn't go to him, I just couldn't, the tears start to fall. I can feel his hands rubbing my back; it hurts to know that I was trapped here and couldn't leave.

What hurts the most was that after a time, all I could think of was that he didn't want me anymore. I was never going to be saved and be forever trapped here alone. The days passed, and then the weeks, and I started to fall into an abyss from which I was never going to escape.

I feel his hands stop moving, and he lifts my chin to look at him. I can see him struggling for an answer that isn't going to hurt me. I know it will, the pain in my body is still crushing me, and I find it hard to breathe with that look on his face. I don't want to hear the answer. How is it that only but a few moments ago, I was taking him to my room, and we were finally going to be happy?

"No, not in the first few weeks; I was so mad at you; I couldn't understand why you didn't tell me. I could not bear to think of you, but everywhere I looked, I saw you. I could smell you in my room, in my bed, and I couldn't get you out of my head. I couldn't stand to say or even think of your name. It just hurt too much, and then one day I got your letter."

"My letter?" How could he have gotten that? It was in my room.

"I found it under my door, and I thought that you had slid it under there because I could smell your perfume." But I don't wear perfume, oh he means how I always smell like flowers.

"When I read it, I went straight to your uncle, and he started to train me." He holds my face in his hands and brings his lips to mine; he pulls back. I can see that his eyes are wet.

"I was such an idiot the day I walked out on you. I have hated myself for it, but that day I got your letter 'love always and free-falling,' which was the day I told myself that I was coming for you. That I would stop at nothing until I had you in my arms, as I have you now. But of course, there was meant to be a lot less blood." He kisses me again.

"That's okay, and we can have a bath together." His next kiss is longer.

"But just one thing, what does that part mean? Love always and free-falling," I smile and let out a small laugh. I press myself against his chest.

"I was free when I fell in love with you, and I am still falling, and the best part is that I am once again free to keep falling in love with you." Eric runs his hands through my hair; he rubs his thumbs along my ears, sending shivers through my body.

"Tell me, little elf." I think my heart just stopped, little elf? "Tell me that you forgive me."

"There is nothing to forgive; it is I that hid who I am." I reluctantly look up at him, and the instant that I do, he starts to kiss me. In between kisses, he breathes my name.

"I love you, my sweet Layla."

"I love you too, my Eric." I drag him up the stairs to my room.

I stand in front of my door, becoming increasingly worried, and I feel Eric's arms wrap around me from behind; his lips are on my neck.

"Layla." I breathe in deep and turn the handle to my bedroom. I let the door swing open; he removes his lips from my shoulder and stares at my room.

"You have a forest in your room!"

I knew it would surprise him. Who wouldn't it surprise? I mean, my room is just covered in plants and flowers and climbing vines. It's a little hard not to when I control all living plants. It truly is a sight to behold; you wouldn't think that this was my room, not when the plants from the balcony are encroaching in on my room and that there are plants next to every piece of furniture.

All the flowers are in bloom and are making the room smell fresh and sweet. I guess everything turned green and started to blossom when I could have Eric in my arms again. Eric walks over to my desk and runs a hand along the top of my desk.

"How did I get your letter if you didn't give it to me?"

"Good question." I walk over to him and put my arms around him. I think about that day that my mother had come to my room just after I had finished Eric's letter. I had escaped to my balcony. I must not have realized that she was still in my room, reading it as I didn't leave the balcony for several days. When I finally came back inside and looked at my desk. I noticed that the letter was missing. I thought my father had come into my room and taken the letter.

"When did you get it?"

"About two weeks after you left." I could feel the smile spread across my face.

"It was my mother. I had finished writing it about two weeks after I returned home." He turned in my arms and put his arms around my waist.

"I am delighted she did, or I may never have found you."

"But there are still so many strange things that had happened as well, for one, I don't know how your shirt got here."

"And I could say the same about your red dress and shoes." I laugh. It takes a moment for it to click, but I think I know who did. I will have to thank Stell when all of this settles.

I grab hold of my sword that is still sheathed on his belt and pull it out.

"Time to put this away." I walk over to my bed and stand on it. I walk across my bed till I get to the head of it, and above my pillows on the wall are two hooks that hold my sword. I place it there and admire how my room now looks complete and whole once again. I walk to the middle of my bed and kneel facing Eric. He is still standing at my desk, watching me.

"Why did you give it to the Fey?" My sword? I stare at my beautiful, crafted sword.

"I made it a long time ago; I placed it above my bed. I was never going to use it. I don't even know why I made it.

One day, my father comes into my room, takes one look at it and demands it destroyed. I couldn't do it, so I gave it to the Fey; more importantly, I gave it to Stell of the royal court. I asked that she keep it safe until it's returned to me and its rightful place." Eric looks at the sword resting above my bed, then looks at me. Our eyes lock, and my heart starts to beat faster. I can hear the blood pumping in my ears. I want Eric in my arms and my bed. I undo the ties that are holding me into my dress.

"Stop!" Eric leaves my desk and walks over to stand in front of me. He puts his hands on my shoulders over mine to stop me from lowering my dress.

"Not yet." He runs his hands through my hair. He pushes my hair behind my ears to expose my pointed ears. He gently runs his fingers over my ears. I instinctively close my eyes and start to purr at the incredible sensation rippling through my body.

"Enjoying that are you?" I can hear the smugness in his voice at being able to melt me with just a touch.

"Could you please not hide these anymore?" He leans in and kisses me on the ear. A deep moan escapes my lips if he keeps going like this. I am to succumb very quickly.

He starts to trail kisses along my neck. My hands move to his bloody shirt; well, what's left of it, and I remove it from his body and throw it over the other side of the room. Eric pushes me down onto the bed, his hands searching my body, my hands holding his body tightly.

"My sweet Layla." He whispers in between kisses, moan after moan escapes my lips. I arch my body into his, begging for more.

"I love you so much, my sweet Layla. Please never leave me. I promise that I will always come for you."

"I love you too, my Eric, and I promise never to leave you,

so you never have to come and find me." I know that our life together has just started, and I know that our realm will be in turmoil, but I will have Eric beside me now, and I will be able to survive anything that comes my way. I allow myself to slip into sweet oblivion in Eric's arms.

Epilogue

I can't concentrate. My back is killing me, and the noise from downstairs is starting to reach my office. I take a break from my paperwork, and I begin to remember the morning after that blissful night with Eric.

"Can I ask a favour of you?" being held in Eric's arms, I keep pinching myself. I still can't believe that we get to be together.

"Yes." I will grant him anything he wants, and I am so deliriously happy I would say yes to everything and anything. He hesitates for a minute. I look up at him. I can see that he is worried, but he asks nevertheless.

"Can I have the brown hair and the storm over the ocean grey eyes?" he says it barely over a whisper. I laugh at his request; I am happy that I can grant it.

"Yes, but you will have to wait until I take the realm. Do you prefer brunettes?" He squeezes me closer to him.

"Yes, and your blonde hair and all, but I fell in love with the girl next door to me that is the real you."

I smile at the happy memory, but I am quickly snapped out of it when I refocus on the report that Bayloss has sent me.

"Has been spotted."

Those three words keep jumping out at me again and again, my father banished to the barren lands, but it wasn't long before he had been spotted within the Eastern or Western Realms. Bayloss and I had been sending out patrols to try and find him, but to no avail. This last report states that he is within the Western

Realm, but that was all.

It has been five years since the day that Eric stormed the castle, as it were, and for nearly five years, reports of my father have been coming in, but he is yet to do anything, and I am starting to get worried and anxious. As I re-read the same lines repeatedly, I can hear feet running in the hallway just outside my door. The door burst open, and I see a small girl with long brown hair, blue-grey eyes and little pointed elf ears, but she isn't wearing the dress I put her in.

"Mamma, look what Uncle Gareth got me." My sweet little Riona bounces on her toes and holds out her dress to show me just how pretty it is. My face softens, and a smile naturally spreads across my face. She twirls around and comes running over to me. I hold out my arms to her; she happily throws herself at me; I place her in my lap.

"Where is your uncle?"

"With Grandpa Sheamus, Grandma Lillian and Grandpa Geoffrey, and they are talking with Grandma and Daddy."

"No, Daddy is here." I look at the doorway to see my husband of five years and counting. Eric has not changed since the day he came for me. He has kept his promise of never leaving me. We set our affairs in order back in Skyhaven and returned here to the Northern Realm to live. It was that first night we spent together that he stopped ageing. It was also the night I fell pregnant with Riona.

Riona jumped off my lap and ran straight for Eric. She threw herself at him; he caught her in mid-air and held her close to him.

"Everyone is waiting for you. Are you feeling okay to come down and celebrate?" I get up and place both of my hands on my hips, and try to stretch out the pain in my back. Only to be rewarded with a kick to my ribs. I sigh and waddle over to Eric and Riona.

“I can’t wait for this little one to be born. My back and ribs are killing me.” Eric puts our little girl down, who runs away, screaming for Gareth. Eric takes hold of my hand, and we walk hand in hand towards the ballroom.

Tonight is to celebrate five years as ruler of the Northern Realm and four years of the council’s formation, but like always, I am worried about my father, what he has planned for my family and me. Eric can see that I am afraid, and he knows that it’s not about the baby.

“What is it, Layla?”

Do I tell him now? No! It can wait. I don’t think he needs to hear about my father and the frequency of his sightings outside the barren lands or that I think he is getting closer to causing an all-out war against the four Realms, well, not tonight at least. So instead, I squeeze his hand and smile at him.

“Nothing that can’t wait till tomorrow.” I hope.